Angels In Red

By Adelle Laudan

Two very different worlds collide the day Jack saves Jenna from a near death experience. The fact Jack has isolated himself in a cabin in the middle of nowhere, or that Jenna is the daughter of one of the country's wealthiest men, never comes into play as they fall deeply, and passionately in love.

Their happy-ever-after is interrupted when Jenna is called home to say her final good-bye to her father on his death bed. Will Jack lose her to the allure of high society she's accustomed to? Does the discovery of her deceased mother's well-kept secret keep her in a world where money and money and status can and does buy anything?

Or does she learn the one thing she wants most in life money can't buy.

Angels
In
Red

Adelle Laudan

Angels In Red
Adelle Laudan

Cover Art : Adelle Laudan

Revised and expanded version of Dear Angel

Adelle Laudan
http://adellelaudan.com

Dedicated to a Special
Angel watching over me.

My Mother

1930-2008

Thank you
Kim McGilvery
For being my 2nd
Set of Eyes

Chapter One

Everyone who was anyone filled the spectacular estate ballroom. If the air of self-importance got any thicker, Jenna imagined oxygen masks dropping from the ceiling like on airplanes. Women wore gowns by top designers, ranging from silky chiffon with plunging necklines by Gucci, to Anthony Vaccarello cut out gowns that had far more *cut out* than gown. Thousands of dollars worth of diamonds sparkled on slender fingers pinching the stems of crystal champagne flutes.

She'd bet money most of the ladies thought the birthday boy to be a ridiculously wealthy, egocentric ass. Yet, to *not* come risked the chance of missing out on all the juicy gossip amongst the wives and girlfriends of some of the richest men around.

The man of the hour, Kenneth Blackburn the Third, spared no expense to throw his yearly, over-the-top party. With it being so close to Christmas, he insisted there would be no festive decorations, cards, or shortbread baking until the day after his celebration. He wanted nothing to detract from him being the center of attention, and everyone knew what her father wanted, he got.

Host extraordinaire stood talking to one of her least favorite people. The two men couldn't be more different. Her father was impeccably dressed in a black tux, sporting his signature silk cravat of hand-spun gold. He wore his lush, dark hair combed back with a liberal application of pomade to keep things perfectly coiffed. Harold Meed, on the other hand, wore an ill-fitting, off the rack suit, even though he could easily afford custom made to fit his rotund shape. His shirt strained across a belly more than likely accrued from far too much drink. He wore his hair military short, making his already round face appear that much more voluminous.

"Jenna!"

She shrieked as her best friend, Buffy, grabbed her by the waist and spun her around. "Earth to Jenna. Where were you just now?"

Jenna tried to slow her racing pulse. "What are you trying to do, give me a heart attack?"

Buffy cast a curious glance in the direction she'd been entranced by. "I never knew those two were that close?" Swarovski crystals embellished her friend's designer ball gown, casting shimmering bursts of light whenever she moved. "What are the two of them talking about?" She smoothed down the wave of her Marilyn Monroe inspired hairdo.

She shrugged. "I don't know, but I'd bet anything dear old *Dad* is up to no good."

What does he possibly have to talk about with that asshole?

Yes, Howard was invited to all social functions, but her father never paid the man much attention aside from a firm handshake and a practiced smile at the door. His stone-face made it impossible to read if his laughter was genuine, unlike Howard's beady eyes that darkened with foreboding, belying the phony grin pasted on his plump face.

Just then, the two men raised hands in a toast and tossed back the contents of their glasses. As expected, a server appeared out of nowhere to replenish.

With new drink in hand, her father sauntered to the middle of the vacant dance floor. "If I could have your attention, I have some wonderful news to share."

The room fell silent. As the guests moved closer to the host, she took a few steps back.

"Jenna, could you come here please?"

Damn! Tendrils of dread slithered up her spine as the crowd parted, and she reluctantly closed the distance between them. "What's going on?" she asked out the side of her mouth.

Harold Meed appeared at the other side of her father, flashing a devilish grin as he brazenly undressed her with his eyes. She'd never wanted to physically hurt someone as badly. He'd have a hard time ogling anyone with his eyes swollen shut.

The ignoramus had never kept his overly-zealous obsession with her a secret. On a couple of occasions, he even went as far as to *accidentally* grab her ass in passing. Only after she threatened to call the police did he finally stop sending her gifts, asking her out to dinner or suggesting overnight jaunts to Paris.

"I'm sure my good friend, Harold Meed, needs no introduction," her father began. "Today, he has given me the best birthday gift. Today, he has asked for my daughter's hand in marriage." He glared into her eyes. "And I have given my blessing."

"You what?" Anger set her pulse racing, and heat rushed to her face. Her quick temper, often attributed by her flaming red hair. "This is a joke, right?" Jenna gawked at her father and then at Harold Meed. *They're actually serious.*

"Jenna, you're making a scene. We'll discuss this *after* the party. Got it?" He grabbed hold of her hand and held it out to Howard.

The harder she tried to pull her hand back, his grip tightened. *This can't be really happening.* The cold slide of a gaudy diamond engagement ring on her finger made it crystal clear it wasn't just a bad dream.

The element of surprise enabled her to break free from her father's iron grip. She couldn't take the ring off fast enough, all the while glaring directly into Howard's brooding eyes. *You know where you can shove this, don't you?* Jenna arched a brow and dropped the solitaire into his drink. The amber liquid splashed up in the very red-face of the jilted, wannabe groom.

"You *will* be mine. Your father made a deal. There is *no* turning back." He spoke as loud as he dared. "I promise, if you don't smile and put this ring back on, you will live to regret it."

She tilted back her head and laughed. "It isn't gonna happen, no way...no how, asshole."

"Jenna!" Her father swiftly slapped her across the face. "You will not talk to our guest that way. Apologize this instant!"

Her initial shock and anger quickly turned to rage. She wanted to scream obscenities at the top of her lungs, but the unexpected slap rendered her speechless. Her burning cheek warmed beneath her fingers as she turned and raced toward the door.

You can both go to Hell.

"Whoa there, kiddo." Charles, her father's personal assistant and her most trusted confidant, blocked her path. "You need to calm down and quit making a scene."

Jenna's eyes filled with angry tears. *First my father side-lines me, and now Charles? Am I getting punked?* "Let me pass or I'll throw a hissy fit right here and now." She shook her head. "Like I give a shit what any of these people think of me."

Buffy scurried to her side. "Please, Charles. Let me take her upstairs."

He heaved a sigh and stepped to the side. "Don't say I didn't try when your father *deals with you* later."

Jenna raced blindly up the grand staircase toward her suite. Buffy's footsteps followed close behind, taking two steps to her one. An overwhelming sense of betrayal had her clutching the bodice of her hand-embroidered dress.

At the last second, she turned and made a bee-line toward her father's wing of the house. Though she'd been forbidden in this part of the estate, which included her mother's sitting room off the master bedroom, her father's deception made her desperate for the closeness of her mother, even if only to sit in her chair amongst her things.

"Jenna? What are you doing? Don't you think your father's angry enough?"She panted. "If he finds you here, God only knows what he'll do."

"You saw what happened back there...do you really think I care how that monster feels?" The threat of tears prickled the backs of her eyelids as she reached the sitting room door. She paused when her gaze fell upon an array of pill bottles next to her father's bed.

"Whatever it is you're doing, you might want to hurry it up."

The sense of urgency in her friend's voice urged her forward. "You don't have to wait for me."

Buffy huffed and stormed back to the master bedroom entrance. "Just hurry up."

A fleeting moment of hesitation stopped Jenna from placing her hand on the crystal knob. She quickly shook the unease away and opened the door, only to freeze on the spot.

A thick layer of dust coated every surface in the room. Nothing had been touched since her mother's death five years ago. She closed her eyes and inhaled the lingering scent of Lily-of-the-Valley perfume.

Oh God, how I miss you...

"Jenna! I think somebody is coming up the stairs."

Her friend's warning abruptly ended the bittersweet memory. As much as she wanted to stay, she feared her father might abuse this moment, threatening to get rid of everything if she didn't marry Howard.

Darting her gaze around the room, she sought something, anything that might make her feel close to her mother. *Of course.* Jenna took two long strides to her mother's writing table, careful not to disturb anything, and opened the center drawer. The leather bound journal she'd seen her writing in on a few occasions sat atop a number of papers and pens.

"Jenna!"

She grabbed the journal and pushed the drawer shut, hard enough to send a cloud of dust upwards making her sneeze. Part of her still wanted to lock the door and remain in the midst of her mother's memory. Thoughts of her father using all of these treasures for blackmail gave cause to take one last, quick glance around before following the same footsteps she'd left imprinted in the plush carpet.

Before closing the door, she glanced back over her shoulder.

I'll be back, Mother.

"Oh! What are you doing here?" Jenna gasped, startled by Edna's presence in front of her. "Don't even bother to try and stop me."

The longtime housekeeper smiled and gently laid her hand on the diary. "I wouldn't think of it. I heard everything, and I'm so sorry you were put in such a...uncomfortable situation."

"Does he really believe I'll agree to marry that drunk?"

"He isn't thinking of your feelings, Jenna. Your father is only thinking of himself. I wouldn't blame you one bit if you got away from here for a while."

Jenna hugged her dear friend. "I love you, Edna. Maybe I will take off for a while. I can't even stand the thought of seeing him right now."

"You do whatever your heart tells you to do." The plump woman stepped back and dabbed at her eyes with the hanky she always had tucked away in the sleeve of her uniform. "I love you. You better go. The last thing you need right now is for your father to find you here."

Jenna nodded and kissed the flushed cheek in passing. Buffy stood in the hallway and practically dragged her away. There was no sign of anyone, making her wonder if there really had been someone coming up the stairs. Her best friend pushed her into her bedroom and slammed the door shut behind her. A click of the lock preceded Buffy's long-winded breaths.

Jenna spun on her heel. "Can you believe the nerve of my father? *Howard Meed?*" She shuddered, utterly revolted by the mere thought of being married to the creep.

"Hey, I'm on your side. I'm just so scared for you." Her platinum curls bounced with each step she took to sit on the end of Jenna's bed. "Maybe you shouldn't have made a scene? I've never seen your father so angry."

She could hardly believe her ears. "So, you think I should've played nice, and smiled in all the right places?"

"Well, yes." Her bare shoulders rose and fell. "You could have flipped out on him in private. Don't you think?"

Without giving it a second thought, she grabbed Buffy's arm and led her across the room. "Get out!" Jenna flipped the lock and yanked open the door, pushing her childhood friend out into the hallway. She paused momentarily to look into far too big blue eyes filled with confusion. "Why don't you go downstairs and *play nice* with Howard Meed. Maybe he'll marry *you*, 'cause he sure as hell won't be marrying me."

Buffy opened her mouth to speak, but Jenna wanted no part in hearing anything she had to say. She slammed the door in her face, flipping the lock before leaning back heavily. Her chest heaved as the tears fell.

"Please, Jenna. Don't be like that. Let me in so we can talk about all of this."

She resisted the urge to give in. *I don't want to deal with anyone right now!* Maybe she was being unreasonable, but if one more person told her to placate her father she'd surely lose what little control she had left over her faculties. She set the journal on her bed and slipped out of her dress, letting it pool around her ankles.

Her bedroom was bigger than the ground floor of most people's homes, and she still felt like the walls were closing in on her. "I need to get away from here."

She rushed to her closet and dressed faster than ever, casually in jeans and a sweatshirt topped with a lightweight parka of royal blue. Jenna then grabbed her mother's diary and tucked it safely away in an oversized pocket of her coat before pushing her feet into fur-lined boots.

Maybe I should pack a bag... No, I can buy anything I need. Jenna checked her wallet for credit cards before throwing her purse over her shoulder. She rolled back her shoulders and left the room, running past her best friend who pleaded for her to reason. Charles stood at the bottom of the staircase with arms folded across his broad chest.

"Just where do you think you're going? They're calling for a lot of snow this evening, Jenna. Quit being so childish and come with me, we can talk over a cup of coffee in the kitchen,"

Jenna shrugged his hand from her shoulder. "Please, Charles, just let me go. You of all people should understand why I need to put some distance between me and my father."

His big hand pressed against the door above her head, barring her way. "I get it, Jenna. I really do. Can you at least take Buffy with you?"

She turned, and made her features soften as she stepped toward her best friend.

Buffy opened her arms. "Thank God. You'll be able to think more clearly once you have a chance to calm down."

Jenna spun around, catching Charles off guard, she ignored their shouts from the front doorway as she trudged through the snow to the carports housing a fleet of cars. She opened the glass-encased peg board and snatched her keys before letting herself in the port reserved for her Jag.

Charles still stood at the front doors when she pulled up and lowered her window. "I'll call later."

He descended the stairs, but she took off down the cleared driveway from the house. He grew smaller in her rearview mirror, completely out of sight by the time she pushed a button on her key ring and drove through the parting front gates. She'd never done anything remotely this defiant in all of her twenty-two years.

I'll just give him a little time to come to his senses. Once he realizes how serious I am, he'll rescind the offer of my hand in marriage...won't he? She grimaced into the mirror. *You better hope so, girl.*

Jenna stopped for coffee-to-go at the Canada/USA border—separating her from her father back in Thunder Bay, and the serenity of Eagle Ridge ski resort in Minnesota's Lutsen Mountains. The taunting strains of 'I'll be Home for Christmas' filled the car. Despite the steady snow fall and poorly lit road, it didn't take a genius to figure out she'd taken the wrong mountain access to the resort on the summit of Moose Mountain. A light on her dash flashed red, warning her gas was running low.

"Oh God, please don't." *You idiot, why didn't you fill up at the border?*

Suddenly, two green orbs of light pierced the darkness. Her heart pounded as she swerved to avoid the fear-stricken deer in her headlights. The steering wheel slipped through her fingers as the Jag slid out of control. Her body jerked forward as the crunch of her front end bursting through the guardrail ravaged her eardrums.

Plummeting down the side of the mountain, Jenna screamed as the door flew off and sucked her out into the frigid winter's night. Forcing her arms up to protect her face, she spiraled down into a vast expanse of nothingness.

Silence...

Her eyes fluttered open, momentarily blinded by a wall of white. Only the rush of blood sounded in her ears. Incredible pressure restricted her from moving. Her mind scrambled for a thread of memory.

Cold...white... I'm alive...

Oh my God! I'm buried in the snow...

She teetered on the edge of hysteria as her memory slowly unraveled...the deer...crashing though the guardrail.

How long have I been here?

Jenna made a futile attempt to move. Her muscles contracted, but her legs wouldn't budge under the heavy snow. *How much is on top of me?* She couldn't tell, but luckily there seemed to be an air pocket in front of her face. It made no sense, but she thanked

God for it. If the snow continued to fall, it was only a matter of time before the pressure strangled the flow of blood through her veins. Her teeth chattered, never had she been as cold.

One of her arms lay beneath her. An attempt to move her fingers brought tears to her eyes. Daggers shot up the other arm resting against her side. The wall of snow in front of her stained red, spreading from ice-numbed skin she couldn't. She wasn't sure how long she'd survive like this, but she was smart enough to know she was in *big* trouble.

Jenna faded in and out, fighting to stay awake, scared if she fell asleep she might never open her eyes again. Tears froze on her cheeks until, unable to fight any longer, she closed her eyes and succumbed to the cold tiredness invading her limbs.

Chapter Two

Jack Davis looked through his telescope at the stars when a sudden flash of light stole his attention. He steered the lens down just as a car smashed through the guardrail and over the mountain ridge.

"Holy shit!"

He dashed around the cabin to the front, knowing with each passing moment the chances of finding the driver alive grew slim. He fumbled with harnesses and hooked up the two dogs to the sled, battling the biting winds and blowing snow. By the time he reached the destination, the sports car was completely engulfed in flames, squelching any hope of finding someone alive. Through the inferno, he noticed the driver's door was missing.

Did somebody make it out before it hit the ground?

The light attached to his hat illuminated the snow-covered land between his sled and where the car came down. Snow continued to fall heavily, and as the wind picked up even more, the possibility of there being a survivor became less than likely. If the driver had been ejected, there was no way of telling where he or she landed.

"Sasha, Tito...search and find." He unclipped their leads, and the two dogs bounded atop the snow effortlessly. The only chance of finding someone alive relied entirely with his Huskies. In between litters, he worked hard with them for just such an emergency.

The dogs suddenly stopped, ears twitching, snouts stuck up in the air. They'd caught wind of something and took off to the base of the mountain, clawing at a mound of snow.

Jack saw no sign of life in or around the area they were digging through. No footsteps, no nothing.

"There's nothing here, you two. Come on. Let's go."

Sasha and Tito ignored his command and continued digging at a frantic pace. He angled the light on the front of the sled on them. His brow crinkled, knowing they wouldn't dismiss him without reason.

Jack lunged forward and dropped to his knees, burrowing through the snow with his gloved hands. A piece of blue fabric urged him to pick up speed. Someone lay face down—no way of telling if they were alive or hurt.

Sweat dripped from his brow, his throat ablaze as he gasped for breath. He grabbed a hand shovel from the sled and dug out trenches on both sides of the body, removing enough snow for him to slip his hands under and lift it out, carefully flipping the person over to lie on the snow face up. For a split second, he was awestruck by this sleeping beauty with a sweet smile on her bluish lips. Jack pulled his glove off with his teeth and put two fingers to her ice-cold neck, breathing a sigh of relief to find a pulse.

His hand came away wet and sticky, but he couldn't tell where she bled from. He *did* know if he didn't get her warm, fast, nothing else mattered. A gust of wind passed through the spot he'd dug out, revealing an object in the middle of blood-stained snow. Half-hidden by a drift, he picked up a book and stuffed it in the inside pocket of his vest.

"Sasha, come. Lie down." He snapped his fingers next to her and the dog stretched out beside the woman, inching in as close as possible. Another snap of his fingers and Tito followed suit on the other side. "Stay."

He took off his scarf and secured it as best he could across her face, covering her nose and mouth loosely before trudging to his sled. The wind pelted his now exposed face mercilessly as he fought his way back; the blowing snow obstructed the light, making it impossible to see past the tip of his sled. Living in the middle of this vast, snow-covered expanse where everything looked the same, he'd acquired an incredible sense of direction.

Luckily, the light on his hat enabled him to at least see what his hands were doing. In a matter of minutes, he had the woman on the sled with a blanket tucked tightly around her slight body and his scarf secured. From what he could tell, she bled from the back of her head. The sooner he got her home, the faster he could tend to her.

In a matter of minutes, the dogs were hooked up and they flew across the snow toward the log cabin he called home.

Jack paused; his hands trembled as he quickly assessed how to go about undressing this woman with as much decorum as possible.

Get to it! You need to get her in dry clothes, now.

With a definitive nod, he proceeded to exchange her wet clothing for a new pair of flannel pajamas, wool socks, and heavy down comforter.

The bleeding came from a nasty gash at the back of her head. Fortunately for her, he kept a first aid case filled with supplies for every possible scenario, and he applied liquid stitches, securing the gash closed before bandaging her head. As far as he could tell, she'd broken three fingers and had a badly sprained wrist, so he made a splint for her hand. An ugly patch of bruising spread across her ribs, making him fear she'd broken them, too. He wasn't a doctor, but he could find nothing more to validate this fear. Still, to be safe, he wrapped a tensor bandage around her battered ribcage.

Once satisfied he'd done all he could, Jack stepped away and added wood to the fire. He rubbed down and fed the dogs before settling in a worn armchair next to the warmth emitted from the cast iron insert he'd salvaged from an old farmhouse along the way.

Rubbing his stubbled jaw, he drank in the sight of his unexpected guest. It had been quite some time since he'd been this close to a woman, or any other human for that matter. After the skiing tragedy, he'd brought his breeding business out to this uninhabited land between the Lutsen Mountains and the Canadian border. Far enough from the popular ski resort and any main roads that he didn't worry about unwanted visitors. The only contact with the outside world over the past five years came when *he* wanted it and made the trip to Grand Marias for supplies.

She lay there so calm and peaceful; he shuddered to think what might have happened if the Huskies hadn't found her. He settled back in his chair and crossed his long legs. All of his hard work training them had definitely paid off tonight. Sasha and Tito now lay in front of the crackling fire, their heads resting on their front paws, completely sated after finishing off a bowl of venison stew given as a reward.

There was a variety of pain and antibiotic medicines he could give his unexpected patient, but not knowing her medical history, and the fact she didn't seem to be in any immediate discomfort, persuaded him to wait until she came to. The lady had enough strikes against her without giving cause for an allergic reaction.

Jack usually didn't keep the fire so big, but she needed the warmth. Albeit fortuitously, they'd found her in time to eliminate any fear of hypothermia or frost bite. From what he could tell, the impact of her fall let loose a shelf of snow, burying her. But the way the snow was blowing and accumulating...

Jack left his sleeping beauty and set about rinsing her wet clothes in the sink. He checked her pockets, but found no clue to her identity.

The book.

His vest hung on a hook by the door where he fished the sodden book from the pocket. It appeared to be some kind of diary, but he found no names on the inside cover. He could have read further to find answers, but from what was legible of the neatly written scroll gave the impression the entries were private. For now, he parted the pages as best he could and set it on a shelf above the stove to dry. As long as she didn't worsen, he felt no sense of urgency to try and decipher the badly stained pages. Anything else she had in the car was gone. No doubt someone would be looking for her, but he didn't want to leave her alone in order to alert the authorities, at least not until she regained consciousness. True to form, his two-way radio proved to be useless in the storm.

What the hell was she doing up there to begin with?

Nobody drove those roads this time of year. Especially not in some fancy sports car. The winding road only led to more of the same, and forest land mostly inhabited by deer, which drew a crowd of hunters each season.

She certainly didn't fit the bill of a hunter, not with diamonds that size in her ears and an expensive watch on her wrist. The pink bra and lacy thong he couldn't bring himself to take off her didn't come from any low-end department store.

A faint murmur from his patient brought him to his knees beside her. He cupped the side of her face and waited for any sign of her coming to. Her flawless features remained expressionless, her breathing slow and steady. The corners of his mouth twitched with the threat of a smile as he gently smoothed down the red hair framing her face.

Jack snatched his hand away as if scorched by fire.

No way, don't even think of going there. Quickly reminded of the pain caring could inflict, he'd best keep his distance. Out here in the middle of no-man's-land was no place for some upscale princess from the big city.

As he started to leave the room, Sasha and Tito raised their heads expectantly.

"Sasha, stay."

The silver and white dog relaxed back to her former position, while Tito stretched and padded behind him to the bedroom. Sasha would alert him if their mystery woman awoke.

Chapter Three

"What do you mean you don't know where she is?" Kenneth Blackburn the Third paced back and forth across a one hundred year old Persian carpet. He puffed out smoke from a big, fat cigar he periodically wedged in the corner of his thin lips.

Charles sat at the edge of his chair, rubbing his hands together. "Jenna left here the night of the party, madder than a wet hen. She tore off in that Jaguar and I haven't heard nor seen her since."

Kenneth paused. "She took the Jaguar in this weather? Is she crazy?" His face reddened as he continued to pace. "You'd think that kid would be grateful for all she has." He waved his hands at the space in front of him. "Not our Jenna. She gets all bent out of shape when one of the richest men in Devon Falls wants to marry her...who, by the way, she *will* marry!"

Charles followed his boss's tirade in silence, as he often did. He didn't blame Jenna one bit for taking off. Harold Meed was at least fifteen years older than her, and a far cry from the GQ model type she dated. In fact, some might call his pocked face and bulbous nose repulsive. Not to mention, he never once saw the man without a drink in his hand. He shuddered, completely repulsed by the thought of the oaf's filthy hands roaming Jenna's slender body.

"Where could she have gone? Have you tried to track her down?" Kenneth cocked his head and looked down his nose at him.

"Of course. Nobody knows where she is. It's like she vanished." Charles scowled. *She's been gone two days and* now *you're suddenly concerned?* He'd known Jenna all her life, and had come to love her like a daughter. Sure she was a little hot-headed, but he'd yet to meet a redhead who wasn't.

"Call Chief Swanson and have him put out an APD, or ACF, whatever it is, on her." He clasped the banister and lowered his head. "Jenna didn't just vanish. Somebody had to have seen her somewhere." His employer drew in a ragged breath.

"Are you okay?" He readied himself in case the man passed out.

Kenneth raised his head, his cheeks stained red. "What are you doing just sitting there? Get on with it!"

Charles left the room. *Of course he's okay, idiot. Only the good die young.* He shook his head. *It's Jenna who needs you now.* He'd already talked to the chief earlier that morning and sent in a recent photo of Jenna. A search of her credit cards only revealed they hadn't been used in over a week.

He gazed out the window at the falling snow covering the meticulously manicured grounds of the estate in a blanket of white. It hadn't stopped accumulating over the past couple of days.

A knot tightened in his stomach. *The Jag certainly isn't the best car to be driving in this mess.*

Charles ran a hand over his smooth head. *Come on Jenna, pick up the phone and call like you promised me.*

Radiating warmth told she no longer lay beneath the snow.

Jenna blinked rapidly until her eyes adjusted to the dim light. She tentatively wiggled her toes and exhaled shakily. Her eyes burned as they welled up with tears of relief.

I'm alive...but where am I?

The second she tried to shift her weight, searing pain shot through her body like a bolt of lightning. She gently laid her head back onto a soft, puffy pillow and remained perfectly still until the pain faded to a dull roar. It took a few minutes to realize her hand was confined somehow. The back of her head throbbed from under some kind of band pulled taut around her head, and her ribs felt like someone used her as a punching bag.

She appeared to be alone, but a crackling fire made it clear someone lived here.

Jenna didn't sense any danger, but had no idea where she was. Out the window, snow, white and pure, floated down from a light, cloud-filled sky.

Something so beautiful almost buried me alive.

From where she lie, she saw a small kitchen and two doors slightly ajar. The creak of a door opening set her pulse zipping. She took a deep, steadying breath and closed her eyes.

"Come on you two, get in here. You're letting all the heat out. Do you want to sleep in the barn tonight?" A man's voice accompanied a bevy of clips and clicks on a wood floor.

Jenna dared to open her eyes a sliver and found two beautiful dogs, one with a silver and white coat, and the other black and white. Both danced at the feet of their master. They looked like those Husky sled dogs she'd seen in movies.

The man disappeared from her line of sight. She strained to decipher the sounds of a zipper, followed by the rustle of clothing and a thump like something hit the floor. *Probably his coat and boots.* She focused on keeping her breath slow and even, not exactly sure why she feigned still being out of it; she didn't get a bad vibe like he was a serial killer or worse. It was more apprehension about dealing with a stranger.

A dark shadow blocked the light over her eyelids. She wanted to take another peek, but didn't dare, sensing he was very close.

Is he looking down on me?

Her blood pumped so loud in her ears, she feared he'd hear it.

Suddenly, a cool hand touched her warm forehead. Jenna pressed her lips firmly together to stifle the gasp rising up in her. Fingers, still cold from being outside, pressed against the pulse at her wrist. Then her hair was smoothed back from her face—a touch so gentle it caught her off guard, and drew a moan under her breath.

"Hey, little lady, can you hear me?" His warm breath whispered across her face. "You have nothing to be afraid of. I'm here to help you."

The man remained close to her in silence for several minutes. Cool air brought bumps to her skin as the man heaved a sigh and shuffled away from her side.

"Well, kids, I think I'll make a nice pot of chicken soup for when our guest wakes up. She'll probably be mighty hungry after being out of it for so long."

* * * *

Sasha's head shot up and her ears twitched. She stood and padded over to the couch where their guest lay, and licked her face.

Jack lunged forward to grab the collar. "Sasha, get out of there."

The woman sneezed, and cried out in pain. Her head lifted off the pillow and fell back down. Jack hurried to her side to find a trail of tears slipping into her hairline. She stared at him with green, fear-filled eyes.

He searched her face for any sign of being in pain. "Do you remember anything? What's your name?"

She nodded slightly, and her lips parted. "Jenna...Jenna Blackburn." A tremor laced her voice.

"My name is Jack Davis. Are you in much pain?"

"Yes," she whispered hoarsely. "Where am I?"

"You're safe. Let me get you something for the pain. We'll have plenty of time to talk when you're up to it."

He opened the first aid case beside the couch.

"Are you allergic to anything?"

She closed her eyes and mouthed the word no.

He filled an eyedropper with pain medication. "Okay, Jenna, I'm going to lift your head a little so this medicine can slide down your throat. It's probably going to hurt." He slipped his hand between the back of her head and the couch. "Ready?"

"Yes," she whispered.

Jack carefully lifted her head, hating to be the reason behind her pain-filled eyes and creased forehead, marring her otherwise flawless skin. Her lips parted, and he gently laid the dropper on her tongue, squeezing the liquid into her mouth. She swallowed easily, and he slowly set her head back down.

The corners of her mouth lifted slightly. "Thank you."

Within seconds, her eyelids started to droop.

"The medicine will make you sleepy. You don't have to worry about a thing." He smiled down at her as her facial muscles relax and her eyes close.

Chapter Four

Jenna opened her eyes to darkness, except for the low flame burning in the fireplace. She'd dreamed about being buried in the snow...white snow turning red. She shuddered. It wasn't *just* a dream.

The doors were closed, and only one of the dogs snored softly next to the hearth. If memory served her correctly, she owed its master her life.

How did he find me buried under the snow?

The horror of crashing through the guardrail flashed in her mind. There hadn't been anything she could do to stop her car from dropping over the side of the mountain.

Jenna drew in a ragged breath and blinked back the tears.

I truly thought I was going to die.

She shivered. A picture of her father and Charles replaced the horrific accident that would surely haunt her dreams for quite some time to come. She remembered the party, her father announcing Harold Meed had asked for her hand in marriage—and he'd given his blessing.

Her stomach churned at the thought of being married to such a man. Not only was he much older, he was a drunk—a drunk who didn't know how to keep his hands to himself. *Maybe if my father knew the ogre has been obsessed with me for quite some time...*

It serves dear ol' Dad right if he's worried about me, but Charles...and Edna. Both were her saviors for as far back as she could remember. One, or sometimes both, often stepped in, sparing her from yet another argument with her father. Since her mother's death five years ago, Kenneth Blackburn the Third had changed into an angry, bitter little man who seemed to take great pleasure in dictating her life. His mission since she'd turned twenty was to marry her off. *Oh how I miss the man he once was... the father, he once was...*

How long have I been here? The urge to pee became a nuisance. *How did I go pee before now?* She shivered. *Maybe I don't want to know the answer to that one, or how I ended up wearing these oversized pajamas and thick wool socks.*

The distance between the sofa and where she believed the bathroom to be didn't seem too far away. *Maybe if I take it slow...*

Jenna braced for the pain as she lifted her head. It definitely hurt, but not even remotely close to the excruciating pain from her first attempt. Even so, there wasn't an inch of her body that didn't cry out in protest as she moved her legs to the side of the sofa and let them fall over the edge. "Erg!"

She held her breath. The dog by the fire lifted its head and looked directly at her.

Shit.

The need to pee increased tenfold. "Go back to sleep, boy," she whispered hoarsely and brought her body up to a sitting position. She remained perfectly still until the room stopped spinning. When it did, she noticed the dog was now at her side, licking her hand.

At least he's not trying to eat me. Or is he deciding if I taste good?

Once she was convinced the dog liked her, she planned her next move. *If I can get around to the back of that big chair, I can hang onto it.* After that it would be only a few feet to the one open door.

Jenna took a deep breath and, using the arm of the couch, pushed herself upright. A burst of fire ignited from under the bandages that covered her two fingers. She breathed deeply for a moment until the pain ebbed a bit. Sweat dripped from her brow. All she'd managed to do was stand up, and it felt like she'd run a marathon.

A bark shattered the silence.

"Hush! Good boy, come here." She tried to coax him to her, but he was having no part of it, and continued to bark relentlessly.

The second door flew open, startling her backwards. The rigid jarring knocked the breath from her, and she cried out as her body collapsed over the arm of the couch, searing pain blazed throughout her. Her legs now hung over the side and her back on the cushions, akin to the position she had to get in at the gynecologist—only now there was no cold, metal foot stirrup or red-faced doctor, only intense pain and her own face growing warm at being caught in such a predicament.

"What do you think you're doing?"

The man, Jack, hurried to her side and helped her—painfully—to a sitting position. She noticed he wore only jeans, not even the belt done up, bare chest and feet and sandy blond hair disheveled from sleep.

Her bottom lip trembled; she hated the weakness at not being able to stop the tears from falling. She'd cried more in the past few days than she had in years.

The fire's light played on his perfectly sculpted chest and washboard stomach. Jenna feigned interest in something on her pajama bottoms, suddenly very aware of how close he was to her. He lifted her chin with a finger —entranced, she had no choice but to look into his baby blues.

"Listen, you're recovering from a very serious accident. If you fall, you could do some damage to your already fragile physical state. I'm here to help you."

"I was trying to...er...I just needed to..." She nodded in the direction of the doors.

He chuckled, further intensifying her embarrassment.

"I'm glad one of us finds this amusing." She lowered her lashes, now thoroughly mortified.

"Come on, I'll give you a hand to the bathroom. Let's take it slow." He helped her to stand and tucked her arm around the crook of his. With every step her muscles were forced to take, darts of pain shot off like firecrackers. Finally, they reached the destination, and he took her inside the small room.

"Do you think you can manage on your own now?"

Truth be known, she was weak as a babe, but if she had any hope of salvaging even a thread of dignity, his help had to stop at the door.

"I think so," she said, though she still couldn't look him in the eye.

"Okay, I'll be right outside here if you need me." He bowed and closed the door.

Pulling down her bottoms proved to be a monumental task; she still had on the same panties she wore the day she left the house.

Jenna carefully sat and relieved herself.

"Jack? Where exactly am I."

"Well, the nearest city is Grand Marais, Minnesota." He paused. "I guess you could say my cabin is a little, isolated."

Isolated? That's on odd choice of words.

"So it's safe to say you're not some mentally deranged recluse who is going to chop me up to feed to your dogs?"

His laughter made her smile.

"Seriously." He laughed some more. "If I was some nut job, do you really think I'd tell you first?"

Her laughter came to a full stop as she grit her teeth against the hurting as she kicked her legs through the pajama bottoms, leaving her lacy thong to hang from her foot.

Now what the hell do I do?

She couldn't reach down; she couldn't stand up. Like it or not, she needed help.

Tired, and more than a little frustrated, she pulled her top down to cover her privates and begrudgingly called, "Okay, you win."

Jack peeked through a crack in the door. "Are you okay?"

Her shoulders sagged. "I need your help." She tried to be strong, but simply didn't have any strength left.

He probably thinks I'm a great big wimp.

The door opened and he seemed to access the situation while stroking his jaw. "What exactly are you trying to do?"

"I wanted to rinse out my...my panties." Her cheeks heated.

"I see. I'm sorry, but I don't think mine will fit you."

She looked up to find a grin spread across his rugged face, his eyes sparkling in amusement.

Her lip trembled. Never had she been so physically and emotionally defeated. "Can you please just help me?"

His expression changed to one of concern. "I'm sorry." He stooped over, took the thong off of her foot, and set it in the sink before guiding her feet back into the pajama bottoms and pulling them up to rest on her knees. "There, will you be okay now to...um, rinse them out?" He rolled his eyes as his cheeks stained pink.

Having the tables turned, even for a moment,

broke the tension, and she smirked. "Yes, thank you."

Jack backed out of the bathroom and closed the door. His act of kindness touched her heart. A man in tune to a woman's needs was a rare breed indeed. Most men wouldn't even think to let her finish what she had started on her own.

Thankfully, she could reach the sink and turn on the water from her position on the toilet. After wetting a bar of soap, she set about trying to wash her thong without getting her bandages wet. Not that there was much fabric to wash. After rinsing them out, she laid them over the side of the sink to dry.

The warm water running over her hands reminded her that her panties weren't the only thing not washed in quite some time. She could feel where the blood had dried and caked around the back of her neck. Night sweats had left behind an odor she could seriously live without.

Moving carefully, she gradually pulled up her bottoms as she straightened. She stepped back enough to open the door.

Jack stood to one side with his arms folded across his bare chest. He simply smiled and offered his arm, of which she gratefully accepted.

The couch seemed a mile away. By the time her head hit the pillow, and he'd helped her under a blanket, she was worn right out and unable to stop her eyes filling with moisture.

"What's wrong, Jenna?"

The genuine concern in his expressive blue eyes moved her. She sighed wearily. "I really wanted to wash up, but I just didn't have the strength to do it."

He fell silent for a second before his eyes lit up. "I can bring you some warm water and soap, a towel maybe, and you can wash up right here. Would you like to try?"

Embarrassed at needing assistance for such a simple yet personal matter, she avoided eye contact. "If you'll help me, yes."

"Of course I will. I'll be right back."

Jack eyed his patient one more time, then quickly returned to the bathroom, filled up a basin and opened a fresh bar of soap. He grabbed a clean towel and carried it out to her. "So, how do we go about this?"

"If you could help me to sit up and wash this dry blood away, I'd feel much better."

I'm such an idiot...of course the crusted blood would be uncomfortable to say the least. "I'm so sorry. When I brought you home, my main concern was to bandage you up and keep you warm."

He gently helped her to sit, and propped a couple of pillows behind her back. When she unbuttoned the pajama top, he turned his head, not wanting to add to her discomfort.

Jenna tapped his shoulder. "Don't worry. I'm not going to get all naked." Her laughter was cut short by a big yawn. "Oh my, as you can see, I'm beyond tired, so sex is out of the question."

Her silliness eased his tension, but did little to stop the heat warming his cheeks. She sat with his pajama top pooled around her waist, her arms folded modestly across her pink lacy bra. The firelight played up her creamy skin, making it appear deliciously...edible.

He swallowed, hard, wishing she hadn't said the word sex, even in jest.

"Let me wash your back and neck first."

Jack welcomed the reprieve to rein in his wayward libido. He kneeled on the couch behind her, lathered the face cloth and brought it up to make circular moves up and down her back. He rinsed out the cloth with shaky hands, and then parted her hair to expose her neck, holding the warm cloth over the caked on blood for a second before gently washing it away. Her body shivered under his touch.

A desire he thought never to be ignited again sparked.

Easy does it big guy. Now is definitely *not the time.*

In his mind, he knew this, but the increasing tightness behind the zipper of his pants told just how attracted he was to this woman.

Then she purred.

"I can't begin to tell you how good this feels."

Ditto. "I'm glad." He smiled; surprised at the degree of pleasure her reaction brought him. "I'm going to go change this water for you."

He picked up the plastic tub and left without waiting for a response. In the bathroom, he dumped the dirty water down the toilet and went about re-filling the basin with warm water. He opened the hand-made wooden cabinet and frowned at his reflection in a mirror affixed to the back of the door.

Blushing? How old are you, for God's sake? You'd think you never saw a pretty girl before. Though, it had been a very long time since ....

He splashed water in his face and patted it dry with a housecoat hung on the back of the door, then filled his lungs and blew the air out slowly. "Grow up," he scolded his reflection.

Jack returned and set the container down within her reach, handing her a fresh face cloth. "I'll leave you to take care of the...er...front," he stammered.

Her slight giggle drew him to her emerald green eyes. The instant her gaze met his, she quickly turned away. It brought him a certain degree of satisfaction in knowing she appeared to be as uncomfortable with the situation as he.

"I'll be in my room. Give me a shout when you're done."

She flashed him the slightest of smiles before picking up the facecloth and swishing it around in the water with a soft, "Thank you."

Jack took long strides to his bedroom and shut the door behind him. He flopped back on his bed and closed his eyes, breathing in and out, nice and slow until he regained some semblance of composure.

The poor woman was buried alive in snow, Casanova. Get hold of yourself.

He rolled to his side, and his gaze settled on the silver frame on his bedside table. A rush of guilt curbed his desire, and he quickly rolled back to stare at the ceiling.

I have no reason to feel guilty...or do I? She's a virtual stranger...how can I be so attracted to her?

Perhaps she'd feel up to a bowl of soup, offering him the chance to know his mystery lady a little better...

"Jack? You can come back now."

He jumped off his bed and paused for a second before opening the door. Jenna lay back on her pillows with her eyes closed. As quietly as possible, he took the basin and things away.

Her eyelids fluttered open upon his return, and he smiled. Not realizing how disappointed he'd been to find her asleep until her eyes opened.

"Do you feel better now?"

She nodded.

Jack scanned her face. "Do you want something for the pain?"

"Not right now, it puts me to sleep."

"How about some soup first. Maybe after, we can try and figure out what to do about taking you to see a doctor and getting hold of your family."

Her belly growled a response.

"I'll take that as a yes." He smiled.

Mere minutes later, Jenna sipped at the soup from the side of her spoon, all ladylike. Her eyebrows arched ever so slightly. Then proper etiquette went out the window as she dug in like she hadn't eaten for days.

Most probably because she hasn't.

It pleased him to see her attack his mom's recipe with such relish.

She dropped the spoon in the empty bowl and wiped her mouth with a napkin.

Jack took the dish from her. "Do you want some more? I have lots." He pointed to the big pot on the stove. "My mom used to say it's better than any medicine a doctor can prescribe."

"Your mother was a very smart lady. Maybe I'll have some more a little later—a cup of tea would be lovely, that is if you don't mind." She settled back on her pillow, smiling sweetly.

As if I could deny you anything when you smile at me like that. "Of course, I'll put the kettle on for you."

"Thank you."

Jack took the dishes to the kitchen and filled the kettle, setting it on the stove to boil while he went about finding a tea pot he'd never used. He blew the dust off of a fancy tin filled with teabags—given him by the ladies at the post office shortly after he moved in.

Jenna's eyes opened upon his return.

"I'm sorry, were you sleeping? We can always do this later if you'd like?"

"No, don't be silly. I was just resting." She pulled herself up to sit with her back against the arm of the couch.

Jack set the tray down and took the pillow wedged under her backside, plumping it up for her to lean against. "How's that?"

She reached up and cupped the side of his face. "My knight in shining armor, how will I ever repay your kindness?"

Her tender touch moved him and he swallowed hard. "You just worry about healing. I'm sure anyone would have done the same for a damsel in distress."

"I doubt..."

His finger against her lip stopped her in mid sentence. "Please, you've already thanked me." He took her hand from his face and quickly turned away, busying himself with their tea. "Sugar and milk?"

She nodded. "Yes, please."

Thankfully she indulged his unspoken desire to change the subject.

"I should warn you, I have no idea what kind of tea this is." He looked over the rim of his steaming mug.

"Seriously? You save my life and now you would have me drink something that could potentially kill me?"

Jack took a drink and set the cup down on the coffee table. "Wait five minutes. If I keel over and am rendered unconscious...don't drink yours."

Jenna laughed and immediately reached for her side, her face contorted in pain. "Ouch! Don't make me laugh."

He grinned sheepishly. "I'm sorry."

She waited a few seconds before picking up her drink and tentatively sipping from the side of her mug, and closed her eyes. "Mm, mm, good. My guess is, Earl Gray."

The room fell silent, aside for the crackling fire as

she appeared to enjoy the tea.

"So, what do you do for excitement out here in the boonies?" Jenna put her cup down and settled back against her pillow. "I mean, don't you ever get bored?"

"Actually I don't. I have an extensive collection of books in my room, and of course, these two are great company."

The dog's ears twitched as they raised their heads, looking back and forth between them.

She chuckled. "I think they actually know you're talking about them."

Jack shrugged. "I guess since we're in each other's company pretty much 24/7 we've grown in tune to each other." He rubbed the tops of both dogs' heads in turn while their tails thumped against the hardwood.

"Impressive." Jenna shifted and cringed at the pain shooting up her arm from putting weight on her hand.

Jack kneeled beside her. "Are you okay? Can I get you something more for pain?" He pushed back a few wayward curls from her face.

The gesture sent chills up her spine. She shook her head, and shivered.

"Are you cold?" He made a move to stand and she grabbed his hand.

"No, I'm fine, really," she replied, stifling a yawn.

"Maybe you should close your eyes and rest."

She held his face in her hands and gazed deeply into his expressive blue eyes. "Thank you for saving my life." Completely on impulse she kissed him. A sweet kiss, of which she would've gladly continued if encouraged. His sudden silence made her uncomfortable and she pulled away. "Oh God, I'm so sorry. I don't know what came over me."

Jack kept his head lowered. She wanted to be anyplace else but here. Utterly humiliated by her forward advance, she blinked back the threat of tears.

His hand touched her arm, and she found him staring her in the eyes with such intense emotion it robbed her of breath.

"Please don't be sorry. I've wanted to do that since you opened your eyes." He moved to his knees and gathered her in his arms. "Let's take things slowly. You still have a ways to go in your recovery. Your health comes first." He pulled away and put a finger under her chin, tilting her face up so she'd look at him. "If you ever feel the need to kiss me again, I won't stand in your way."

Her cheeks grew warm, and she inwardly cursed the color of red she knew her face must be. "Thank you. You really are a special man. I'm not glad I went over the side of the mountain, but I am more than glad to have met you."

Jack pressed his warm lips to her forehead, lingering longer than she expected.

"I'm going to get you a couple of pain pills. I want you to try and have a sleep." He eased her back against the pillow and smiled. "I'll be right back."

Jack hurried to the kitchen area, welcoming the timely diversion to compose himself against the unexpected thrill in knowing the attraction was mutual. He reached for a pill bottle on a shelf above the stove when his hand knocked over Jenna's book he'd set up there to dry.

Shit! I forgot all about this.

He shook out two painkillers from the bottle and then took down the journal.

"Hey, Jenna, I forgot to tell you..." He crouched to pass her the book. "This was under you in the snow."

Her head popped up off the pillow, and as her eyes sprung open, she clenched her chest. She took the leather bound journal from him with shaky hands.

He didn't begin to understand the depth of emotion welling up in her eyes as she turned the book over in her hands.

"I'm sorry. I completely forgot with all that was going on. I take it's important to you?"

Jenna let out a breathy shudder. "Words aren't enough to thank you for this."

Jack passed her the pills and glass of water. "Here, take these first."

Despite how curious he was about the origins of the book, he had startled her awake and sensed her need for privacy to look inside. He rubbed his hands on his thighs and stood. "I have to tend to the dogs. Can I get you anything before I head out?"

She pressed the book to her chest. "Thank you. You've given me exactly what I need right here."

He swallowed hard; the intensity of the moment had him fighting the threat of tears. *Keep it together, big guy. The last thing she needs is a blubbering fool sprawled out on the floor beside her.* He coughed into his hand. "I shouldn't be too terribly long. Promise me you won't try to wander around on your own."

She quickly diverted her gaze; the corner of her mouth twitched with what appeared to be the makings of a smile.

"Promise me, Jenna. I'm not leaving until you do."

Her eyelashes fluttered as the slightest of smiles curved her lips. "I promise."

Chapter Five

Only after she heard the door close behind him did Jenna let loose the myriad of emotions welling up inside of her. She wiped her tears on the corner of the blanket covering her before taking a look at her mother's diary.

The outer leather casing was badly stained. On closer inspection, she realized it was by her own blood. Her stomach lurched as she opened the book to find more of the same. Almost every page was stained so bad it left the writing illegible.

It broke her heart to think her mother's innermost feelings were lost forever. She clung to hope the remaining entries would shed some light on their content.

The date on the first page was smudged so bad she couldn't make it out. Her eyes grew heavy as she scanned the first entry. She tilted the book toward the light from the fire, and her finger followed the lines of a short, barely legible passage.

It finally happened today. I've been counting the weeks to feel the first flutters of her in my tummy. It was like the whole world stopped moving and all that was left, me with my Angel. I was almost asleep again when I felt a tiny little tap, tap, tap from inside. It was as if she was saying hello for the first time, letting me know she was really there.

Not long after the tapping subsided, I was roused from sleep, only to learn I am very ticklish on the inside too, I couldn't help but burst out laughing, not able to control the tickling feeling any longer. Needless to say, not much sleep happened for the rest of the night. I didn't want to miss a second of her first movements inside of me. It didn't matter how she was conceived as much as her being my living, breathing baby ... my little girl.

The page ended there, the following entries completely wiped out. Most were stuck together as if bound by cement, but she found a legible short entry near the end...

I'm so excited to be going on a real date. I know at my age I should've been on at least a few before now, but life seems to be playing out of order for me. I can hardly call my time with him so long ago a real date.

Should I tell him my secret right away? No, I don't want to scare him away. This man is so different. He's such a gentleman...K.

That was it, nothing else was readable. She'd never been more confused than she was in that moment. *Was her little girl the secret? Who is K?* There were many pages between the first entry and this short snippet. It didn't add up. *Who was she dating after she had me?* What about my fa... Her mouth went dry. *Could the K be Kenneth? Did my mother have me before she married him? Does it mean he's not really my father—a welcome possibility given his behavior of late.*

She read the entries over and over again, only managing to further confuse herself. Her head buzzed from the pain pills.

"Jenna?"

"Oh!" She bolted upright, a burst of fire raged through her skull. "Ow!" The diary fell to her lap as one hand flew to her head while the other to her chest. Her heart raced beneath her fingers.

Jack knelt beside her. "God Jenna, I didn't mean to scare you. Didn't you hear me come in?"

Sasha and Tito pressed their cold, damp snouts against her arm.

"Hey you two, go lie down." Jack snapped his fingers and both dogs obeyed with their heads bowed.

"It's okay. They're fine. I must have zoned out for a bit."

"I thought you were going to have a heart attack right here and now." His gaze moved to the book clutched against her chest. "Did you read something upsetting?"

"Most of it is ruined." Her bottom lip quivered. "What I could make out left me a little confused, is all."

He arched a brow. "Are you sure that's all it is?"

"Yes, I'm sure."

"I'm going to let it go, but for the record..." He wiped a tear from her cheek with the pad of his thumb. "You're a terrible liar."

Jenna's breath hitched and her eyes widened at his statement.

"How about another cup of hot tea?" He got up from his knees and looked down at her. "Then we can talk more."

Jack caught the roll of her eyes as he turned toward the kitchen, not to mention the quick disposal of the journal under her pillow. It was pretty obvious she didn't want to talk about what was on the badly stained pages.

He put the water on to boil and put tea bags in two clean mugs before he turned his attention back to his patient. "So, tell me, Jenna. What exactly were you doing on that road to begin with?" He walked over and sat in the armchair across from her to put more wood on the fire.

She lowered her lashes. "I was trying to get to the ski resort. I guess I got a little lost."

Jack chuckled as he brushed the shavings from his hands and eased back in the chair. "I'd say you got a lot more than a *little* lost."

Her cheeks flushed.

"Your family must be going crazy wondering where you are, especially with Christmas just around the corner."

Jenna feigned interest in the crackling fire. "I doubt it. My mom passed a few years back, and my dad is busy chasing women who are far too young for him, and orchestrating the rest of my life." She shrugged. "Charles and Edna and my best friend Buffy...are probably the only ones concerned about my absence."

"What about a boyfriend, husband maybe?" He hoped he didn't sound like he was fishing for info because he was interested–even though that was the absolute truth of the matter. He'd be a fool to fall for a girl like Jenna. There was no denying the attraction between them, the kiss validated his hope the feeling was mutual. The fact remained, she definitely wasn't the type to want to spend the rest of her days here, and he had zero desire to rejoin the moneyed society of the elite as the diamonds in her ears attested to.

She cocked her head sideways. "Are you trying to get rid of me?"

The shrill whistle of the kettle interrupted them. He continued the conversation as he poured water into the mugs. "Of course not, that's not what I meant. I just thought someone like you would have the SWAT team out looking for her."

She arched a brow. "What do you mean *someone like me*?"

"Forget I said that. I just have to wonder what you were doing headed to a ski lodge this close to Christmas, and at that time of night."

Jenna sighed resignedly. "Are you sure you want to know?"

He shrugged. "Only if you want to tell me."

She wrapped her hands around the mug he gave

her, sipping at it tentatively while he was seated.

"Where should I start?" She eyed him curiously.

"How about the beginning?"

Jack sat quietly while she told him about an estate and an ogre of a father who arranged a marriage for her to the town drunk, who just happened to be much older and loaded. The union, she believed, must be part of some business transaction between the two men. Jenna went on to tell him how the diary was her mother's and she'd taken it from the *forbidden* sitting room before leaving the estate.

As he listened to her story, the floodgates opened. It was as if she gave herself permission to talk freely for the very first time, the accident stripping her of all her riches, awakening a beautiful, desirable woman.

Carly's passing taught me the biggest life lesson. Money can't buy everything. In fact, the most important things in life are free.

Jenna cleared her throat, waving a hand between them. "Hello? Jack?"

"Yes, oh, em... I'm sorry. From what you've told me, I don't blame you for wanting to get away from there. And I get why you're not in any hurry to go back. Will you be looking for another place to live once you're up to it?"

"I can't think that far ahead right now." She shrugged. "I kind of like it right here for the time being. That is, if it's okay with you...that I stay...just a little while longer."

Her words slurred, telling him the pain medication had kicked in. He got up and kneeled beside her, fussing with her blanket so it covered her properly. Acute pleasure in that she wanted to stay made it impossible to curb his desire. Jack leaned in and kissed her eyelids shut, pausing to emblazon the moment to his memory.

He pressed his cheek lightly against hers and whispered into her delicate ear, "I know my cabin is nothing like the grand estate you're accustomed to, but you're welcome to stay as long as you want to. I have to ask, why do you want to stay here when you have the world at your disposal?"

"I like being in your world." Her eyes remained closed. "Everything I want or need is right here, right now. Okay?"

Jack abruptly pulled away and folded the blanket up under her chin. "Okay." Yet, unable to resist, he lightly kissed her forehead.

He knew he was setting himself up for heartache, but whatever spell this beautiful creature thrust upon him had cast, made him powerless to resist her feminine airs.

What have you done to me?

Chapter Six

Garland swags draped down the grand staircase—the house abuzz with preparations for the annual Christmas Eve party. Charles shook his head in disgust. They hadn't heard from Jenna in almost a week, and her father carried on like there was nothing amiss.

At times, he felt like picking the man up by his scrawny little neck and giving his head a shake. The police had come up with nothing, not even activity on her credit cards. As far as he knew, she hadn't packed a bag. Surely by now, she'd need a change of clothes. The Jenna he knew and loved never wore the same outfit twice.

No, something isn't right.

Kenneth descended the stairs looking extremely pale, most probably brought on by too much drink the night before. Aside from his pasty complexion and atypically fragile disposition, nothing changed. He didn't have to open his mouth to still ooze arrogance.

"Good morning, sir." Charles shook his boss' limp hand. "We still haven't heard from Jenna. I'm getting pretty worried."

Kenneth clicked his tongue and waved his hand nonchalantly. "You worry too much. Jenna is a young girl. She probably decided to go on a shopping spree to spend all of my money because she's upset with me."

He frowned. "I don't think so. Like I already told you, she hasn't used any of her credit cards."

Jenna's father stopped and looked back over his shoulder. "Can't you see I have a lot going on? I pay you enough money, so I'm sure you're capable of tracking down a twenty-two year old having a tantrum."

It took everything in him to stop from lunging at the seedy excuse of a man. He obviously didn't give two shits about his own daughter. Maybe she *was* the only smart one with a good head on her shoulders. Maybe she found a way to leave all of this behind.

Please let that be the case.

Cool air swirled around his ankles as the front doors opened wide and workmen brought in a massive evergreen. They stood it up beside the staircase; the top almost reached the second floor.

"What is this?" Kenneth shouted, his hand flailing in the direction of the tree. His face turned red.

Pedro removed his toque and folded it in his hands. "It was the biggest one they had, sir."

"Bullshit!" He pointed a shaky finger in the Spanish worker's face. "If you want to keep your job, I advise you to pick up a chainsaw and find me a *Christmas* tree. Get this piece of crap out of here now!"

Without uttering a retort, the worker shouted orders in Spanish at his bewildered team. The men immediately sprung into action, taking the rejected tree back out the doors it came through only moments before.

Kenneth swayed in the entryway to the living room, briefly placing his hand on the ornate wood casing before throwing his hands in the air. "Idiots!"

Charles shook his head in disgust. *Asshole!*

A blood curdling scream had Jack jumping out of bed and flying into the living room.

"Let me out! Please God, let me out!" Jenna's hands thrashed about.

He ran to her side and brought her hands together, gathering her in his arms. "Hush, Jenna. It's just a bad dream." He smoothed down her hair and rocked gently back and forth as he whispered against her ear. "Easy now, it's over. You're safe...shhh."

She hiccupped and startled awake, gasping for air. "Oh my God, Jack, it was so real. The snow kept falling, burying me deeper and deeper. I couldn't breathe." She laid her head against his bare chest and released a windy breath.

Jack pressed his lips to the top of her head. This was the third night in a row she woke up screaming. His protective instincts were quickly growing for this woman. He held her close until her breathing slowed and her body relaxed. "Jenna? Are you okay now?"

She pulled away, looking disheveled and more than a little embarrassed. "I'm sorry. I don't know what came over me. You have to believe me, I'm not normally this...weak."

Her choice of words surprised him, and he gently persuaded her head to turn so he could gaze into her eyes. "I never once thought you were *weak*. It's been a little less than a week since you regained consciousness after your accident. I don't know of anyone who wouldn't have a few bad dreams after being through what you have."

"Why are you being so nice to me?" she asked in all seriousness.

Jack shrugged and eased her back, forcing a cool expression to hide the overabundance of emotions battling inside of him. "I'm sure anyone who pulled a woman out from under the snow would do the same."

She shook her head. "I don't think so. You're quite a guy, Jack."

He signaled under the table for Sasha and Tito, who had been standing back, now pushed their noses between them. Jack laughed to mask his ruse. "I think somebody is a little jealous. You have to forgive them.

They're not used to sharing me." *I'm not used to sharing me...*

Jenna buried her face in Sasha's soft coat. "They are beautiful dogs."

"They make beautiful puppies, too. In fact, if I'm right, there will be a few little paws prancing around early spring." He rubbed behind Tito's ears. "They're the ones that found you out there. I would never have known you were under the snow if it wasn't for them."

The firelight caught her tear-filled eyes as she pressed a kiss to both dog's snouts. "Thank you."

Jack's body responded to her tenderness, reminding him he sat next to her wearing just his boxers. He shifted to hide his growing *discomfort*, and coughed out the side of his mouth. "I guess I should put on some clothes."

Her hand touched his arm before he could stand. "Don't do so on my account."

His breath caught in his throat. *Did I hear her right?* He turned his head to find her grinning from ear to ear.

She pointed at him and laughed. "If only you could see your face right now."

Jack took a pillow and lightly smacked her. "Ha, ha, aren't we funny." He couldn't help but join in her laughter. "I'll just be two secs, and then I'll put on some coffee."

"Please, let me."

He cast a sideways glance. "Do you think you're up to it?"

Jenna threw her blanket aside. "If you'd give me a hand, I'd like to try. You've been waiting on me long enough."

He saw the determination in her face and nodded. "Don't try to stand on your own. I'll be right back."

Jenna smiled as she watched him retreat to the

bedroom. How wonderful it must be to live such a serene life. A welcome reprieve from the tension-filled days on the estate she called home.

She tugged at her bottom lip with her teeth. Charles must be going out of his mind with worry, but she couldn't bring herself to ask about contacting him. She wasn't anywhere near ready to forgive or go home...or leave Jack.

He hadn't moved quite fast enough to hide his *condition* a moment ago. He really was a fine specimen of a man. It brought a small, hesitant smile to her lips just knowing he found her desirable.

What brought a man like him to live a life alone? Did he suffer a loss, or maybe he was just tired of modern-day society? She glanced out the window to find the snow was still coming down hard. How long has it been snowing like this, did he say almost a week?

Jack returned fully dressed. It took a little maneuvering, but he managed to help her slowly make her way to the kitchen. She leaned heavily against the counter while he made his way back to replenish the fire.

"How long have you lived here?" she asked, fumbling with coffee cups—her splint being a royal pain in the ass.

Jack tossed a few last splinters of wood in the fire and brushed the sawdust from his hands. He reached her side just in time to grab a coffee mug before it rolled off the small kitchen table in front of the window. "Come sit. I'll take it from here."

Jenna didn't have the strength to argue. "You win." She was relieved not to have to ask for help, and admit she had no clue how to make coffee like he did. Her brave knight pulled a chair out for her, not leaving her side until she was seated comfortably at the table.

He went about preparing the coffee pot and putting it on the stove to brew. "I've been out here for almost five years, breeding those two. Their puppies are used as rescue dogs. Places like the Eagle Ridge ski resort you were trying to get to pay good money for purebred Siberian Huskies."

When the vintage percolator let out its final gurgles, he filled their mugs and put the coffee pot back on the stove.

"Don't you ever get lonely?"

He glanced out the window. "Not really. I have Sasha and Tito to keep me company, and once a year, four or five puppies for a few months. I apologize for not having a phone at your disposal. My two-way radio doesn't work so well when it's snowing this hard. Usually, if I feel the urge to have a conversation, I just hook up the sled and make a trip to town for supplies."

She sipped at her coffee.

"Do you think you're up to a trip to town to see a doctor? We can contact your family while we're there."

Jenna squelched the panic rising up in her. "I thought you said...I mean, didn't you say I could stay for as long as I needed to?" She huffed. "There's something about this place...I haven't felt this at ease in a very long time—you see, everything changed after my mother passed, and not in a good way. I'm not sure if you understand what I'm trying to say."

"I understand better than you know." His gaze drifted out the window. "Of course you're welcome to stay."

"Thank you."

An amiable silence fell between them. His smiled faded, though, as he slumped a shoulder against the window pane.

I hope nothing I said is to blame for the sudden sadness in his demeanor. She opted not to ask him for fear she'd only make things worse.

Jenna tried to scratch her itching palm beneath the splint on her hand. "How long do I have to wear this get up? I'd love to have a shower?" She looked around the cabin. "I noticed a shower in the bathroom, does it work?"

Jack chuckled, flashing a dimple she hadn't noticed until now.

"Yes, it works."

"I didn't really take a good look at it. I guess I was too busy trying not to fall off the toilet." She laughed, pleased to see his mood shift.

"You'll have to wait until I kick in the generator that heats the water. It takes about twenty minutes." He pushed away from the table. "I'll go turn it on, and then we can take a look at your hand, and your head while we're at it."

Jenna smiled her thanks, her gaze following him from the room. Just then, she realized she hadn't once looked, or thought about looking in a mirror. *How can that be? I'm still the same girl who never goes anywhere without make-up...or am I?*

She held out her hand to inspect her nails. They were definitely in need of a little TLC, but for whatever reason, it didn't bother her. Having such a close brush with death had her reassessing her life and what was most important.

Jack came out of the bathroom. "Give it half an hour and you'll be good to go. Unfortunately, I don't have an endless supply of hot water. You get a ten minute shower, *if* you're lucky."

"I'm sure it will feel amazing."

Jack picked up his case beside the couch and

brought it to the table. "How about laying your arm out so I can take a look?"

He worked quickly, with a gentle touch. Soon she felt air against the skin that had been wrapped up—her fingers were black and blue.

"Try and move them."

She did as asked and immediately sucked air through clenched teeth. She'd expected it to be painful, but...

"Hang in there with me...I need to feel how the breaks are healing."

Jenna nodded and pressed her lips firmly together, looking the other way.

"Your fingers seem to be healing nicely. I think we can ditch the splint and just tape these three together." He mindfully cleaned the glue from the bandages and applied medicated salve of some type, then held the three fingers together—his brow wrinkled as his gaze shifted from her fingers to his medical supplies and then to her face. "Hold your fingers together for me. Not too hard now..."

It surprised her to see her hand shaking as she complied. It wasn't because of the pain, or being unsettled about her injuries. Having him this close, his touch so gentle...

Suddenly Jack's face came into view; a look of amusement lifted the corners of his far too sexy mouth. She'd obviously been lost in her own thoughts.

How long has he been waiting for me to zone back in?

She quickly dropped her head and once again cursed the heat rushing to her face. "Oh my...I'm sorry."

He didn't tease her like she expected him to, and went about taping her fingers together before covering them in plastic for the shower.

Jenna turned her hand over and back in between them. "I take it you've done this a time or two? I hardly felt a thing."

He sat back in his chair and sipped at his coffee. "Actually, I'm winging it. Other than putting a bandage on me a time or two, you're officially my first patient."

"I'm impressed." She looked up to find him gazing into her eyes, not at his handiwork. Her pulse quickened and she feigned interest in something out the window. She'd have to be dead not to feel some serious chemistry between the two of them. The realization made her happy and scared shitless in the same moment.

"I'm sorry but I can't promise removing the bandages on your scalp won't be painful."

She squeezed her eyes shut. "I'm ready."

He chuckled. "It's not going to hurt less with your eyes closed."

Cut it out! How old are you, twelve? She cussed the tell-tale warmth to her face returning.

"Ow!" His pulling on the bandages tugged on her matted hair and sent a sharp pain through her skull and down her neck.

"I'm sorry. The worst is over for now." He cut a circular shape out of a bigger bandage to cover the head-wound. "You need to be real careful when you wash your hair. I'm not sure if this will hold or not, but if you get any soap on this you're going to know it. Go ahead and take the tensor bandage off from around your rib cage. It will probably be tender, so be careful not to bump into anything or bend over too quickly."

Jenna grabbed hold of the back of the chair and stood on her own. "What about these?" She pulled at the flannel shirt. "How long have I been wearing this?"

"A week...no, more like five, maybe six days?" He pondered, and raised a finger. "I think I have another pair still in the package. I'll be right back."

Six days? She did the math in her head. *Is tonight Christmas Eve?*

Jack returned with pajamas the same as she had on, only blue. "I know they're not what you're used to, but they'll keep you warm."

"They're perfect." She smiled and took them from him. "I just realized its Christmas time. Maybe Santa will bring me a flannel nightgown."

Her legs started to wobble and she tried to sit back down without raising any suspicions of not being as strong as she wanted him to believe.

"I'm afraid Santa doesn't stop out here," he said matter-of-factly, and picked up his empty coffee cup. "Do you want a refill while the tank heats up?"

"Sure." Jenna set the pajamas on her lap. "So, what do you do for Christmas? Do you have family nearby to spend the holidays with?"

Jack set a fresh coffee in front of her. "No, no family. Christmas is just another day around here." He shrugged. "What about you? Are you sure you don't want to be home for the big day?"

She laughed. "Very sure. I can't believe I don't care about what's under the tree. It's like I'm two people—Jenna before the accident and Jenna after the accident." The near death experience had apparently changed her list of priorities. Material possessions now placed real low on the scale, and just being alive and breathing came first.

"Well, I didn't know the old Jenna, but the new Jenna is pretty cool."

He quickly turned away, but not fast enough to hide his visibly flushed face at being just as surprised by the compliment as she was.

"Water should be hot. I, um, need to take the dogs out. I won't be long if you need help with anything."

"Thanks." She got up, fully intent on making it to the bathroom on her own. After one painful step without any support it became crystal clear it wasn't an option.

Without making a big production of it, her knight came to her aid, yet again. He put her arm through his and set off toward the bathroom.

"Don't forget, ten minutes. You might want to wash your hair first." He gave her a subtle wink before opening the door and, waiting a few seconds after she stepped inside, closed it behind her.

A cool draft wafted up from under the bathroom door, followed by the sound of the outside door closing. Clean towels, a bar of soap, shampoo, toothpaste and toothbrush still in the package sat in a neat pile in the sink. There wasn't another surface he could have put them aside from the toilet.

Jenna undressed and carefully removed the bandage to reveal a bruised and very tender rib cage. She turned the water on for a couple of seconds before stepping into the warm stream.

Ahhhh, heavenly!

It was a far cry from the luxuries afforded her at home, but in the short time she'd been in the cabin, she'd discovered there was no price tag on how she was feeling right now. *Alive.*

True to Jack's words, she'd barely finished washing and rewashing her hair when the water ran cooler, and cooler...to cold. Her teeth chattered as she dried off as best she could in the cramped space and put the clean PJ's on.

Feeling reasonably human for the first time in days, she opened the door to ask Jack to help her to the sofa—she wasn't even going to try doing it herself. The shower not only washed away the caked on blood from her hair, but also stripped her of what little energy she had left.

"Jack?" Jenna frowned to find the cabin empty, no Jack, no dogs.

Oh great!

She took in her surroundings, lost as to how she could get from point A to point B without falling flat on her face.

What the...?

One of the chairs from the dinette set sat up against the wall directly beside her.

It wasn't there before...of course, Jack. Just when I think the guy can't get any better, he pulls a stunt like this.

She sniffled, failing to stop the few tears from falling. Exhaustion, coupled with his sweet acts of kindness, equaled no chance in hell of not being a crybaby.

Jenna inspected the chair. *Should I sit and wait or can I...?*

She grinned mischievously, knowing Jack would have a fit if he walked in on her. She gripped the outer rungs of the chair and straightened her body, until her slow-to-heal ribs made it painfully clear to stop.

It can't be more than six feet to the back of the sofa. I can do this.

Using a short shuffle-and-push step she made it to the couch. She eyed the seat of the chair longingly. *No, if I sit now, I'll never make it on my own.*

She summoned a fresh surge of energy...ignoring each muscle's cry out in revolt of the final steps. If she had an ounce of strength left, she would have done a victory dance having made it on her own. As it was, she dropped the second half of her descent to the couch and closed her eyes until the streak of pain the action took on her ribs subsided

Completely and utterly spent, the crackling fire captured her attention—mesmerized by red turned orange, she watched gold tips snap like the crack of a whip, sending sparks up the black metal pipe.

Jenna stared at the fire until her pulse returned to normal.

There's a fireplace in almost every room of the estate, and not one of them, even remotely makes me feel as warm or comforted.

She lifted her legs to stretch out on the sofa, tucking the blankets under them as best she could. The heat of the fire soon warmed her outstretched hands and chased the goose bumps from her freshly scrubbed skin. *It feels so good to be clean.* She splayed the fingers on her good hand and pushed them through her wet hair.

"Ouch!" It was going to take forever to work through her unruly, tangled curls. She huffed and leaned back against her pillows. The effort of taking a shower left her completely wiped out. *If I don't address the knots while it's wet I'll have a much bigger problem on my hands.*

Jenna slowly sat up again and repeated the process, only to snag another tangle.

"Ohh!" She dropped her hand and flopped back. "Ouch! Crap!" Her ribs were on fire, having pushed them to the limit.

A cool breeze ended her tirade, and she looked over the back of the sofa to find Jack grinning at her.

"Are you okay?" He chuckled.

"Just peachy, thanks for asking." *No, do not cry. You made it this far without tears.*

"Would you like to use my brush?" He took off his coat and boots and ducked into his bedroom, reappearing in seconds with the item in hand.

She saw that he took notice of the kitchen chair still sitting behind the couch, but he said nothing. No scolding, no smart-ass remark, no congrats on making it on her own. The sting of disappointment for not being praised for her accomplishment came unexpectedly.

More than a little embarrassed, Jenna gratefully took the brush from his hands, fumbling with a way to hold it with her fingers taped together.

Jack snatched the brush back from her.

"Hey, why'd you do that?"

He rounded the couch to stand beside her. "Scoot up a bit."

"What?"

"I'll brush your hair if you scoot up so I can sit behind you."

His offer left her without words. It would never have crossed her mind to ask for help with her hair from him, or any man for that matter.

He sat behind her and wedged a pillow between them for her to rest back against.

"Are you sure you can handle this? I've got a big mess going on up there."

"I think so."

His fingers brushed the back of her neck as he lifted her hair. She shivered.

"Are you cold? Should I put more wood on the fire?"

Warm breath against her skin made her tingle all over. "No, I-I'm fine," she murmured.

He lightly worked through her hair, not once pulling so it hurt. She closed her eyes, the motion, soothing. "Tell me something, Jack, did you ever like Christmas?"

He stopped mid-stroke. "Um, it's not that I don't

like Christmas, I just don't see the point in putting up decorations, or stuffing a turkey for just me and the dogs."

Jenna shrugged. "That's actually quite sad. I can't imagine not at least having a Christmas tree. There's something almost...magical about a decorated tree."

Her hair, silky as a newborn pup's slid through his fingers easily. Now tangle-free, he continued brushing it dry. "I guess I've never looked at it that way."

The scent of floral shampoo and body wash lingered in the cabin. Jack hadn't realized how much he'd missed the scent of a woman. She eased back closer and closer to him—her breathing grew slow and steady.

Sleeping?

He didn't have the heart to wake her, and if he was honest with himself, quite enjoyed having her close. Gently, he tugged the pillow out from between them and eased her back to rest against his chest. Once he rearranged the blanket to cover her, he folded his hands at her waist and closed his eyes.

She's the perfect fit...almost too perfect.

His feelings were growing for this woman, and if he was right, that worked both ways. She'd be going home soon. He was a fool to allow himself to fall in love, but he'd grown powerless to stop. Her presence stirred up memories he'd tucked away for quite some time now, the good parts—laughter, the joy in a simple conversation, self-worth that came from being appreciated, things he'd forgotten after Carly's death.

Maybe Jenna would break his heart, but at least he'd have times like this to look back on during those long lonely nights in his foreseeable future.

Jack pressed his cheek against the side of her head, committing the scent and feel of her hair against his skin to memory. But most of all...the warmth of her body next to his.

Chapter Seven

"A car went through the guardrail..."

It's Jenna.

The chief went on about road conditions, but Charles heard all he needed to hear. The tightness in his chest and the swell of emotions rising up in him made the conclusion, undeniable—Jenna, the girl he loved as if she were his own daughter, had been behind the wheel of the car that crashed through the guardrail.

"We haven't positively matched the paint and chrome. It might not be hers." Chief Swanson spoke from behind his cluttered desk.

"I hear you, Chief." He bowed his head. "I know it's her Jaguar. I don't expect you to understand, but when you find a piece of your heart missing..." The vintage wooden chair creaked under the weight of him shifting.

"Have faith, my friend. We should have some answers soon."

Just then, the door opened and an officer passed the chief an envelope. "The results are in."

He tore it open, and read the paper.

Silence...spoke loud and clear. Charles pressed his face in his hands and drew in a ragged breath. *I'm so sorry, Jenna. I should have tried harder to keep you from leaving.*

A firm hand on his shoulder kept his emotions in check. He shook his head and straightened in his chair. "So, what happens now?" Charles stood and walked to the window. "Send out a search team?" *Is there any chance you could be out there, kiddo?*

Chief Swanson shook his head. "Unfortunately, there's not much we can do right now." He slapped the results down on his desk. "If she did go over the side, I'd say the chances of her surviving are pretty slim, and even if she did, she's been out there in some pretty nasty weather, for days..."

Charles swallowed the lump in his throat. *I can't stand around here and do nothing.* "Let me at least see for myself."

"Okay. I can make that happen."

Should I phone her father?

No, not until he checked it out. Besides, Kenneth would just tell him to take care of things and call when there was something concrete to report.

Charles rushed out the door after the officer. Part of him wanted to know for sure, but the other half wanted to run the other way.

He stepped out of the precinct into a virtual Christmas Wonderland. The whole town was abuzz with preparations for the Christmas Eve celebrations later that night.

Jenna loves Christmas.

He looked up at the sky. *Please let it be a Merry Christmas.*

Jack had just tied down the tree to his sled when he caught movement from the corner of his eye. He took out his binoculars to find two police cars with lights flashing over the break in the guard rails. They'd find no sign of the Jag. It was completely buried under several feet of snow by now.

He tucked the binoculars away and quickly finished tying up the tree. He'd woken sometime later that afternoon with her still in his arms and, on a whim, managed to slip away without waking her. So focused on his surprise, he'd completely dismissed the fact Jenna had family. And whether she believed they cared or not, surely someone had to be praying she'd make it back for Christmas.

There has to be. No woman like her goes through life unloved.

Should I tell her? Am I selfish not to, at least until after Christmas Eve? She didn't seem to be too concerned it was Christmas; in fact, she'd asked to stay longer. He looked back up the mountainside to find one of the cars gone, but the two remaining men seemed to be deep in conversation, standing on the ridge overlooking the steep incline.

Even if they did match the paint to Jenna's car, they wouldn't be able to search with this much snow. He couldn't even ride the sled out there right now. They'd have to wait for some of it to melt. Nothing would be conclusive until at least after the holidays.

I'll have to play it by ear. For now, he hoped Jenna would be pleased with a Christmas tree—the first one he'd had in over five years.

The mouth-watering scent of bread baking reached him before he got to the cabin telling him she must have put the loaves he'd left to rise in the oven.

Once he let the dogs off their lead, he put them in the barn to wind down and be out of the way. His mouth went dry with the realization he was excited to see her reaction to the tree. He felt like a kid with a secret.

He shook the snow from the branches and opened the door. "I'm back. Look what I found?"

Jenna turned from setting two golden brown loaves on a wire rack; her eyes grew big. "A Christmas tree?" She took a couple of shaky steps, using the counter edge for leverage, and touched the boughs and sniffed the scent from her fingers. "It's beautiful."

You're beautiful.

Her peaches and cream skin had a fresh-scrubbed tint and her now dry hair shone from a good brushing, falling in ringlets to frame her sweet face.

Jack's elation quickly dissipated as unease clouded her otherwise vibrant green eyes. Not exactly the reaction he'd hoped for.

"I've been thinking, maybe I should at least make a phone call to let Charles know I'm okay."

His heart sank. It became painfully clear to him what he viewed as an intimate moment hadn't evoked in her the intense emotions he'd experienced.

I'm an idiot.

"Of course you'd want to be home for Christmas. I'll just take this back outside."

"No wait." She leaned heavily against the countertop. "Come sit with me for a second."

Jack's walls went up, brick by brick with every step he took toward her. Was it empathy or pity he saw in her eyes? Either way, he didn't want her to stay because she felt sorry for him. Though it had only been mere days, he'd been a fool to think that he alone would be enough for a woman like her.

"You don't have to say anything. The dogs need a short rest, and then I can take you to town. You could be home in time to spend Christmas Eve with your family."

She furrowed her brow. "Do you *want* me to leave?"

Jack quickly turned away, shrugging indifference as he grabbed the tree trunk. "I'll go check on the dogs. Why don't you get ready to go. You have fifteen to twenty minutes."

He hefted the evergreen up and pushed it back out the door.

Jenna's eyes filled as she lumbered to the table and sat in stunned silence. Her heart ached knowing her life-changing time with Jack had just come to a crashing end.

I don't want to leave here...to leave him. But he doesn't want me to stay. How could I be so wrong? Didn't we just share a special moment, even though he thought I was asleep? All she had wanted to do was call Charles so he could share the news with Edna, and Buffy, so they wouldn't be worried about her on Christmas.

Feeling lost and defeated, she looked around the room. "What does he expect me to wear?" She stopped and reined in her fragile emotions. *Get it together. If this is what he wants...so be it. I will not beg to stay.*

Jenna used the kitchen chair to go to the door and open it wide. "What am I supposed to wear?" she called out to Jack.

He glanced up from hooking the dogs. "Your things are in the closet in my bedroom." He avoided eye contact and turned back to what he was doing.

Jenna pressed her back up against the closed door. Thunder Bay might be in a different country, but not too far away in actuality. It would only take Charles a couple of hours to come pick her up...*and take me...home.* Her eyes burned, on the verge of tears. *I don't want to go home, and Jack doesn't want me here...*

Despite the frustration urging her forward, her body quickly reminded her she was exhausted and far from healed. As she paused outside his bedroom door to catch her breath, all of her hurt and pain turned to anger. She pushed open the door and stepped into his orderly bedroom. One wall was completely filled with neatly aligned books on floor to ceiling shelves.

A picture on his bedside table caught her eye. "Son of a..." She turned the frame around. Jack smiled at her, his arm draped around a pretty blonde with a winning smile.

Why didn't he tell me? Where is she?
It doesn't really matter now, does it?

She yanked open the closet door. Her clothes were in a neat pile on the top shelf with her coat hung on a hanger under them and her boots lined up on the floor. Other than a few light blood stains, it was obvious he'd cleaned them to the best of his ability.

Jenna shed his pajamas right there and awkwardly pulled on her clothes with her taped fingers. After a whole lot of cussing, she pulled up her jeans. Doing them up was another story. She fumbled with the button; tears of frustration and confusion spilled over her lashes. She gave up and pulled her sweatshirt down to cover it.

I'll be damned if I'm going to ask for his help.

By the time she put on her boots and coat and made it back into the living room, she was sweating like crazy, pausing to sit on the chair she'd been pushing around and slow her breathing. She reached down and grabbed the journal from under a couch cushion, stashing it in her coat pocket.

Maybe Charles can make sense of what I read.

The door opened a crack. "Are you ready in there? Let's go."

Jenna hardly recognized the stern voice. She wanted to storm out of the house, but her battered body thought otherwise, forcing her to slowly and painfully make her way to the door and outside. The distance to the sled might as well have been a mile. If she put one more foot in front of the other, she'd surely slip on the snow and ice.

Up until now Jack kept his back to her. He glanced back over his shoulder and shook his head before taking a few steps closer and offering his hand. Reluctantly she accepted, and leaned heavily against him the short distance to the sled. The realization this might be the last time she'd stand this close to him sent a searing pain in her heart, like someone had plunged a knife in her chest.

"You can sit here." He held out his arm for her to use for leverage.

Jenna purposely avoided looking at him, and summoned the last of her shattered resolve to lower herself to sit in the sled where he'd tied down a couple of bedrolls for a back rest.

"Wrap this around your legs, and cover your nose and mouth with this scarf." He tossed a pair of gloves and the scarf on top of the blanket before taking his place behind her. "Ready?"

"Um, hello?" She held up the items he'd given her. "Give me a second, will ya?"

Once outfitted and settled, she held up a shaky hand. "Ready."

Without a response, the sled lurched forward, taking her away from everything she'd grown to cherish... and love.

Chapter Eight

With a heavy heart, Charles got out of the car and sifted through the snow toward the diner. Any hope of Jenna surviving the fall had vanished as he peered down the mountain ridge. He rubbed his eyes and coughed into his hand as the chief's radio crackled and squawked behind him.

"Charles!" The chief honked his horn. "Forget the coffee and get back in the car. We found her!"

He hardly believed his ears as he dashed back to the car and jumped in the passenger side. "Where is she? Is she hurt?" he asked breathlessly.

"Some guy took her to Grand Marais. Apparently, she just tried to call you. One thing led to another, and the authorities there called the station looking for you."

"Thank God! What are the odds of something like this happening?"

"Santa Claus came early, my friend."

Yes, he most certainly did!

Jack originally planned on taking her to the cops he'd seen on the mountain brow, but he'd looked through his telescope while Jenna dressed to find they'd already left the scene. He decided on handing her over to the care of a couple of doting postal workers.

Though he prepared himself during the trip to town, actually leaving her proved far more difficult than imagined. A profound sense of loss shrouded him, comparable to the heartache of losing Carly. It took everything in him to give her a quick hug and leave the post office without actually looking at her face. Even seeing her in the window robbed him of breath, bringing him to his knees next to Sasha and Tito. It took some doing to get them to stop barking after Jenna and settle down. They'd grown *very* attached to her in such a short time. *He'd* grown *very* attached to her.

Jack closed his eyes and recalled the scent of her hair, the sound of her laughter...after losing Carly, he swore he'd never let another woman in his life...in his heart...and then came Jenna, buried under a mound of snow. He'd known as soon as he set eyes on her he was in trouble.

It hadn't been easy to act as if he wanted her to go, but it was for the best. She had a life before him, and he'd been a fool to think she wouldn't want to go home for Christmas.

Jack exhaled a long breath, cut short by a cop car screeching to a halt in front of the post office.

The officer and a big guy with a bald head rushed up the steps two at a time. Through the window, he saw the man lift Jenna in his arms. Her pain-filled cry out brought him to his feet. He stopped himself from rushing to her aid, and watched her arms go around him, her eyes closed as she rested her head against his broad chest.

Breathing into his gloves, Jack choked back a sob framed with jealousy and heartache. Without another moment's hesitation he positioned himself on the sled. "Let's go, Sasha, Tito. Let's go...home." His voice cracked as he passed the post office, leaving his beautiful snow angel behind.

* * * *

Charles sat open-mouthed, understandably shocked by Jenna's harrowing recount of plummeting off the side of the mountain and being buried alive in the snow.

"I wouldn't be here today if it wasn't for Jack and

the dogs. He...they saved my...life." She swallowed hard, struggling to keep it together.

"Where is this Jack fellow? I owe him a big debt of gratitude?" He perused the room.

The last thread of her resolve snapped and she crumpled against him. *What am I supposed to do now? I'm not the same woman I was before I met Jack. I can't go back to my life in Thunder Bay as if nothing has changed.*

She welcomed her dear friends' strong hands on her arms, guiding her to a seat in the waiting area of the post office.

He pulled up a chair to face her and clasped her shaking hands. "Jenna, do you need to see a doctor?"

She shook her head as she struggled to gather her composure. "I...I don't want to go..."

"What do you mean you don't want to go? I'm here to take you home."

"I don't know why he thinks I want to leave him?" Her chin dropped and her breath hitched. *Oh God, I think I love him.* "I need to see him Charles. You have to take me to him."

"Are you sure that's what you want? What if he doesn't want to see you?"

A middle-aged woman dressed in a postal uniform brought Jenna a glass of water.

Each tender moment they shared replayed in her mind. "There are some things in life you can't fake. I only wanted to let you know I'm okay, and he jumped to the conclusion I wanted to leave for good...then I saw a picture on his bedside table. He was standing with his arm around a very pretty blonde woman."

"A blonde woman?" The postal worker took a step back to stand beside Charles. "That's Jack's wife, Carly. She died over five years ago. That's when he built the cabin. He's lived there ever since."

His wife? "What have I done?" She jumped up, immediately regretting the sudden move. She grabbed hold of Charles and looked around the room frantically. "Can someone take me back to the cabin?"

Chief Swanson joined them. "We'd have to arrange for transportation. As you know, it's not exactly down a country road."

Jenna laughed through her tears, the huge knot in her stomach slackened somewhat. "No it's not. It's in the middle of paradise."

"Let me make a couple of calls. I'll get right back to you." The chief left the building.

Jenna slumped back in her chair, suddenly exhausted.

"I don't understand, Jenna. Why call me if you didn't want to come home?" Charles bowed his head, feigning interest in his clasped hands.

"Jack nursed me back to health. Until today, I wasn't well enough to make the trip here, and he didn't like the idea of leaving me alone in such a fragile state." She cupped the sides of his face and raised it up to look into his eyes. "Please don't be angry with me. I love you, and I didn't want you worrying about me ruining your Christmas."

His expression softened. "I love you, too, kiddo." He took her hands in his and kissed her forehead. "Nothing's been the same at the estate since your mother passed. As much as it pains me to say so, you're good to be rid of it...all of it."

Charles squeezed her hands. "Do you have any idea how worried we've been since you left the house?"

Jenna searched his misty eyes. "*We?* Does that include my father?"

His gaze dropped. "Of course he's worried..."

"The truth..."

"You know your father. He's not one for open displays of emotion. Besides, I don't think he's been feeling well."

She tossed back her head, her laughter dripping in sarcasm. "Who are you trying to kid? The only reason he wants me found is so I can marry that beast, Harold Meed. He doesn't give two shits about me." The memory of sneaking into her mother's sitting room and the pills on his bedside table flashed back... *Maybe he really is sick?*

"I'm not going to lie for your father, but have you forgotten the people back home who *do* love you? Edna is sick with worry."

A wave of guilt washed over her. She'd been so caught up in her own needs; she'd completely blanked out the woman who was more like a mother than a housekeeper. Not to mention Buffy; her best friend must be going crazy with worry. She never intended to hurt anyone. "And you?"

"It's no secret how much you mean to me. I love you like a daughter." He sniffled and looked away.

"I know you do, and I really am sorry for causing so much worry. You do understand why I had to leave, don't you? Does my father actually believe I'm going to agree to marry that man?"

"I hear ya, kiddo. I think there's more to the story than either of us know. Harold Meed has been to the estate every day since you ran off."

Her stomach churned, and she swallowed the sourness rising up the back of her throat. "He has? What does he want?"

"I'm not sure, to be honest. His visits with your father are behind closed doors." He rubbed her arm. "If I were to venture a guess, your hand in marriage is part of a business deal, or perhaps blackmail of some sort. Whatever the deal is, Harold expects you to marry him."

"I don't care what he expects." *Blackmail?* Her hand pressed against the diary in her coat pocket.

Cold air filled the room as the police chief walked in and joined them. "We can leave for Jack's place in half an hour or so."

Jenna used Charles' shoulder to stand, and hugged him. "Thank you." Her face warmed in the reflection of his reddening cheeks.

"Ah, erm...I'll be back as soon as the snowmobiles arrive and are ready to roll." He backed up as he spoke, seemingly in a hurry to escape her sudden display of emotions.

Jenna eased back down to her chair. Her hand pressed against her bruised ribs, the pain reminding her she was still healing.

Charles reached out to her. "Are you okay?"

She sniffled, chuckling at herself. "I'm more than okay."

An image of Jack taking the Christmas tree back outside flashed in her mind. Jenna straightened in her seat, an idea forming in her mind. *Perfect.*

Charles eyed her quizzically as she grabbed his arm.

"I need you to help me do something before we head back to the cabin..."

* * * *

Jack thrummed the table top as he stared blankly into the dwindling fire. Everywhere he looked reminded him of Jenna. She'd only been there a short time, but his heart ached like he'd known her his entire life.

The dogs sniffed every inch of the cabin for her. Sasha tilted her head sideways at him and whimpered. He half-expected to see a tear slip from her sad eyes.

"I'm sorry old girl, she's gone." He scratched the

patch of snow-white fur under her chin and sighed. The sadness in the room was almost suffocating.

Rather than assume their usual places in front of the fire, both dogs sat at the back door. *It's all my fault.* He'd jumped to all the wrong conclusions. Of course she'd want to go home sooner or later.

Jack gazed out the window at the setting sun, and how it cast a purplish glow on the snow. *There is something magical about this time of night. I wish Jenna were here to see this.*

He rubbed his eyes on his shirtsleeve. For the past five years he'd been content on his own with the dogs. *Now, I don't think I've ever felt so alone.*

Sasha and Tito began whining and scratching at the door.

"Knock it off you two. You're not making this any easier. She's not coming back."

Light flooded the room as a snowmobile passed his window, and then another. "What the..."

Jack quickly slid his feet into boots and opened the door. Tito almost knocked him over as he bounded over to a trio of sleds.

He put his arm up over his eyes, momentarily blinded.

"Did you really think I'd let you off of having a Christmas tree that easy?"

Jenna? His heart raced. "Jenna?"

"You were expecting who? Santa Claus?"

Jack ran to her and lifted her off her feet, spinning her around. He tilted his head back to laugh. "I'm so glad you came back."

He set her down. "Shit! Are you okay?" Her excitement overshadowed the lines of pain etched between her beautiful eyes.

The dogs pranced about their legs as she laughed and grimaced in the same breath.

"Yes, are you sure it's okay I'm here? I didn't want to leave you, Jack. Did you really want me to go?"

"None of that matters right now. You're here, and I am not letting you go again."

"Umm, hello?" Charles tapped her shoulder.

Jenna laughed at her friend's not so subtle reminder he was there. She turned her attention back to Jack and smiled, rubbing her hands together. "If you don't invite us in nobody is leaving. We'll all freeze to death."

"I'm so sorry." Light from the sleds revealed him blushing. "Of course, come on in. I'll put more wood on the fire."

Jenna nudged Charles forward. "Jack, I want you to meet Charles Wylder. Charles this is Jack Davis, the man who saved my life."

He shook Jack's hand heartily. "Thank you doesn't seem to be enough."

"No thanks necessary. Besides, it's actually these two who deserve the credit."

Charles went down on one knee to see the dogs. "Who do we have here?" The Huskies were more than happy to accept a good rubbing behind the ears, even from a stranger.

"The black and white one is Tito, and this is Sasha." He stoked her gleaming coat.

"You two are beautiful." His depth of gratitude cracked his voice. "Thank you for rescuing our girl."

He turned to face Jenna, just in time to catch her from falling to her knees. "Shit! Are you okay?"

"I-I'm just tired." Her words slurred.

Jack was quick to pick her up in his arms. "Of course you are. You must be exhausted." He moved toward the door, and called back over his shoulder. "Please, follow me inside."

"Shouldn't we be taking her to see a doctor?" The

man's depth of concern came across loud and clear.

"Let's get her inside and warm before we decide our next step." He paused to look directly at Charles, waiting for his nod of approval before moving forward.

Officer Dan scurried past him to open the cabin door wide.

Once inside, Jack quickly stepped out of his boots and carried Jenna to the sofa. He tucked a blanket in around her and searched her face. "Are you okay? Did you hurt yourself again?" His fingers gently feathered her fragile rib cage.

"No. I just think I might've overdone it." She smirked. "I'll be okay once I catch my breath."

He smoothed the hair back from her face and kissed her forehead. "I'll put more wood on the fire."

The warmth of Jack's lips lingered as Charles quickly took his place at her side. "Why didn't you say something while we were in town? You could've seen a doctor."

Jenna smiled sweetly. "There is only one doctor I'm interested in seeing." She winked at Jack before closing her eyes, breathing in the scent of wood burning. *There's no place like home.*

It took less than an hour before she caught her second wind and sat up to pay a little attention to two very happy dogs. Her face was immediately lathered in sloppy kisses as they wiggled about in excitement.

Jack patted both Huskies' sides. "Come on you two. Go lie down or it's out to the barn you go. They aren't going to let you out of their sight. You won't be going anywhere if they have anything to say about it." He sat on the arm of the sofa and nuzzled the side of her face. "Welcome home, my snow angel."

Jenna would have been quite happy to stay in this moment forever, but they weren't exactly alone. "I think there's something missing here, don't you?" She accepted Charles' offer of his arm to help stand.

Jack frowned. "Just where do you think you're going? Whatever you need, one of us can get for you."

She put her hands on her hips and stared down her nose at him. "I think there's a Christmas tree in need of saving."

His smile lit up his handsome face. "Yes, Ma'am."

"I'll give you a hand." Dan jumped up and followed him outside.

"Did you bring them in with you?" she asked Charles as she sat at the kitchen table.

"No. I'll nip out and get them," he whispered.

Jenna giggled. "I don't think he can hear us from outside. Be careful he doesn't see you."

Charles grunted in passing to put on his coat.

The house grew quiet with only the sounds of Chief Swanson making a fresh pot of coffee. She wanted to dance and shout out her happiness, but her body definitely didn't agree.

A few minutes later, the scent of coffee brewing filled the cabin. She wrapped her arms around herself and smiled. *It feels...right.*

The guys returned with the tree and proceeded to set it up. Holiday scent of pine made it feel even more like home.

Jenna used the table to push herself to stand and stroked her jaw. "Something's missing?"

Jack snuck up from behind and enfolded her in his arms. "I have everything I need right here."

The tender moment abruptly ended with a gust of frigid air from the open door.

"Ho, ho, ho! Merry Christmas." Charles held up two shopping bags.

She glanced back over her shoulder. "Whatever could that be?"

Jack planted a quick kiss to her cheek before letting her go, and grabbed the bags from his hands. "You're all terrible actors." He reached in and pulled out strings of shiny cranberries, twisted silver garland and a strand of twinkling lights—a small box contained tiny birds to clip to the branches. He laughed like a kid on Christmas morning. "I can't believe you did all of this."

"Why not? You didn't think I'd spend Christmas here without a proper tree, did you?" From another bag, Jenna carefully lifted delicate crystal snowflakes in various sizes.

Jack's smile warmed her heart.

Charles stood with a string of garland strewn from one hand to the other. "Um, a little help here would be nice."

The two men kept busy decorating the tree, giving her the opportunity to retrieve a brown paper bag from one of the shopping bags and hand it to the chief unnoticed. Chief gave her a thumb up and proceeded to sneak over to the fridge and hide her surprise without Jack being the wiser.

"It's beautiful." Her breath caught, and she blinked rapidly. "But something's not quite right. Is there another package in those bags?" She winked playfully at Jack.

He shook his head, flashing his very sexy dimple as he picked up the last box and opened the lid.

"You're something else." He smiled and carefully lifted the porcelain angel from the package. "Will you do the honors?"

She shook her head, heeding her body's current limitations. "How about I watch from here."

"Are you okay?" Concern doused the excitement in his eyes.

"Yes, I just need to rest for a while. I feel like I've

ran a marathon."

Jack quickly stepped up on a chair and positioned the shimmering angel on top of the tree.

A rush of emotion welled up in her as she took in their masterpiece. "It's perfect," she said breathlessly. Her heart so full of happiness made it impossible to stop the tears from falling.

Jack moved in behind her and whispered in her ear. "You're perfect."

Jenna leaned back to rest against him, and shivered as his warm breath caressed her neck.

"I hate to be a party pooper, but I have a couple of kids at home waiting for Daddy to hang their stockings." Chief got up from the couch; his officer followed suit.

Jenna stepped into Charles outstretched arms. "I'm so glad to see you, Charles. I hope you know how sorry I am for worrying you, and understand why I'm not going back."

"Of course I understand. I'd be lying if I said I'm happy about saying goodbye though." He kissed the top of her head before letting go. "If you had a bigger place, I'd be staying, too." Her dear friend extended his hand to Jack. "You take good care of my girl."

"I will. You're welcome back anytime."

Jenna gave Charles one last hug, and wished them all a Merry Christmas before the men boarded the snowmobiles. Jack stood next to her in the doorway and waved good-bye.

The door barely closed behind them, and he had his arms around her again. "I'm sorry, Jenna. I didn't mean to make you leave. I thought that was what you wanted."

"I thought you didn't want me here, and when I saw the photograph beside your bed..."

"Let's sit by the fire and talk. You look like you're

in pain. Do you want something for it? "

"Maybe later." She smiled. "I think there's something in the fridge for us. Would you mind getting it?"

Jack didn't leave her side until he'd laid a blanket over her knees and plumped up a pillow and slipped it behind her.

"What did you get?" He opened the fridge. "Oh, very nice. I do believe a toast is in order. After all, it is Christmas Eve."

Jenna watched him open the bottle and take two wineglasses down from the top shelf in his cabinets. He wiped them clean before filling them and putting the bottle back in the fridge. She remembered the night he came to her aid in his boxers, and how she'd admired his physique. Her pulse started to pick up its rate in anticipation of what the night might bring.

He smiled as he handed her a glass and sat next to her, fussing with the blanket so they were both cozy in front of the crackling fire. "You look so beautiful sitting there. I'm so happy you're home."

"Home. I like the sounds of that. Let's not dwell on the misunderstanding between us. We both know we jumped to conclusions in haste. Maybe we can drink to *us*, from this day forward." Jenna raised her glass.

"To us." Jack clinked her wineglass and took a sip.

"I'm glad you met Charles. I wish he could've stayed longer."

"He's a nice guy. I bet he was pretty surprised when you decided to come back here."

Jenna sighed and took a sip of her wine. "Since my mother passed away, he's been more of a father to me than my real one. I don't think there's anything he wouldn't do for me. I've been very blessed to have him to lean on over the years."

"I'm sure he feels the same way about having you in his life. How do you think your father will react to the news?"

She shook her head. "I really don't think he cares if I'm there or not. All he cares about is marrying me off to Howard Meed. Charles said Howard has been to the estate every day since I left. He's very determined my father live up to his end of whatever deal they made. I promise you, there is no way in hell I would even consider marrying that man." She felt her anger rise. The last thing she wanted was for thoughts of Howard Meed to invade this special time between them.

"Is he really that bad? I'm not saying you should. I'm *definitely* not saying that." He brought her hand to his lips and kissed her fingertips. "I'm just curious why you loathe him so much."

"I'd rather not talk about him at all, and especially not tonight. Let's just say the man has a thing for me, bordering on obsession. About six months ago, I reached my limit and threatened to get the police involved if he didn't back off." Jenna drank the rest of her wine in one gulp. "I really thought he got the message, that is until my father suddenly announced my engagement to him and he tried to put a ring on my finger. That's when I left the estate...and you know the rest of the story."

"God, I'm sorry, Jenna. Maybe I should mention that creep in town in case he shows up asking questions about where you are." He put his arm across her back and pulled her closer to him. "As long as I'm here, he won't get anywhere near you, I can promise you that."

"My knight in shining armor. You've already rescued me once. However can I ever repay your kindness?" She fluttered her eyelashes.

Jack kissed her hand once more. "When you look at me, so vulnerable, so beautiful, the walls around my heart come crashing down, leaving me raw and exposed. No matter what you ask of me, I will move heaven and earth to make it happen. From this day forward, I will do whatever it takes to ensure I see only happiness in those mesmerizing eyes of yours."

Jenna couldn't have stopped the tears if she tried. Never had anyone spoke such beautiful words to her. "You're amazing. All that I am, and all that I have is yours. I promise to do whatever it takes to make you a very happy man."

He leaned over and lightly kissed her lips. "*You make me the happiest man in the world by just being here with me...*"

Jenna pressed her mouth to his and playfully tugged his lip with her teeth. "I think we've done enough talking. If we don't go to sleep soon, Santa won't stop here."

"Oh, oh I'm sorry, Jenna. Of course you must be exhausted"

It was like someone flipped the off switch. One moment she was trying to seduce him, and in the next, he worried about how tired she was.

What happened? Doesn't he see where I'm going with this?

"I insist you take my bed, I'll sleep out here." His speech rolled out a tad too fast, showing how flustered he'd become. He made a move to get up and she pulled him back down by his shirt tail.

"I think your bed is big enough for both of us, don't you?" She smiled seductively.

Jack's eyes grew big, and slowly filled with desire. He gazed deeply into hers. "I think I've loved you from the moment I laid eyes on you."

Her body tingled in anticipation. "I love you, too,

Jack. I think I've loved you since I realized you make a wicked pot of chicken soup."

His laughter filled the room as he stood, scooped her up off the couch. "You're one of a kind, Jenna, my snow angel, and I wouldn't have it any other way."

She laid her head against his chest; his heartbeat thumped in her ear. "Take me to bed, Jack. My days of sleeping on the couch are over."

He kissed her soundly and padded to the bedroom, Sasha and Tito on his heels. He stopped in the doorway. "Go lay down you two."

"Aww, don't shut them out," Jenna joked, every nerve ending in her body abuzz.

"No way, you are *my* Christmas present, and I'm definitely not sharing, not even with them."

Jack laid her on the bed, so gently, as if he feared she'd shatter in a million pieces if he set her down too hard. Mere minutes ago there wasn't a place on her body that didn't cry out in pain—now, it cried out for a very different reason.

He smoothed back the hair from her face and held her gaze captive. What she saw excited and scared her all in the same breath. What she saw...was a man in love.

"I'm so happy you came back to me, Jenna."

Jack pressed his face into her hair, inhaling the sweet scent he missed the moment he walked into the empty cabin after he took her to town. He rained kisses from her earlobe down her jaw line, her skin so soft against his lips.

"I couldn't bear the thought of never seeing you again." Tears spilled over her long lashes. "I thought you wanted me to go...but I had to be sure...I'm so sorry..."

Sorry? "Oh, my sweet angel, you have nothing to be sorry for." He brushed her tears away. "When you said you wanted to call home, I was reminded about how vastly different my ways are from yours on the estate. I could never compete with the life you're accustomed to."

Jenna held his face in her hands. "Don't you get it? Just because it's the life I'm accustomed to, doesn't mean it's the life I want."

"And just what is it you want" He noted the unexpected tremor in his voice. If there was any doubt before, there wasn't now...

I'm in love with this woman.

With trembling hands, she began unbuttoning his shirt, hampered by her taped fingers. She huffed, and dropped her hands in frustration.

Seeing her struggle, he took over and unbuttoned his own shirt. He guided her hand underneath and placed it over his thumping heart.

"Make love to me Jack...."

Her words ignited a fire in him he'd almost forgotten. After Carly died, so did his sex drive, until now. He kissed her deep, and his arousal hardened against the zipper of his jeans. It took every ounce of restraint to pull back.

"I'm so sorry, Jenna," he panted. "I want you so bad, but I'm afraid of hurting you."

"I promise I won't break." Her voice echoed how very sexy she looked in that moment, skin flushed, eyes bright.

"In that case..." He tugged at the waist of her jeans. "You have far too many clothes on."

Without hesitation, he helped her undress, being careful of her injuries. When she lay naked on the bed, the moonlight illuminated her peaches and cream skin. Her chest rose and fell with each shaky breath, and her eyes grew big as he stood, undid the button on his jeans and took them and his boxers off in one fluid move. The lust in her eyes, coupled with his own growing desire, sent him in a slow sensual spin, further heightening the yearning he thought never to feel again for any woman.

"Please, Jack." She reached out for him. "I need you now."

Jack crept up from the end of the bed until he lay on his side beside her. He thoroughly enjoyed hearing her quickened breaths as he lightly feathered the swell of her breasts with his fingertips.

Jenna put a hand on his chest, and he lifted it to rest above her head. She winced, barely audible under her breath, but he caught the flicker of pain in her eyes before she managed to chase it away with a flutter of her lashes.

"I'm sorry, Jenna."

"Sorry? For what?"

"I want to make love to you, but not like this." He shook his head.

Even in the moonlight, he saw her lip tremble.

"It's okay. You're not hurting me."

The corner of his mouth lifted. "You're a very bad liar." He lay back and pulled her to his side. "We have all the time in the world, angel. I want our first time to be memorable because of the experience, not for the pain it causes you."

Jenna laid her head on his chest, and melded to his side. "I thought you wanted me?"

"I *do*, and I will have you...but for tonight, I am completely satisfied holding you like this, knowing that when I close my eyes to sleep, you'll still be here when the sun rises on a new day."

Her body lost all tension; she yawned. "I promise I will make this up to you."

Jack smiled and kissed the top of her head. "Look at me." He hardly recognized his own voice, so thick with emotion.

Jenna lifted her head; her tear-filled eyes glistened in the moonlight.

I almost lost you. He swallowed hard, *Never again....*

He raised her chin with one finger and brushed the droplets away with the pad of his thumb. "I love you, Jenna Blackburn."

Tears flowed freely now. "I love you, too."

He kissed her softly. "No more tears, please Jenna. You need to take care of yourself and do everything in your power to heal...*quickly*." Her laughter, as he'd hoped, eased the tension in the room. "I fully intend to make up for lost time when you're able."

Jenna laid her head back on his chest. "And I fully intend on letting you."

"No matter how long the winter, spring is sure to follow" -Proverb

Chapter Nine

Watching Jack help Sasha birth her pups was a beautiful experience. The dog lay panting on her side as he carefully persuaded the fourth one out. The new mother set right to work licking the placenta off the newborn while the first three pups squirmed next to the teats they'd be suckling before long.

As she loaded the woodstove, Jenna tucked her hair behind her ear and glanced sideways at her man. "Is that the last one?"

He pressed Sasha's tummy, then sat back on his heels and wiped his sweaty brow on his shirtsleeve. His undershirt stuck to his lean frame like a second skin. God, she loved his body.

"Looks like three, maybe four more," he said

Any other time, the snap and crackle of the fire, coupled with the way his shirt hugged every ripple of his sculpted chest, might've had her eyeing the straw bed in the rafters with interest. Her face warmed, and not from the almost unbearable heat of the barn.

Jenna knelt beside Jack's faithful companion and ran a hand down her damp coat. "You're doing a great job, Sasha."

The new mother made brief eye contact before laying her head down, resting for the next birth.

Two of the pups were silver and white like her, and the third dark gray and white like its dad, Tito.

"How about I make a fresh pot of coffee?" She slipped in behind Jack and squeezed his shoulders. "I'm guessing this might take a while?"

He leaned back and turned his head to her. "I'll

give you about an hour to stop that."

His forehead was damp against her lips. "We'll have none of that while you're on duty, Dr. Doolittle."

Jenna snickered while wrapping her cloak tightly around her to brave the inevitable rush of cold. She stepped outside and quickly closed the door behind her. The night's chill swirled around her ankles, bringing bumps to her skin. Even though the days were becoming increasingly warmer, spring had not fully awakened, leaving cold nights.

Jenna hurried in the house, stopping for a second to scratch behind the anxious father's ears. "Hang in there, Tito. She still has a ways to go."

As if he understood her words, the dog huffed and rested his head back on his paws. The Husky hadn't moved from his spot at the door since Sasha went into labor over four hours ago.

She'd witnessed another side of the man she loved today. Jack had remained calm and cool, assisting Sasha, the new mother's well-being first and foremost on his mind.

He'll make a great father one day.

She'd just filled the coffee pot with water when something drew her attention to the window. A headlight gradually approached the cabin. Jenna wiped the moisture from the glass with a dishcloth.

Now, who could that be?

She set the coffee to brew before stepping into her boots and hurrying outside. The quad's bright headlights momentarily blinded her.

"Charles!" she squealed, happy to see her dear friend.

He climbed off, setting his helmet on the seat and pulled his gloves off with his teeth. "Hey, kiddo." He fished a hanky from his pocket to wipe the sheen of perspiration from his head before opening his arms wide. "Where's my hug?"

Jenna laughed and flew into his embrace, knocking him back a couple of steps. "What a wonderful surprise!" So thrilled by her unexpected visitor, she chose to ignore the dark shadow that stole the sparkle from his eyes. "Come in out of the cold," she urged. "I just put a fresh pot of coffee on."

"Where's the boss?"

"He's in the barn. Sasha is having her litter. Four so far, and probably four more to come."

Charles attempted to rub the cold from his hands before taking off his boots. "So, how are you making out in the middle of nowhere?"

"We can discuss that later." She recognized his avoidance of a more serious matter. Small talk had never been his forte. "I'm sure you didn't come all the way out here just to ask if I'm okay."

The wooden chair he sat on creaked precariously under his large frame. "It's your father, Jenna." He shook his head. "It's not good news. In fact, he could go any day now."

"He could go where?" Jenna swallowed the lump in her throat. A picture of the prescription bottles on his bedside table flashed in her mind. She turned her back to him and grabbed hold of the countertop. "What does Dr. Harvey say?"

"He was initially treating him for a bladder infection. After two weeks of the antibiotics not working, he ran a series of tests. Your father has stage four colon cancer, and it's too far gone and spreading. They're keeping him as comfortable as possible, but he's weakening rapidly. In fact, I'm taking a chance leaving there at this time, but I thought you should know."

She'd spent the first weeks at the cabin wondering how her father reacted to her decision to stay. A part of her even hoped he'd reach out to her. As the weeks passed by, she gave up waiting, and accepted the harsh truth. Her father simply didn't care enough about her to make the effort.

Now he's sick, dying of cancer...

Jenna fumbled with the coffee mugs; one slipped out of her hand and hit the floor, breaking into several pieces. "Damn!" She stooped to pick up the shards, slicing her finger on a jagged edge. "Now look what I've done..." Tears rolled down her cheeks.

Sure, she had every right to be angry, and more than justified in not wanting anything to do with the man, but he was still her father...

Charles stooped and grabbed hold of her arms, guiding her to stand. He took her bloody finger and ran it under cold water. "It's going to be okay, kiddo. You're not alone."

Jenna sniffled. "I know my father can be an asshole, but nobody deserves to die from that horrid disease."

Her dear friend picked up the broken mug and threw it in the garbage. "Got another cup?"

She sucked on her finger and nudged him out of the way with her hip. "Go on, I got this." After taking another mug from the cupboard, she filled all three with steaming coffee. "I need to take one of these out to Jack."

Charles smiled reassuringly. "Mind if I come? I've never seen a dog giving birth."

She offered him a weak smile, grateful he sensed her need for a diversion. "Thank you."

Charles hated being the bearer of bad news, but he hoped to talk Jenna into coming home for a few days. He hadn't counted on the eight new arrivals. There was no need for words between the young couple, working together seamlessly, like a well-oiled machine. A brush of her hand against Jack's arm and the slightest of smiles tugged at the corner of his mouth in response—the pair obviously very much in love.

Maybe it wasn't such a good idea coming here and disrupting their lives.

"Well, let's give our girl some privacy with her new pups." Jack wiped his hands. "It's good to see you again, Charles."

They returned to the main cabin and settled in around the fire before he brought up the topic again. "I'm sorry I'm not here under more pleasant circumstances."

Jenna sat on the arm of Jack's chair.

"What's wrong?" His gaze shifted from Charles to Jenna, and back again.

"Jenna's father is very ill. He could go at any time now. I thought she should know."

Jack took her hand and steered her to sit on his lap. "I'm so sorry. Are you okay?"

She sniffled. "I think so. I haven't been close to my father in a very long time."

"He's still your dad, so I get it." He rubbed her back. "How long will you be gone?"

Jenna frowned and brushed his hands away. "Who says I'm going anywhere?"

"I am. You'll regret it for the rest of your life if you don't go." He smiled reassuringly. "It won't be long, and you can help Charles tie up any loose ends. I'd come with you, but Sasha needs me here. I have to make sure all the pups are being nourished. You just don't know from one litter to the next how the mom is going to do. So far, she's been doing great, but it could go bad very fast."

Charles ran a finger along the inside of his shirt

collar. It felt a little like he was intruding on a very personal moment. A quick look around showed nowhere to bow out and give them some privacy.

"Don't you need me here?" She pouted.

The same pout Charles remembered from when she was just a little girl.

"Of course I do." Jack brushed his lips across her knuckles. "I'll manage. You'll only be gone a couple of days, right Charles?"

"Oh, uh, yes," he stammered, surprised his presence was acknowledged. "I would think three or four days, depending on how long he..."

He pressed his lips together. Yes, the man had acted like a complete ass the past four or five years, but he'd worked alongside Kenneth for many years now. His life would have turned out very differently if he hadn't hired him.

Charles cleared his throat noisily. "I'm not sure how he did it, but your father has pre-arranged everything. The will is to be read the day after his death, naming you as executrix. I imagine there will be a few details to take care of in regard to the house and staff."

Jenna held up a hand to stop him. "Okay, I'll go. I'm not crazy about leaving here, but I guess I should be there."

Her knuckles turned white as she tightened her hold on Jack's hand and moved closer to his side. Even so, Charles couldn't help being happy she'd decided to return with him. Selfish or not, he looked forward to spending some quality time with her. He still wasn't used to not seeing her every day.

He hoped the old guy hung in there long enough to see his daughter, but in the same breath, he prayed she wouldn't bear the brunt of his nasty disposition.

Chapter Ten

The Lutsen Mountains gradually faded into the horizon. They'd been on the road less than an hour and Jenna already missed Jack so badly her heart hurt.

She'd spent so much time justifying her right to be angry with her father, she never once thought of things from his point of view. There was no disputing the *arrangement* he'd made with Howard Meed was wrong. It was her who ran off, not him who abandoned her. *Was he hurt? Did he shed a tear over me behind closed doors?*

Jenna put down the visor to block the blinding sun. "Did my father ever talk about me?"

Charles shifted in his seat. "Every now and then, I guess."

She narrowed her gaze on him, sensing there was something he wasn't telling her. "How did he react when you came home without me at Christmas time?"

He blew out a rush of air. "What do you want me to say?"

"Is it that bad?"

He shrugged. "No, he just thought you were punishing him for setting you up with Harold."

"Well, I *was* pissed off. Who wouldn't be?" She shook her head in disgust. "I guess it was pretty dumb of me to think he might have missed me, even just a little."

"I'm sorry, kid."

What a fool I am to have entertained the thought he actually cares about me, not just as part of a ridiculous business deal. How much was my hand in marriage worth to him? She shook her head and straightened in her seat. *No more. I will not set myself up, only to be shot down by his indifference toward me.*

Jenna recalled the diary entries. "Did I tell you about my mother's diary?"

Charles shook his head in response as he maneuvered around an old lady who seemed to be sightseeing at thirty mph.

"Before I left the estate the night of my father's birthday party, I snuck into my mother's sitting room and took a diary from her writing desk." She saw the surprise on his face. "Yes, I know I was treading on forbidden territory, but at that moment in time I didn't give a shit what my father wanted. So, when Jack and his dogs found me under the snow, he also found the diary underneath me. It wasn't until I woke up and began healing that he gave it to me."

"I didn't think anything was recovered from your car?" He kept his eyes on the road.

"I had stuffed the diary in my coat pocket." She shrugged. "Unfortunately, the book was near ruin from blood stains and being soaked from the snow." Jenna shuddered. "I could only decipher two entries...one at the beginning and one at the end."

"That's too bad, kiddo. So, what has you so confused? What did it say?"

Jenna situated herself to face him. "The first entry was about her experience, feeling me in her belly for the first time." She swallowed hard. "It was the last entry that really made no sense. She talked about being excited to go out on a first date, and debating whether to share her secret so soon."

"A first date *after* you were born?" Charles' brow knit.

"I know. The only secret I can think of is, having me. The strange thing is, she started to write out the mystery man's name, but all that was left was the letter K."

His eyes grew big. "K?"

"Yes. Now you see why I'm so confused. There were at least one hundred pages ruined in between the two entries. I thought maybe it meant she had me before she met my father, but I remember seeing pictures of him holding me in the hospital room." She flopped back in her seat. "When I get home, I'm going to look around and see if I can find more diaries. I know she wrote in one every night before bed."

Charles scratched his bald head. "I'm sure you'll find something to make sense of it all. I highly doubt your mother had you before meeting your father. I came to live on the estate shortly after you were born. I remember the big write up in the paper about their wedding at least a year before then."

They sat in amiable silence for quite some time. It wasn't until they hit the border the reality of going back to Thunder Bay hit her. In less than an hour's time, she would face the man who was her father, possibly moments before his death.

Jenna settled in her seat and shuddered.

"Are you going to be okay?" He reached over and squeezed her hand.

She stared out the window. "Sure I am."

As the landscape grew more and more familiar, her anxiety rose. They passed a sign that read WELCOME to THUNDER BAY. Her hands trembled as she flipped down the visor to look in the mirror. *Why am I so scared to face my father? I'm not the same girl who ran away in a fit of anger, what seemed a lifetime ago. Will he be able to tell how much I've changed just by looking at me?*

Before long, Charles turned down the winding driveway to her childhood home.

"How about once you're settled and have paid your father a visit, we'll sit down to a nice meal and talk about what happens next?"

The screech of tires assaulted them, the air filled with the stench of burned rubber.

"What the..." Charles spun in his seat and groaned.

Jenna followed suit just as the back door of a silver Lincoln flew open and a very red-faced Howard Meed lunged out.

Her stomach churned in distaste. "Oh God... I can't deal with him right now." She locked her door and hunkered down in her seat.

What the hell does he want?

Charles patted her hand. "Stay down out of sight. I'll take care of him."

He pushed open the door and sprung out of the car. "What the hell do you think you're doing?"

Howard stormed toward him, shaking his fist. "Kenneth made a deal with me, and I've come to collect."

Jenna swallowed the sour bile rising up the back of her throat. *He's got to be kidding.* She pushed herself up just enough to see between the seats. Howard stood in Charles' shadow.

"Listen up, buddy. Listen good." Charles jabbed a finger in the man's chest. "I don't know what kind of deal you made with Mr. Blackburn, and I don't really care. What I do know is your business partner is lying on his death bed, and his daughter has come to be by his side."

As Charles spoke, he continued to jab Howard's chest, forcing the big oaf to take a step back every time.

Howard opened his mouth, and Charles stooped until his face was mere inches from his. "I'd choose my words very carefully if I were you. I strongly suggest you get in your car and leave the premises.

You need to do so now. Got it?"

The chauffeur opened the back door of the Lincoln.

"Okay, I'm going, but I promise you one thing." He poked Charles chest. "You haven't heard the last of me. I *will* be back, and Jenna *will* be my wife."

Charles grabbed hold of his chubby finger and bent it back, rewarded by Howard's pain-stricken cries. "You'll have to go through me first. Be warned, I will stop at nothing to keep you away from her. Now get out of here before I break this finger, amongst other things."

He shoved the man so hard Howard stumbled back into the backseat of the Lincoln. His grunts and curses carried all the way to her ears.

The chauffeur closed the door behind him and smiled at Charles, tipping his hat. "Thank you for that. Please extend my heartfelt condolences to Miss Blackburn." With a nod of his head, he opened the driver's door. Moments later, the Lincoln drove out of sight.

Jenna got out of the car and clapped her hands in applause. "You were amazing." She chuckled lightly. "I think you made the chauffeur's day."

Charles shook his head, reaching into his pocket for a hanky to wipe the sheen from the top of his head. "Can you believe that guy? It took everything in me not to kick his ass right then and there."

"What kind of deal could my father have possibly made with that man?" She squeezed her eyes shut for a moment to rein in her anger.

Charles walked over to her and tucked her hand in the crook of his arm. "Don't worry, we'll deal with him later."

Jenna nodded her approval while taking in the grandeur of the house—worlds away from the cabin...and Jack. She blinked rapidly. "Let's get this over with."

He ushered her inside, not letting go until they stood on the shiny marble floors of the foyer. Everything looked the same as it did when she stormed out only a few short months ago—a lifetime ago.

I feel like a stranger in my own home...in someone else's home.

A familiar clicking preceded Edna's descent down the grand staircase. Jenna had never seen the woman look so frazzled and scared. The housekeeper was more like a mother than one of the help. She rushed to her aid and gave her a quick hug, sensing her urgency.

"Thank goodness you're here! I think it's almost his time," she cried out breathlessly.

Charles reached for her hand. "Calm yourself. We'll go up and see him right now."

The older woman's red-rimmed eyes pooled as she kissed both of Jenna's cheeks before dashing off toward the kitchen.

He held out his hand. "Remember, I'm right here for you."

Lost for words, Jenna took his hand and followed him up the stairs. The stench of disinfectant and urine had her covering her mouth and nose before reaching the room.

Charles paused at the door. Tiny, tell-all worry lines sprouted between his eyes. "Take a deep breath, in through the nose, out through the mouth."

Conflicting emotions dueled within her...nervous about her father's reaction to seeing her, concern it might be too late to salvage any kind of relationship with him, but mostly sadness for the loss of the loving father he once was.

She squared her shoulders and blew out a rush of

air before nodding her readiness to go in.

He opened the doors, and tiny dust particles rode the stream of sunlight that poured in through a small gap between the curtain panels. Her father lay in his over-sized, four-poster bed—a mere speck in a sea of plush, white bedding. She let go of Charles' hand and inched her way to the bedside. His chest rose and fell as if it took every ounce of his energy to do so.

"Father?"

His eyes moved behind paper-thin eyelids before they fluttered open, their usually vibrant hazel color now milky and deep in sunken dark circles. His gaze traveled toward the sound of her voice, but it was as if he looked through her. Her lip trembled. It saddened her to see a shadow of the man whose very presence once commanded attention.

He parted his chapped lips, emitting the slightest murmur.

"I think he's trying to say something." Through misted eyes, Jenna glanced over at her father's right-hand man.

Charles lightly squeezed her shoulders. "He's been doing that for a few days now. Nobody can make out what he's trying to say."

Just then, her father convulsed in a coughing fit that rattled his chest as well as her fragile disposition. She fell to her knees and rested her head gently against his frail chest. His shallow breathing permeated the room, and once again he tried to speak.

She raised her head, positioning herself over her father's mouth. "Talk slowly, Father. I can hear you." Her heart swelled with hope...hope to hear this man truly did love her.

"You..." His words were nothing more than a whisper.

Tears slipped from her eyes, dampening his

cheek.

"Are..." he continued breathlessly.

"You are... I hear you, Father."

"Dead..."

The temperature in the room dropped, raising the hairs on her arms as she tried to swallow.

"To...me..."

Jenna gasped in horror and jerked back from his venomous words. "H-how can you be so cruel?"

A slow smile spread across his gaunt face as her father closed his eyes for the last time.

Chapter Eleven

Jenna backed away from the bed. Charles watched the color literally drained from her face as he whisked her off her feet and cradled her in his arms, her body melding to him like putty. If he hadn't witnessed it for himself, he'd never have believed a father could be so cruel, not even Kenneth. His eyes clouded as he clenched his fists in anger. The insensitive prick had actually waited so he could plunge a knife in his only child's heart before he died.

Edna reached the top of the staircase just as he made his way to Jenna's bedroom.

"I'm going to need a hand here."

She fell in behind him, matching step for step. "What's wrong with her? Should I call a doctor?"

"Let's get her to bed first, and then I'll explain everything."

The housekeeper hurried past him to open the bedroom doors and turn down the blankets.

Charles set Jenna down, and Edna removed her shoes. She curled up in a fetal position as he tucked the plush bed covers around her like a cocoon. He stood back and let out a long breath before motioning Edna to follow him just outside the bedroom door.

"Her father passed on."

"Oh, the poor girl. She'll need some time to heal."

He put a hand on her shoulder. "There's more. Our *boss* had a few chosen words for his little girl before he died."

Her hand flew to her chest. "What could he possibly have said to upset her this much?"

"His exact words, '*You are dead to me.*'"

Edna gasped and her lower lip trembled. "Oh, my God. The brute!" Her gaze settled on Jenna. "I know he could be a terrible man, but to do something like that...to his own daughter?"

Charles made no attempt to hide his aching heart. He rubbed his eyes with the heel of his hands. "I don't think I'll ever understand how that man could be so cruel, especially to a girl like Jenna."

"You've always been more of a father to her than he was."

He turned away and coughed into his hand. Over the years, he'd wished that were true so many times, and how he'd always wondered if Jenna thought of him in that way.

This is no time to be falling apart. Jenna needs me, now more than ever.

He cleared his throat noisily to mask the overwhelming rush of emotion battling for free rein.

"Maybe we should wait for her to bring up the subject of her father...when *she's* ready to talk about it." His words caught in his throat. *She might not ever want to, and I can't say as I blame her.*

"Don't worry about Ms. Jenna. I won't leave her side."

Her kind words curbed his anger, and he stooped to kiss the intuitive woman's flushed cheek. "Thank you. I'm going to make sure he's gone before she wakes up." *Even if I have to throw him in the back of my truck and take him away myself.*

Edna slipped back into the room, offering him a slight smile before quietly closing the door behind her.

That woman is a godsend. If I've been like a father to Jenna, then she definitely stepped up and filled the void of mother.

Charles stormed down the stairs. *Son of a bitch. What I wouldn't give to turn back the clocks, even a few minutes.*

The coroner arrived within minutes of him

threatening to leave Kenneth at the end of the laneway for pick-up. Shortly after, he summoned the staff to the front foyer. Not one tear was shed with the announcement of their employer's demise.

"It's not my place to tell, but Kenneth had a few hurtful words for our Jenna before he took his last breath. To say I'm disgusted would be putting it mildly. Edna is watching over her while she sleeps."

A murmur of empathy rippled over the employees.

"I don't know how much time we have before she awakens, so we have to work fast. I want every window opened wide, and every picture of, *that man* taken down. I have flowers being delivered as we speak. I'll let you ladies decide where they should go." He held up his hand. "Before you go, I think you all need to be aware of a man who is causing some serious problems for our Jenna. I want security alerted if anyone sees any sign of Howard Meed on the property. They will immediately escort him off the premises. The man is not to be trusted, so I think it's best if you all refrain from confronting him on your own. Are there any questions? If not, let's get moving."

Not a moment's hesitation passed before the staff disbursed and went about doing as he asked. Some of the heavy drapes hadn't been opened in years, stirring up quite a bit of dust. In spite of Kenneth Blackburn the Third's death, there was an air of release about the estate. The darkness cast upon the house lifted, and before long, sunshine and the sweet scent of flowers replaced it.

He'd have to do his best for her. It had always been a priority to keep her out of harm's way. The one person who had hurt her most was now dead, robbing him of the chance to kick his scrawny ass.

Jack grimaced as he swallowed a mouthful of coffee. He didn't know what Jenna's secret was, but it made his java taste like crap in comparison.

He stared longingly out the window as he sat at the table. She'd only been gone a matter of hours, and he was already lost without her. To make matters worse, he couldn't shake the feeling something was wrong, something more than the death of her father.

Funny, she'd never really talked about her dad, making Jack wonder just what type of man he was. It eased his mind somewhat knowing Charles had her back. Even so, the memory of finding her in the snow after her car crash sent a shiver down his spine.

Please be okay, Jenna. My life is nothing without you.

Jack surveyed the small cabin. He knew just how vastly different this life was from the life she'd known on the estate. Before building the cabin, he had an incredible wife and beautiful home in a prominent neighborhood, every room tastefully decorated to exemplify his wife's passion for interior design. After Carly's tragic death, none of the material possessions mattered without her.

I can't possibly go back to that way of life. Is that going to be a deal breaker? Jenna never complained about much, aside from not having a way to communicate if there were an emergency. *Maybe not.*

What I wouldn't give for a phone right about now, though.

With a decisive nod, he left the table and set his cup in the sink. As soon as she returned, they'd look into phone service. For the last five years, he'd preferred the isolation, only having to associate with society as he deemed fit. He loved the fact no matter which way he looked, there wasn't a paved road in sight.

Everything changed with Jenna.

Jack stepped into his boots and trekked across the dewy grass where Tito thumped his tail against the barn door. He scratched his old friend behind the ears.

"Well, c'mon. It's time to visit your family."

For the first little while, he only allowed Tito in when he was there to watch over things, just to be on the safe side while the new mother bonded with the pups. So far, the new dad seemed content to just see them, not venturing too close.

Sasha raised her head to acknowledge their presence and went right back to being a mom. Her eight pups fought blindly for a teat to suckle. They squirmed on top of and under each other until they found a free teat to latch onto. Their tiny mews filled the barn as he replenished the fire. It was a duty he'd have to keep up with until the pups eyes were open and their instinct to keep warm on their own kicked in.

After the pups had their fill and lazed about, Jack managed to get Sasha to eat. She needed to keep her strength up and a good supply of milk for her brood. This was her third litter, and she showed no sign of disconnecting. It appeared she genuinely loved being a mother.

Jenna will make a good mother, too.

He laughed nervously. "Where the hell did that thought come from?"

The last time he'd entertained the idea of having children, he'd been happily married. Carly had wanted to be a mother in the worst way. He clenched his jaw as the unfulfilled longing tied his stomach in knots.

Having thoughts like that about Jenna scared the supreme crap out of him, but he had about as much control over his feelings for her as he did the weather. He rubbed the back of his neck and rolled his head, his attention drawn to a pair of boxers and one of Jenna's shirts still hanging from a clothesline he'd strung across the barn.

Maybe I could look into a proper washer and dryer, too.

Chapter Twelve

"Jenna, it's time to get out of there. You're going to catch a cold."

"Oh." She startled fully awake to find Edna standing next to the tub with a big, fluffy towel held open for her. It took a moment to get her bearings. "I guess I nodded off. How long have I been in here?"

She remembered slipping into warm, lavender-scented water and letting the tears fall. A ritual she'd performed so many times throughout her childhood whenever something upset her. Not one of those heartaches came even close to the pain she felt now.

You are dead to me.

Jenna shivered, suddenly very aware of the cold water she sat in—her skin resembled goose flesh.

"Too long! Now out with you." Edna's words were stern, but her eyes told another story.

"Thank you." She welcomed the warmth of the towel her caretaker wrapped around her, easing her anxiety.

"I have a housecoat warming by the fire. Hurry and slip into it so we can do something with that hair of yours."

Jenna hurried to the fireplace and slipped on the housecoat, pulling the collar up under her chin and reveling in its cozy warmth. She squished her toes in the plush carpet as she crossed the room to sit at her dressing table. Edna rubbed her hair with a dry towel before beginning the arduous task of pulling a brush through her hair. She tilted back her head and closed her eyes.

"Mmm, that feels so good. I remember my mother brushing my hair dry every night while she told stories about growing up on a horse farm."

Thankfully, for every bad situation life threw at her, there was a good memory to combat it.

"Your mother would be very proud of the strong woman you've become."

Edna's voice always had such a calming effect on her. She focused on the pull of the brush and warmth of the fire. She might not have had her father's love, but the love shown to her by Edna, Grace, the cook, and especially Charles, was far more than most people experienced in a lifetime.

And then came Jack...

She smiled, remembering the first time he'd brushed her hair...*and I fell asleep in his arms.*

Edna setting the brush down abruptly ended the precious memory. She rubbed her upper arms, missing his touch against her skin.

Jenna saw the compassion and worry in the housekeeper's misty eyes as she gazed at her in the mirror while smoothing her now shiny hair. Charles probably told her about what her father said.

Please forgive me, but I just can't talk about it right now.

"Charles would like you to join him for a meal." Edna gathered the damp towels.

Knowing her mentor, he was probably worried sick about her. "Tell him I'll be down in half an hour."

Jenna got up and stood in the doorway of her walk-in closet. She perused row upon row of color-coded clothing sorted by dresses, shirts, skirts and more. Her gaze traveled up to the ceiling of shelves filled with shoes for every occasion and then some.

"Wow."

Back home with Jack, she had a couple shoes and a pair of rubber boots. Her wardrobe consisted of two pairs of jeans, half a dozen tops and two bulky knit sweaters. She flipped over a price tag dangling from one of her dresses—five hundred dollars. It shamed her to think how she'd tossed about money on such frivolous things.

I'm definitely not the same girl who didn't think twice about spending that much on a dress. A dress I haven't even worn.

Jenna rummaged through the closet until she found a pair of comfy yoga pants. She'd just pulled them up when a familiar item of clothing brought a smile to her face. She quickly discarded her housecoat for Jack's oversized sweater she'd put in her bag at the last minute before leaving the cabin. She brought the ragged sleeves to her face and inhaled his lingering scent on the misshaped knit.

It's too bad there isn't a way to communicate with him.

She caught a glimpse of herself in the full-length mirror. Her shiny red hair fell in waves down the front of the forest green sweater. She smiled at her reflection, happy with the woman looking back at her. The only time she glanced in the mirror at the cabin was in the morning when she brushed her teeth. It wasn't a matter of not caring how she looked anymore; Jack gave her all the positive affirmation needed. Without words, he told her with his eyes, usually coupled with a lop-sided grin, just how beautiful he thought she was every single day, and that's all that really mattered to her.

The polished marble tile was cold against her bare feet as she made her way down the staircase to the foyer.

Something is different...

She paused midway.

Father's portraits are gone.

All that remained of the paintings were several large squares of wallpaper untouched by age.

Her nose twitched as the scent of flowers wafted up to her.

What the...?

Her gaze settled on a large arrangement of cheery yellow roses atop a table in front of an open window. The last time she remembered flowers—or the windows opened wide—her mother was alive. It was as if her spirit had been set free in the house once again. A smile played on her lips as she made her way to the solarium, her favorite room on the estate.

"Well, hello there." Charles kissed her on the cheek and held out a chair.

"Thank you."

She caught him giving her attire a once over, but kept any comments he might have had to himself. The quiet of the solarium grew a little uncomfortable. She wasn't quite sure how she was supposed to act. She couldn't be the grieving daughter some might expect her to be, and chanced a look at her friend through her lashes.

"Listen, Jenna, I'm sorry how things turned out. If I thought there was even the slightest chance of something like that happening, I would never have brought you back here."

She straightened in her seat and lifted her chin, willing the hurt and anger away. "We both know what kind of man my father is...was. For a minute, I forgot and allowed myself to think there might be a final heartfelt moment between us." She sipped from her water glass. "Do you mind if we not talk about this anymore?"

"You're quite a gal." Charles took a bottle from the ice bucket at the tableside. "Would you like a glass of wine?"

"Sure, why not." She gazed up at the canopy of stars they dined under. It brought comfort in knowing even though Jack was hundreds of miles away, they shared the same breathtaking view.

Conversation flowed easily as they enjoyed a meal of scrumptious cracked crab. She'd forgotten what an incredible cook Grace was as she eased back in her chair and wiped the butter from her chin.

"What would you like to do with the rest of the evening?"

"Actually, I think I'd like to visit my mother's sitting room and see if I can't find some answers to those cryptic entries I told you about." Now that her father was gone, she could move about the estate freely.

"You'd mentioned wanting to take a closer look, so I took the liberty of having the room spruced up. Are you sure you're up to it?"

Jenna smiled and got up from the table. "Yes, I guess seeing the flowers in the foyer have me feeling a little nostalgic. Thank you, for everything."

"If you're sure you're okay, I'll tend to a few things while you explore." He balled up his napkin and pushed away from the table to stand. "You don't have to do this today."

She wrapped her arms around him and rested her head on his chest. "Don't worry about me. You go do what you need to do."

"I...I'm sorry, I didn't mean to..." he stammered.

Jenna kissed his flushed cheek. "Relax, I'm joking. You need to loosen up, old man. Go get a massage or something." She winked playfully on her way out of the solarium.

Mounting trepidation slowed her pace, however, as she meandered to her parents' wing of the estate.

Jenna mindfully opened the door where, only a short time ago, her father lay dying. She breathed a sigh of relief to find the bed stripped and windows open wide. The sweet scent of freshly cut roses masked any lingering smell of death. She squished her toes in the lush, white carpet, worlds away from the rustic hardwood floors of the cabin, and forced her gaze away from the spot her father had discarded her.

The sitting room door opened with a creek, and the breeze from the open window married the scent of roses and lily-of-the-valley perfume. It had to have been Edna's idea to spray her mother's perfume in the room. Her gaze settled on the rocking chair where a fresh, hand-knit throw hung over the arm.

Thank you, Edna.

How many nights did I spend sitting on Mother's lap right there?

Precious memories.

Her eyes misted as she opened the small closet to find boxes and baskets of various sizes and colors lined the shelves. One container in particular caught her eye, a floral hatbox hidden behind a tub filled with an assortment of hair barrettes. She wasn't able to shake the feeling she was somehow treading on forbidden territory as her hand trembled when she lifted the lid.

Jenna sat in her mother's chair and laid the soft knit over her legs. The container was filled with letters in neat bundles, tied with ribbon. The yellowish edges of some told of their age.

She took out what looked to be the oldest pile and gently tugged at the ribbon. The letter wasn't addressed to her mother.

Ursula Jennings?

If she remembered correctly, her mother's mother...a departed grandmother she never knew existed until after her passing.

If they were mailed to my grandmother, why did Mother have these?

Jenna flipped the envelope over to find no postal stamp or marking of any kind.

Hmm...

She carefully took the stationary out of the envelope and unfolded it. Her mother's familiar handwriting sprawled across the page. The letter dated only months before she married.

Mother,

I am a very lucky woman to have a job here at the Ski Resort, but I'm terribly homesick and missing my Angel. I have to keep reminding myself it's only for six weeks and I'll make twenty times the money I would working on the farm.

Jenna furrowed her brow. *Missing my Angel...who?* She knew her mother was raised on a horse farm, but she'd never talked about working at the resort. So far the letter added to her confusion, not answered her questions as she continue reading...

I think some of the men here aren't so interested in skiing as they are in the girls. I don't care for the way they look at me. However, I did meet a rather polite man today. His name is Kenneth. My heartbeat races every time he glances my way. I hope to see him again.

It became obvious this letter was written at the same time as the last entry in her diary. Jenna continued to read the neatly written lines. She could almost feel her mother falling in love, telling the story of the loving man Jenna remembered from her childhood—full of laughter and spontaneity.

She leaned back and closed her eyes, picturing a little girl at the window, waiting for Daddy to come home after a business trip, because she knew he'd have something special hidden behind his back just for her.

Polar opposites of the father who spoke such

hurtful words on his death bed.

An air of melancholy settled in the room, prompting her to take a break. She stood and stretched her stiff body before gathering the letters and returning to her bedroom where she changed into pajamas. She reached for the phone to call the kitchen and stopped, the clock on her bedside table reminding her how late it was.

Jenna dashed downstairs in her bare feet. She'd forgotten how cold the floors got at night. The warmth from the kitchen welcomed her as she swung open the door.

A very startled cook looked up from what she was reading. "Oh, Ms Jenna. What are you doing down here this time of night?" Grace stood and strode across the room to wrap her arms around here. "It's so nice to see you, even in your bare feet." She clicked her tongue like she'd always done when scolding.

"I missed you, Grace." She stepped out of her arms and sat at the breakfast bar. "I couldn't go to bed before I had a cup of tea and your famous shortbread."

The dear woman chuckled, setting her tired eyes to sparkle with pleasure. "Now, that sure brings back some fond memories. I'll be right back."

Grace ducked into the pantry and closed the door behind her as she always did when fetching her shortbread. She had a secret hiding place, and to this day Jenna didn't know where it was. Not for lack of trying, having climbed the shelves many times in search of the treasure.

She scampered over to the stove and turned on the kettle to boil. "Would you like a cuppa tea?" Jenna called out.

Grace stepped out of the pantry with a stack of shortbread in hand. "What do you think you're doing?

That's my job."

"That *was* your job. I'm not a little girl anymore." She opened the cupboard door. "Did you want some or not?"

The cook sighed wearily. "Oh, not this late for me or I'll be up half the night peeing." She giggled behind her hand.

After a brief battle over who would carry the bedtime snack upstairs, Jenna was off with her goodies in hand. She'd just set the steaming mug down when there was a light rap on the door, and Edna appeared in her housecoat and hair wrapped for the night.

"What are you doing up at this hour?"

Edna waddled across the carpet and fussed with her blankets, folding them down for her to get in. "I could ask you the same thing. I ran into Grace on my way to my room..."

She laughed and held up her hand. "Don't worry, she already scolded me enough for both of you."

"I'm sorry, but..."

Jenna quickly kissed her cheek and climbed under the blanket. "No need for apologies, I'm quite capable of making myself a cup of tea."

Edna sniffled, shaking her head. "You've changed some since you've been gone."

"I hope that's a good thing." She sat up against her headboard and reached for her tea.

"You've grown into a lovely young woman. Your mother would be very proud."

Tears stung her eyes at the mention of her mother. "If I never thanked you for being there for me after she passed..."

"You were so young and heartbroken." Edna shook her head as she scurried to the door. "Good night, Ms. Jenna."

Jenna recognized the quiver in her voice. Her rush from the room undoubtedly preceded having a good cry. "Good night, Edna."

She got comfy and reached for the hatbox on the other side of the bed. The next letter she took out wasn't addressed to her grandmother, but to her mother's sister Rose, who passed away many years ago.

Dear Sister,

Kenneth has offered to pay for her to stay at one of the best facilities who cater to people like her. She'll have everything she'd ever want or need. All of the things I could never afford to give her. He'll pay for it all, even her clothes. How can I say no?

All he asks is to keep Angelina a secret between us. No one can know she exists. Kenneth says it's because his family will never approve of our marriage if they knew I had a child out of wedlock.

Jenna dropped the letter to her lap and stared off into space.

A child? Out of wedlock?

"I have a sister?" Her mouth grew dry and her heartbeat quickened. "I have a sister!" She reread the last two paragraphs to be sure she'd understood correctly. Her heart ached for her mother.

How did she endure all those years without being able to talk about her own child...my sister?

The term, "people like her" left her unsettled, not knowing what it could possibly mean.

Jenna tossed the blanket aside and shifted to sit in the middle of her bed, her bum resting against her heels as she read the last page for the third time.

Somebody has to know something. Did Father continue to pay her expenses after Mom died?

One thing was certain: she had far more questions than answers.

"Where could she be?" She owed it to the memory of her mother to find her and make sure Angelina was still being cared for. Surely, once Jack learned of this unexpected revelation he'd understand why she needed to stay a little longer.

Jenna hugged her pillow and closed her eyes. "Don't worry, Mama, I'll make sure Angelina is okay." She flopped back on her bed. "Wow, I have a sister." Tears of happiness filled her eyes.

I wonder if she looks like me.
Does she even know I exist?

Chapter Thirteen

A jumble of possible scenarios scrambled in her mind, least of which, her father might have deleted her from the Will, and she wouldn't have the resources to find her sister. She didn't want or need the money for herself; Jack provided her with everything she could possibly need.

Outside of her father's den, she came to a full stop to steady herself. "I really wish I knew what to expect."

Charles shrugged. "I wouldn't put it past your father to leave everything to a stranger just to piss us off."

Jenna smiled despite thinking it was a definite possibility.

He winked at her before opening the doors.

Mr. Bond sat behind her father's impressive desk—hand-carved out of the finest mahogany money could buy. Without fully standing, he nodded toward two empty chairs across from him. "Good day, Mr. Wylder, Ms. Blackburn. Please be seated."

Jenna raised a brow at being seated in her own home, and Mr. Bond cleared his throat and pushed his glasses up the bridge of his narrow nose.

The next half-hour passed like a dream.

"So, as you can see, Ms. Blackburn, you are the sole benefactor and executor of this estate and its considerable holdings. That is, excluding the antique cars, which your father left to Mr. Wylder."

Jenna sat utterly dumbfounded. *I'm not surprised my sister wasn't mentioned, but it makes no sense he'd leave me his vast fortune.* Maybe he didn't intentionally do so.

His last words echoed in her mind. *You are dead*

to me.

I can't imagine he made this decision in the recent months.

"Mr. Bond? Can you please tell me when my father wrote this will?"

The lawyer flipped through the file. "He had this drawn approximately one year before your mother passed away. If she were still alive today, she would've been the sole benefactor. The provision in the event of her death being all holdings go to any children they had together."

"Wow." She crinkled her brow. "I find it hard to believe he never made any changes over the years. He didn't even know Charles back then?"

"A codicil to his will with respect to Mr. Wylder was made last summer when he bought the Rolls Royce."

Jenna summoned the courage to bring up the topic of her sister. Bracing herself for whatever may come, she straightened in her chair and took a deep breath.

"If you could indulge me for a minute, I'd like to share something I discovered last night while going through some of my mother's old journals and letters."

Mr. Bond glanced at his watch and folded his hands on the desktop. "Yes, I have a little time. I must say you've piqued my curiosity."

Charles furrowed his brow. "Is everything okay, Jenna?"

"I think so. I'm a little confused, though. You see, while reading through a letter addressed to my grandmother, my mother talked about a daughter she had before meeting my father." She scrutinized both of them in turn to gage any reaction. "It seems my father agreed to pay for 'Angelina's' care as long as

Mother agreed to never speak of having a child out of wedlock. I think my sister may have some kind of special needs. Which is why my mother agreed, so her daughter got the care she could never afford to give her."

Charles sat with his mouth slightly agape. His genuine surprise at the news reflected in his eyes. "I'm not sure what to say. I had no knowledge of this. Your mother never breathed a word of having another child...at least not that I'm aware of."

Jenna faced Mr. Bond; his stone-face was void of expression.

"You've been my father's lawyer long before he married my mother. Did he ever ask you to draw up a letter for him? Knowing my father, I would think he'd have something in writing so my sister didn't get a piece of the inheritance."

"I can assure you I'm just as surprised as you by this revelation. Your father never spoke a word of this girl... Angelina, did you say?"

"Yes, Angelina. I find it hard to believe Mother never visited or spoke about her to anyone in the fifteen years married to my father. She wasn't that type of person to just drop her own child off someplace, never to be seen or heard from again."

Mr. Bond pushed away from her father's desk, gathered his papers and put them in his briefcase. "I agree. Your mother had a heart of gold. I wish I could be of more help. Like I said, I'm just as surprised as you."

"Do you have any suggestion as to how I go about looking for Angelina? If my father never made provisions with you, I need to find her and make sure her expenses continue to be paid for her care."

He shook his head. "I'm hardly in a position to play detective. When you learn of her whereabouts, I'd be happy to prepare the appropriate documents you might need."

Charles walked over to the door and opened it. "Thank you for coming out today. We'll be in touch."

Mr. Bond paused briefly. "My condolences to you both." He nodded curtly in her direction before taking his leave. The front door banged shut seconds later.

"Well, kiddo, it looks like you'll never have to worry about money for the rest of your life."

Jenna sunk in to her father's chair. "This is all too weird. You were there and heard my father's last words to me."

He dropped to one knee in front of her and held her hands. "Now, you listen to me. You deserve every penny of that money. It's your birthright."

She searched his eyes for answers. "I can't do all this alone. How do you feel about staying on here? You can take care of the staff and the estate while I'm with Jack. I'll even double your wages. I'd like you to continue with the charity work my father was involved in. Maybe you can..."

Charles rose, shaking his head. "Whoa, slow down, kiddo. Are you telling me you intend to go back and live in that cabin with Jack?"

She laughed. "Seriously, can you see Jack being happy in a place like this?"

The corner of his mouth twitched. "You have a point. Why don't we discuss all of this after the funeral?" He took a seat beside her before clasping her hands in his. "Now, you say your sister's name is Angelina, what else did you discover?"

"Exactly what I just told you and Mr. Bond. My mother had Angelina long before she met and fell in love with my father. That would mean Angelina's last name is Freeman. When he proposed marriage, he had one condition—nobody could know she had a child out of wedlock. In exchange for her silence, he'd pay for the best care money could buy and all of her expenses. In essence, give Angelina everything my mother could never have afforded her."

Charles shook his head. "Your poor mother, I can't imagine how hard that must have been for her."

Jenna squeezed his hands. "Think hard, can you recall *anything* she might have said or done over the years that made no sense at the time, but..."

"Nothing comes to mind right now. Maybe we should ask the staff. It's more likely she would've shared something that personal with Edna or Grace."

"I can't think straight. I need a little time alone to process everything." She yawned. "I wish you'd let me help with the funeral arrangements. There must be something I can do."

"It's all taken care of." He leaned against the desk and folded his arms across his chest. "We'll have a very short service on Friday."

Suddenly her eyes grew heavy. The emotional rollercoaster she'd been on was taking its toll on her—how she wished for the simpler life with Jack again. "I'm going to lie down for a bit."

Charles pulled her into his arms, wrapping her in a very much-needed sense of family.

"Why don't you put on one of those pretty dresses of yours and we get out of here this evening? Let's go to The Chateau?"

The last thing on her mind was dressing up and going out, but she saw how happy the thought made him. Jenna shrugged. "Sure, I guess I can do that."

Recent events must've taken a bigger toll on her than she realized; it hadn't been her intention to sleep the day away. One minute she sat on the side of her bed, and the next, the sun was setting on the horizon.

Jenna took a long, relaxing bubble bath before her dinner date with Charles. The Chateau was an extremely beautiful, upscale establishment. Truth be told, she'd much rather be curling up on the sofa with Jack, watching the fire crackle and pop. There was no need to go elsewhere, fully content with being alone in each others' company.

She sighed with longing as she stepped out of the tub and dried herself off. If it wasn't for Charles, she'd be halfway home by now. Out of respect to him, she'd at least stay until after the funeral. Her dear friend had gone to such great lengths to make her comfortable after her father's passing—and there was the discovery of her sister...

Jenna took her time and swept her hair up in a chignon, decorating it with two antique, emerald clips—a gift from her mother on her sixteenth birthday. Out of the many gowns in her closet, she opted to wear a little black dress with no embellishment...only because the dress code wouldn't allow the comfort of wearing jeans.

Standing in front of her full-length mirror, she had an epiphany of sorts. *I don't belong in this world anymore. I belong with Jack, living in his little cabin in our own private paradise.*

She strolled through her suite, reflecting on all the things that had once been so important to her. Floor-to-ceiling shoes, a canopy bed imported from France, and a spa-like en suite that could easily be featured in any high-end design magazine.

Jenna now had the means to bring all of these luxuries to the cabin, but realized she didn't want or need any of it to make her happy. *Well, maybe the bath,* she thought, chuckling lightly to herself.

Slowly, she made her way to the staircase where she found the chauffeur, John, in wait of her.

"Good evening, Ms. Jenna. Charles asked me to take you to The Chateau. He'll be waiting for you there."

"Do you know why he couldn't take me himself?"

"He said something about a meeting he'd forgotten ." John held the door open for her.

It was another beautiful, star-filled night, and as the spectacular city lights grew closer, all she could think about was whether or not Jack was looking through his telescope at the same sky. The sudden stop of the car jostled her thoughts back to the present. She absent-mindedly played with the clips in her hair as John rounded the front of the car.

Jenna got out of the back seat and took in the grandeur of The Chateau. No matter where she looked it oozed money. At one time, this would've been a requirement for her to dine there. Enormous pillars and marble stairs led to an over the-top foyer, dripping in crystals and snobbish airs.

Funny, I remember it being much bigger than this.

The amount of money that went into such things now seemed frivolous and less than impressive.

She paused in the doorway of the dining room. Through the maze of candle-lit tables, she perused the room when her gaze caught on chocolate-brown hair curled above a stark-white collar. Her breath hitched, and she reached for the wooden archway to steady herself. She blinked rapidly and briefly closed her eyes, only to open them to the same unbelievable sight before her.

How is this possible?

Jenna moved forward; the familiar scent of earthy cologne reached her and set her pulse racing. She was close enough to touch when he stood and turned to face her.

"Wh-what are you doing here?"

Jack grinned, a devilish glint in his eyes. "It's nice to see you, too."

Jenna squealed and threw herself into his arms, pressing her lips against his mouth, kissing him soundly.

He held her at arm's length. "I can't tell you how good it is to see you. God, you're beautiful."

She fluttered her lashes and sat in the chair he'd moved closer to his. "What about Sasha and the pups?"

Only after he was seated did she notice all the heads turned in their direction. Jenna smiled and winked at them, quite pleased in the united reaction of shock and condescension.

"We definitely owe Charles a debt of gratitude. Just before lunch time, two residents from the Veterinarian Institute showed up to take care of the dogs. The first weeks of the pups' lives are crucial in training them for sled dogs." He shook his head. "Your friend even sent a car to fetch me so I could be here with you."

"He's such a dear man." She sniffled, deeply touched by Charles' intuitiveness.

"He said you needed me."

Jenna couldn't stop the stinging of tears. How incredibly blessed she was to have two men in her life who loved her so much.

Jack took her face in his hands, using the pads of his thumbs to brush away the droplets. "No more tears, Jenna. You're not alone. Are you going to be okay?"

"Now that you're here, I will be." She dabbed her eyes with corner of a monogrammed napkin.

"I took the liberty of ordering us a glass of wine. I hope you like it."

She arched an eyebrow. "You ordered wine?"

He grinned. "Don't look so shocked. I wasn't always a hermit."

Jenna sipped the golden liquid. An explosion of plump, juicy grapes teased her pallet. "It's perfect. I didn't know you were such a connoisseur of fine wines."

"Hardly." Behind his hand he whispered, "Between you and me, I picked the only wine on the list in English." Jack winked at her playfully and settled back in his chair. Adjusting his tie and rolling his neck uncomfortably. "So, this is how the other half lives...pretty impressive."

Jenna laughed at his admission before shrugging indifference. "It's not such a big deal." She reached over and loosened his tie, undoing the first two buttons of his shirt.

As if her action gave him permission, he unbuttoned his shirt cuffs and rolled his sleeves up to his elbows before he mouthed, *Thank you*. He waggled his eyebrows while he brazenly eyed her up and down. "You really do look beautiful tonight."

"Thank you, but I'd be much more comfortable wearing jeans back home."

He smiled. "I like that."

She cast a glance to either side of her. "Like what?"

"That you called the cabin home." He grabbed her hands and kissed the palms. "Maybe there's hope I haven't lost you back to all of this after all."

A shiver passed over her. His touch rekindled her desire for him. "You can't get rid of me that easily."

He let her hand go and rubbed his thighs. "So, what's good to eat in a joint like this?"

Jenna laughed as he scanned the neighboring tables for what she believed to be menus, a perplexed look on his handsome face.

As if on cue, a waiter appeared at their table. "Good evening. Can I get you another drink from the bar?"

"I'll have a beer. What would you like, Jenna?"

The waiter smirked, apparently amused by Jack's request.

She glared at the stuck-up snob. "We'll both have a beer. Can you handle that? You do know what a beer is, don't you?"

The waiter gasped and stepped back, promptly turning on his heel to make his way to the bar.

"I'm sorry, but I hate assholes like that," she said under her breath, quickly accessing his reaction, not having thought she might've embarrassed him.

Jack snickered, seemingly unscathed by the arrogant waiter. "Remind me never to piss you off." He patted her hand. "Don't worry about it. I don't give a rat's ass what that jerk thinks of me."

Her anger dissipated, quickly replaced by an overwhelming urge to be anywhere but there. "Do you mind if we get out of here?"

Without a moment's hesitation, he balled up his cloth napkin and tossed it on his place setting, pushed away from the table and offered his hand.

"Thank you. I'm sure I can rustle us up something to eat back at my place."

He winked and placed her hand in the crook of his arm. "Or *we* could rustle something up on our own."

Chapter Fourteen

Jack relaxed against the plush seat in the Rolls while Jenna rested her head against his chest as they drove back to her childhood home.

How can a woman so vastly different from me end up in my arms? Compared to this, will she one day tire of the primitive lifestyle of my cabin?

He wrapped his arms around her, rewarded by a soft mew like a kitten. Tonight, he'd show her just how much she meant to him.

The car turned onto a long, winding road leading to a mansion of epic proportion; a home that only existed in movies, until now.

"Wow."

She pulled away. "Wow what?"

"You actually grew up here?" He whistled long and low as he put down the window.

She dropped her gaze. "It's not really as grandiose as it might seem."

Jack kept any further comments to himself as they got out of the car and walked arm in arm toward the mansion. She led him through ornate front doors and stepped onto polished marble tile flanked by a staircase right out of *Gone with the Wind*.

Jenna took his hand and whisked him up to her suite.

Holy cow!

He'd imagined the estate would be posh, but not like this. It was as if the room had been taken off the pages of the most elite design magazine. Light from the fire illuminated the strands of gold woven into the billowing fabric draped around the canopy on her bed.

She stepped out of her heels and gazed back over

her shoulder. "Will you unzip me?"

Her sultry tone stole his full attention. Slowly, he inched the zipper down, making sure his finger skimmed the length of her spine. Jack nuzzled her neck, and the sweetness of her perfume filled his senses. Her breath hitched as he slid the straps aside to give him better access to trail soft kisses along her neck. She quivered under his touch.

He spun her around to face him and eased her dress completely off her shoulders. The soft fabric followed the lines of her body until it gathered around her ankles.

She stepped out of the dress and smiled. "I'll be right back." Her eyes twinkled with mischief as she padded across the carpet to the bathroom. "Don't go anywhere."

Jack growled and shifted to accommodate the growing bulge in his boxers. He sat by the fire and unlaced his boots, his every nerve ending on high alert.

God, what that woman does to me.

Sheer fabric billowed over a canopy bed unlike any he'd seen before. Tapestries hung on the wall that probably cost more than a brand new truck. Sure, he had a healthy bank account, and the matter of Carly's substantial life-insurance payout. He just couldn't justify spending her money, or any money, on something that had no meaning just to hang on a wall.

Light streamed in from the cracked bathroom door. A very feminine silhouette robbed him of breath. "Jenna." Her name came out nothing more than a heated whisper. She opened the door fully as he walked toward her. The silky, pale pink fabric of a tiny slip skimmed the curves of her body. The firelight cast a warm glow over her alabaster complexion.

"Jack, I've missed you so much."

He swallowed hard. Any doubt he had about their future together quickly dissipated with the way she looked at him. *She loves me, plain and simple.*

Jack swept her off her feet and cradled her in his arms, covering her mouth with his in an intense, passionate kiss while he carried her and laid her on the bed. He swept the length of her with his gaze. His body responding to the way her nipples pressed taut against the fabric, begging to be touched.

"Come to bed."

Her sultry voice prompted him to quickly undress. He climbed on the bed and straddled her to look down into her lust-filled eyes.

"You take my breath away." His fingers danced across the swell of her breast, and she trembled under his touch. He teased her erect nipples with his tongue before lightly blowing on the dampened fabric.

"Jack, please...make love to me." She pressed her belly against his erection.

Jack looked directly into her eyes. "Before you go to sleep tonight, you will know with no uncertainty, just how much you mean to me."

The early-morning funeral was a solemn affair; the first one Charles attended where not one tear was shed. Jenna put on a brave front, clinging to Jack like a lifeline. He could only imagine what was going on behind her far too bright eyes.

Thankfully, the service was kept short, and Kenneth Blackburn the Third's ashes placed in a vault. There would be no gathering afterwards. The few people in attendance, business associates and staff, left the funeral home to get on with their lives.

How would his former boss feel to know less than twenty people had come out to pay their respects?

Charles watched the limo pull up out front and set

off in search of Jack and Jenna. Luckily, he didn't have to look very far, as he wasn't sure how much longer he could contain his excitement.

"Jenna, John is waiting out front for the two of you." His attempt to keep a straight face proved difficult.

She scrutinized him from the bench where she sat next to Jack, her brow creasing. "Why? Aren't you going to take us?"

"Can't you do as you're told just once without asking questions?" The corner of his mouth twitched.

She narrowed her gaze on him and stood with her hands on her hips. "What are you up to Mr. Wylder?"

He turned on his heel. "Fine, stay here if you like. I just thought you'd want to meet your sister. My mistake. I'll tell John he's no longer needed."

Her squeal pierced the air as she ran to block his path. "Angelina?" She shifted from one foot to the other. "You found her? How? Where is she?"

Charles took her hands in his. "After you told us about your sister, I thought I'd question the staff to see if they knew anything about her. I learned from one of the housekeepers that your mother left the estate once a month without fail. She'd leave early in the morning and not return until late at night.

"I went straight to John to ask him about her monthly trips. It turns out he did drive your mother, on the same day every month, to *volunteer* at a ranch about an hour from here—a home for the mentally and physically challenged."

Tears spilled down her cheeks.

Her man now stood by her side, smiling from ear to ear. "I'm so happy for you, Jenna."

"Come on. John is going to take you there now." He winked at Jack. "We've already called ahead so they're expecting you both."

"I thought we'd have a real battle on our hands trying to find her." Jenna threw her arms around him. "How can I ever thank you?"

"No thanks needed. It was John who held the key." He hugged her a little tighter; thankful he was the one to give her such exciting news on an otherwise somber day.

Jack stepped up. "Come on, babe. Let's go meet this sister of yours."

Chapter Fifteen

Jenna took in the scenic country road they travelled, alongside lush, rolling green hills littered with wildflowers. Sections of the land were fenced off to allow half a dozen or so horses the freedom to roam.

"I bet coming here reminded my mother of her childhood on her family's horse farm."

John drove under a wooden archway where a sign announcing Rolling Hills Ranch swayed from its chains in the breeze. They drove a good ways down a gravel road lined by majestic maple trees until they came upon a ranch-style house, a few separate buildings and a big red barn standing behind everything. The property was immaculate, and the buildings appeared freshly painted, giving Jenna a good feeling about the kind of place Angelina lived.

"It's quite a set up, isn't it?" Jack squeezed her hand. "Like going to horse camp all year long."

She smiled, relieved at not finding the haunted insane asylum from her wildest imaginings. "Do you think they'll actually let me see my sister today?"

The limo came to a stop, and John stepped out to open their door.

"I guess we'll find out soon enough." Sliding out first, Jack offered his hand.

"Where is everyone?" She didn't see a single soul outside.

He glanced at his watch. "Well, we are a little earlier than expected. My guess is they're still having lunch. Why don't you take a couple of minutes to calm yourself before going inside?" He winked at her. "Let's check out the horses."

She closed her eyes and blew out a rush of pent up

anxiety. "Yes, you're right. I don't want to appear distraught in front of her."

Jack led her over to the enclosure. Two of the majestic animals, nostrils flaring, came right up to the fence and stretched their necks over to have their faces stroked and tops of their heads patted.

She struggled to focus on the beautiful creatures. Jack stroked a jet-black mare—at ease, like he was around horses all of the time. "Obviously, these animals get lots of attention."

"I didn't know you liked horses. You should buy a couple of them to ride back home? There's certainly enough room for them."

"That might not be a bad idea," he stated. "And I hope you meant *we* should get a couple."

Jenna kissed him lightly. "Of course that's what I meant."

Suddenly, it was as if someone flipped an ON switch. Kids scattered in groups of ten or so, led by a leader wearing a red T-shirt with the ranch logo.

Her heart raced behind the hand splayed over it. "Angelina would probably be around thirty-five years old." Jenna leveled a hand across her brow to block out the sun.

"Wasn't there anything at all about her in those letters?"

"No, only the one time before my parents married." *Maybe she kept the journals about her visits with Angelina hidden from my father? Could they still be in her room somewhere?*

An older gentleman with a friendly smile walked toward them. "Hello, it's a beautiful day, isn't it?"

Jenna noted his stark-white hair belied his age as he appeared to be in his late forties and rather handsome. She smiled back. "It sure is."

"You must be Jenna Blackburn. You look like your

mother."

The mention of her mother brought a warm smile. "Did you know her well?"

"She came once a month without fail, up until we read about her passing in the news. She was a remarkable woman." He offered his hand to her and then Jack. "I'm Daniel Meed, CEO of this ranch."

Her stomach lurched. *Meed?* Surely it was only a coincidence. There was definitely no resemblance between the two. "Oh, I, I'm sorry," she stammered. "This is my... my good friend, Jack Davis."

"It's nice to meet you, Jack. Why don't we go to my office so we can talk privately?"

Jenna took hold of Jack's hand. She opened her eyes wide, trying to convey her shock at Daniel's last name. He responded with a slight nod and squeezed her hand reassuringly. As she followed their host, she scanned the many groups of residents, some of which were undeniably physically disabled.

Angelina, are you out there? Please God, let Daniel's same last name be an odd coincidence. Please, it would kill me if I ever learned Howard Meed was anywhere near my sister.

Daniel ushered them inside to his office. A large picture window overlooked the impressive grounds.

"Let's sit over here." He motioned to a comfortable seating area where he sat in a wing-back chair facing a leather love seat.

"Before we start, I have to ask, do you have any relations in the area?" Jack asked pointedly.

Jenna held her breath in wait of his answer.

"No, I'm afraid not. I'm an only child, and my parents have been gone for many years now. I was actually born and raised in Texas and moved here for this job over twenty years ago." He smiled warmly. "Why do you ask?"

Relief washed over her, and she tried to release her breath without drawing attention. *Thank God they're not related.*

"It's nothing really. We know a man with the same last name. Howard Meed, have you heard of him?"

"Afraid not. My life is here on the ranch. I rarely have the opportunity to socialize." Daniel folded a long leg over his bended knee. "Are there any other questions, or can we get to the reason we're all here today."

"Please, tell us about my sister." She firmed her hold on Jack's hand.

"Angel came to us when she was ten years old. She has Down syndrome."

Jenna gasped, not fully comprehending what the syndrome entailed. "How bad is it?"

"There's no reason for alarm, actually Angel is one of the luckier ones. She has none of the more severe medical issues many people with Down syndrome are afflicted with."

"Thank God." She straightened in her seat, eagerly soaking up any information about the disease, fully intending to research a lot more.

"Through no fault of your mother, Angel's significant hearing loss wasn't addressed. They believed her speech and minimal attention span was part of mental retardation. Once we took her hearing loss into account, she flourished. No two people with DS have the same challenges. Angel's difficulty lies not only in hearing, but in processing information. She is very smart, but it takes her a little longer to *make sense* of things."

"Did my father continue to pay for Angelina after my mother's passing?"

Daniel pressed his lips firmly together, seemingly weighing his words.

"When your mother came to us each month, she paid a cash sum. I never questioned the method, assuming she didn't want a paper trail for her own reasons."

"Those *reasons* would have been a result of my father's wishes." *Great, that's just what I needed, another reason to hate my father.*

"I'm sorry to hear that. Your sister is so much a part of our little family here, turning her away wasn't a consideration. She more than earns her keep around here."

Jenna barely contained her anger at her father for such a cruel, heartless decision on his part. Her mother would be mortified if she knew. "I'll make it right. I promise you that."

"Thank you, but there's no reason for you to rush. Angel is a pure joy to have here, and the younger children adore her." He rubbed his palms on his jeans, and folded them in his lap.

Jenna shook her head. "Do you have pen and paper, please?" In spite of his heartfelt words it was only right she paid for her sister's keep.

Daniel took a pad of paper and pen from his desk and brought it to her.

"How much is in arrears?"

He shrugged. "I can't tell you off the top of my head."

Jenna frowned and rifled through her purse for her checkbook. "As you know, my father recently passed away. Though I am executor of his estate, it will take some time before I can access his money." She opened the leather folder and scrawled out a check. "But I can give you a deposit of ten thousand dollars from my personal savings."

"I don't know what to say. Why don't you wait for me to look up the correct amount?"

Jenna then proceeded to write out a note in good faith, promising to donate another two-hundred and fifty thousand dollars once the inheritance became accessible. She reread the memorandum before adding her signature. "Can you please sign as a witness for me?"

"Of course." Jack quickly signed his name without reading it. One more reason the man was so amazing.

She then gave the paper to Daniel. "If you would please sign this and have your secretary make a copy for me I'd be very appreciative."

His eyes grew big as he read the promissory note. "I...I don't know what to say."

"There's no need to say anything. Thank you for caring for my sister in spite of not being paid, I'm certain you will find a way to make this place even more magnificent than it already is." The curator seemed to be weighing his response, and she added quickly, "Please, I'd rather not discuss this any further. I came here to make sure my sister is cared for. I only recently learned of her existence."

Daniel didn't seem to know what to do or say. He walked over to his desk, put the check in the top drawer, and then politely turned to blow his nose and gather his composure. "I'll just be one second to have a copy made of this." He pointed to a small table off to one side. "Please, help yourself to a coffee or water while I'm gone."

Jenna jumped to her feet the second the door closed behind him. "Can you believe my father? How could he do such a thing? For all he knew, my sister was out on the street with no money, and nowhere to go."

Jack stood and pulled her into his arms, squeezing her hard. "It's all going to be okay now. Don't give your father another thought. You've found your sister, that's all that really matters."

She shook her head and gazed into his eyes. "I love you." She lightly kissed his lips before pulling away. "Can you believe his last name is Meed? I almost fell to the ground when he introduced himself."

"It is a pretty common name. I was just as taken aback by it as you were." Jack walked over to the water cooler and poured them both a glass.

"Thank you for asking him about it. I don't think I could have formulated the words at that moment."

He smiled and gave her a drink just as the door opened and Daniel strode back into the office.

"I hope that wasn't too long. You can pick up your copy on the way out." He returned to his seat.

"Do you think I can see her?" Her heart pounded so hard she imagined they heard it. "That is, if you feel it's a good idea." She returned to her seat and slipped her hand in Jack's, her damp palm against his warmth oddly comforting.

"I've thought about this and discussed it with her doctors and primary caregiver." Daniel crossed his legs. "If we were to introduce you to her as a sister, it would only confuse her. She tends to become very emotional with sudden change. She's lived the same routine most of her life, surrounded by familiar faces. When your mother stopped coming, she took it very hard."

My poor sister. The thought of her suffering such a loss alone almost brought her to tears.

"I think if we were to bring you in as a visitor during arts and crafts time, and without making a big production of it, you could approach her, expressing interest in what she's creating. Now that we've met, however, my fear is that she'll see the strong resemblance to your mother and not know how to process it."

Disappointment at not being able to see her now sparked her determination to see her sister, and she rose. "What if I don't approach her? I'd be happy to see her from afar for today. We can work on the rest later. I promise you, this is only the first of *many* visits."

He nodded. "I think that is an excellent idea, and if she happens to come to you, I guess we'll just follow her lead. Give me a few minutes to find out exactly where she is."

The second the door closed behind him, she clenched her hands and stomped her feet, so excited she wanted to shout. "I'm actually going to see my sister. Can you believe this is really happening?"

Jack chuckled. "She's a very lucky woman to have you for a sister."

Jenna froze. "What if she doesn't like me?"

Chapter Sixteen

Jack had caught a glimpse at the amount of Jenna's Promissory note. He'd never given much thought to how much money she'd come into. It must be a considerable inheritance to give away that much without batting an eyelash. Despite being financially stable on his own, it made him feel small, maybe even inadequate, in comparison.

She'd been so happy with everything...he didn't have the heart to mention his unease. Not to mention, there was something about Daniel Meed that didn't sit right with him. It wasn't one thing in particular, more like a bad vibe. There was no reason to believe the man would lie about not having family in the area, but on the same note, there was no reason not to doubt whether he spoke the truth. Still, it was a pretty big coincidence not to at least wary.

Before heading back home, I'll be sure to let Charles in on my misgivings.

Jenna's excitement was highly infectious. He'd never seen her like this, but he liked it. *Very much.* They were told her sister was in the barn, feeding the horses being one of her daily chores.

Jack paused at the barn doors. "Are you ready?"

She expelled a shaky breath. "I think so."

Daniel put a hand on her shoulder. "Don't be scared, your sister's name suits her perfectly, you'll see."

He could've sworn the guy cast him a sly grin as his hand remained on Jenna.

Hands off, buddy. Jack winced as she tightened her hold on his own, squeezing his fingers together. By the time he looked back, Daniel was in the doorway that opened to a dozen empty stalls. The back entry stood open wide where a few people wandered about amongst the horses in a fenced area.

Maybe I'm over reacting. Could it be a little green monster?

Angel wasn't hard to spot; she had the same captivating emerald green eyes he'd seen in pictures of their mother Jenna had shown him last night. And she definitely didn't look ten years older than Jenna. In fact, she seemed younger. She had the tell-tale features of Down syndrome, a small nose and round face. Instead of small, close set eyes, though, Angel's were almond shaped, and her shoulder-length hair was a darker red than Jenna's. Short, stubby fingers held the reins to one of the horses.

"Do you see her?" Jenna nudged his side. "She's beautiful," she whispered close to his ear.

"Why don't you start here and stroll leisurely in her direction. Just smile and observe, maybe ask a few questions about the horses on your way. I'll be right here if you need me."

Her body trembled beneath his hand as Jack guided her over to where one of the smaller children brushed a horse's side.

"Try and relax. We don't want to make anyone uncomfortable."

Jenna mouthed, *Thank you.*

He took a step back as she approached a little blonde girl and squatted to her level.

"Hello." Jenna ran a hand down the horse's smooth belly. "Does he have a name?"

The girl, no more than ten-years-old, turned to look at her with the most beautiful, ice-blue eyes. She showed no sign of fear. "His name is Snowflake."

A smile tilted her lips as her shoulders shook slightly in amusement at the little girl's choice of name for the chocolate-brown mare. "That's a pretty name. My name is Jenna. Do you have a name?"

The girl giggled, bringing two knotted hands to her mouth. "Of course I do, silly. It's Sweet Pea."

Jack's heart swelled as he watched the two interact, all the while keeping a wary eye on Daniel.

"I'm very happy to meet you, Sweet Pea." She offered her hand, obviously touched by the child's look of shock before she gently placed her deformed hand in Jenna's.

He turned to see if her sister paid any attention to Jenna. Angel had stopped filling the troughs and stood frozen, bucket dangling from her hand. Confusion filled her eyes as she stared at Jenna.

He casually stepped forward and tapped Jenna's shoulder. "Angel is staring at you, and appears to be pretty confused."

"Is she looking at me right now?"

"She hasn't stopped."

Angel's stone-face gave no hint of how she was feeling.

Jenna moved slowly, walking toward her sister without actually looking at her, but Jack pulled her back to stand beside him. "I think we should stay here. She seems kind of freaked out."

Daniel rushed to Angel's side, speaking to her quietly until she finally gave him her full attention.

"What do you think they're saying?" Her body vibrated against him, and her words came out a tad too fast.

"My guess is she's a little spooked by how much you and her mother are alike." He rubbed her arm. "It's not going to happen overnight. Remember what Daniel said, we can't push her."

"Okay," she conceded. "I'll let it go for today, but I'm not giving up."

"Of course, nobody's asking you to."

Her disappointment was almost palpable. He

tried to appear positive, yet empathetic to her feelings. Jack slipped a hand across her back and squeezed her shoulder reassuringly. They walked in silence through to the other side of the barn where John waited at the car with the door open.

"Don't be sad, Jenna." He stroked her hair. "Be happy you've found your sister, and at some point, I truly believe you will become the best of friends." Her skin was cool against his lips as he pressed them to her forehead. "Your mother would be very proud and happy about this."

"You're right. I'm being selfish." The tremor in her voice told how dejected she was.

"Give yourself a break, babe. You've been through a hell of a lot in a short period of time. You're entitled to feel whatever you're feeling." He tilted her chin up. "Everything is going to work out. Before long, we'll be home, sitting in front of a crackling fire. We can forget about everything, at least for one night. All there will be is you and me. How does that sound?"

"Mmm." Jenna snuggled up to him and laid her head against his chest.

The slight frown to her lips confirmed his suspicion...she was nowhere near as convinced as she pretended to be.

Chapter Seventeen

Jack found Charles polishing the hood of a most impressive muscle car. He whistled long and low. "Nice ride. Chevy right?"

The other man wiped his sweaty brow, grinning like a Cheshire cat. "Yup. She's a 1969 Chevelle Yenko." He gave the shiny hood one last swipe with a shammy. "You're back sooner than I thought you'd be. How did it go?"

"Well, we did get to see Angelina."

"Really? I bet Jenna is over the moon. Does the sister look like her?"

He shook his head. "She has the same eyes as their mother, but unfortunately, we didn't get to actually talk to her."

Charles set his rag on the midnight black hood, offering him his full attention. "Why not?"

He went on to tell him about their visit and how Angelina reacted. "Daniel believes it will take time for her to accept Jenna in her life. Right now, she's pretty agitated, so we thought it best to leave her alone for today."

"How did our gal take all of this?"

"She's putting on a brave front, but I can tell she's pretty disappointed." Rubbing the back of his neck, he sat on a bench.

"Poor kid, so what happens now?"

Jack shrugged. "I guess we go home as planned and figure out what to do next."

The big man strolled over and sat beside him. He put a hand on his shoulder. "I know how much you want her back home with you, but do you think it's what she needs right now?"

He frowned; not liking the direction their

conversation was headed.

"I mean, the poor girl just buried her father and found a sister she knew nothing about. If I know her, she won't give up on creating a bond with Angelina. She can't do that from way out there in the middle of nowhere."

His gut clenched, and he thread his fingers through his hair. He knew Jenna would come home with him if he pushed the issue, but... *Do I have the right to do so?*

"I can't stay here any longer, Charles. I have my dogs and a new litter to be trained soon."

"I know it's not what you want to hear, but maybe Jenna needs to stay close to her sister for now."

Jack knew he was right, but that didn't mean he had to like it. "Maybe, but I need to ask you to do something for me before I decide what to do."

"Name it."

"We learned the head honcho on the ranch goes by the name Daniel *Meed*." Jack carefully accessed his reaction.

Charles shook his head. "Shit. Are you saying he's related to that asshole Howard?"

He shrugged. "I asked, and he said no, that he has no family in the area." Jack rolled his neck. "There's something about the guy. I get a real bad feeling about him. Do you think you could look into it for me? Jenna says she agrees it's a coincidence, but I have to wonder if she said that for my benefit. I don't want her to know about my suspicions as she's been through enough."

"I couldn't agree with you more. I promise if there's something shady about this character, I'll find it." Charles offered his hand. "You can count on me."

Jack shook it before wandering off, deep in thought.

I know I can count on him...if I didn't, there's no way in hell I'd leave here without Jenna.

Jenna sat up and took the steaming mug of coffee from Jack's hands. She inhaled the delicious aroma. "Mm, if God made anything better than this, he kept it for himself."

He sat on the bed, facing her. "I think we need to talk."

The seriousness of his tone drew her full attention. "Is something wrong? Is it Angel? Has something happened?" She set her cup down on the bedside table and threw her covers to the side. Her pulse raced. His hand on her knee stopped her from getting out of bed.

"No, no it's nothing like that. I've made a decision I don't think you'll be very happy about."

She breathed a sigh of relief, and eyed him suspiciously. "Well?"

He shook his head at her. "I love you, Jenna. I know you feel like you're being pulled in two different directions. So, I'm going to help you out. I'm going to tell you what you're going to do?"

"Oh are you now? Just when did you become the boss in our relationship?" She smirked. Her attempt to lighten the mood failed miserably.

What could possibly have made him so humorless?

"I'm serious, Jenna. I have to get back to the dogs today...and I'm going on my own."

She opened her mouth to speak, only to have him silence her with a finger to her lips.

"Hear me out. I think you need to stay here a little longer. You need to be close to your sister if you have any hope of forging a relationship with her."

Her shoulders slumped, and she sighed

resignedly. She knew he was right, but wasn't crazy about being separated from him again. "Are you sure that's what you want, Jack?"

He got up and slid in beside her, taking her hands in his. "It's not that I *want* to leave without you, I just think you need to be here right now, close to your sister."

Jenna closed her eyes and focused on keeping a calm exterior. She knew this wasn't easy for him to do, and the last thing he needed was for her to dissolve into tears. Slowly she raised her head and looked him in the eyes. "You're right."

He pulled her close and pressed his warm lips to her cheek. "It's not like we'll be worlds apart. I'll only be two and a half hours away."

Jenna burrowed her face in his flannel shirt, inhaling deep, stamping his scent to her memory bank. "When do you have to go?" Her bottom lip quivered, and she tightened the grip on her emotions. *He'll only be a couple of hours away.*

He glanced at his watch and winced. "Um...about an hour ago."

He's sitting right here, and I already miss him like crazy. She shifted to stare him in the eyes. "I love you so much, Jack. You know that, don't you?"

He took her in his arms, answering her question in a slow, intense kiss that literally took her of breath away.

"You kiss me like that again, and I won't let you go anywhere without me." She loved that her response made him blush.

"Um...er, if I don't leave now..." He coughed into his hand and got up from the bed." Listen, I'll talk to my friend at the firehouse. I'm pretty sure I can give you a phone call from there on the weekend. How does that sound?"

Jenna nodded her approval as she shimmied to the edge of her bed and got up. "It sounds wonderful. I guess we'll just play it by ear and see how things go with Angelina."

He stood in front of her and clasped his hands behind her, drawing her close. "I want you to promise me you'll keep your guard up around Daniel Meed. If you feel anything is *off* about the guy, promise me you'll go straight to Charles." His hold on her tightened. "Promise me, Jenna."

"Yes, yes of course I promise you. I don't want you worrying about me, I've got lots of people looking out for me here."

Jack gave her a quick kiss before making his way to the door.

"I love you, Jack. Drive safely."

He tipped two fingers to his forehead. "I always do. Good luck with your sister, and I'll try to call you on the weekend."

Jenna forced a smile. "I'll be waiting by the phone."

"I love you, Jenna."

His final words filled her heart as he walked out into the hallway. God only knew when she'd see him again. She briefly closed her eyes and drew in a shaky breath.

I have to stay focused on creating a bond with my sister. The sooner that happens the sooner I can go back where I belong...

Home to the cabin and in Jack's arms.

Chapter Eighteen

Jenna squinted against the sunlight pouring in her bedroom windows.

"Ms. Jenna?"

Still half asleep, it took a moment to realize where she was. She was just dreaming of being back home with Jack, only to wake up and find him hundreds of miles away. "Edna?" She sat up in bed. "What's wrong?"

"Nothing is wrong. A man named Daniel Meed called from the Rolling Hills Ranch. I told him you were still sleeping and you'd call him back when you got up."

Angel. She opened her eyes wide, completely awake now. "Did something happen to my sister?"

"No, Ms. Jenna. I thought so, too, but Daniel assured me it was nothing bad."

Her rigid body relaxed on a sigh of relief. "Thank God. I don't think I can handle any more bad news."

A light rap on the door found Tara, one of the housekeepers, with a large arrangement of wildflowers.

"Sorry to interrupt, but these just came for you, Ms. Jenna. The delivery man had specific instructions these were to be given directly to you."

Overwhelming homesickness consumed her. Jenna blinked back the threat of tears; recognizing the bright gold flecks on the petals of ruby dianthus, accompanied by lavender snapdragons and vibrant yellow black-eyed Susans, the same wildflowers that littered the countryside back home.

Edna crossed the room and took the flowers from Tara. "Thank you."

Jenna hugged herself, trying to reclaim the

sensation of being in Jack's arms.

"Aren't these beautiful, Jenna? Where would you like me to put them?"

"How about right there in front of the window? Is there a card?"

Edna set the arrangement down on the small table and plucked out a small envelope. She handed her the card, and a small note with the number for Daniel scrawled across it. "How about I bring you some coffee?"

"That would be lovely. Thank you, Edna."

Jenna's chest tightened as she fumbled with the small envelope and finally removed the note.

My Snow Angel,
   Missing you.
      Love, Jack xoxo

She tossed her covers aside and swung her legs over the edge of the bed. *The sooner I get to know Angelina, the sooner I can go home where I belong.*

She paused on her way to the bathroom. "Why did Daniel call?" Jenna went back and picked up her phone from the bedside table and keyed in the numbers. Someone answered after the first ring.

"Rolling Hills Ranch."

"Hi, this is Jenna Blackburn. I'd like to speak to Daniel Meed, please."

"Sure, hang on just a sec."

Every possible scenario tangoed in her mind. *What will I do if Angel doesn't want any part of getting to know me? I can't force her...*

"Jenna?" Daniel asked.

"Hi. I understand you phoned this morning?" she blurted in one short breath.

"Yes. I'm sorry things didn't go as well as you hoped yesterday."

"Thank you. I hope my sister wasn't too upset. Is

she okay now?" Jenna nibbled on the side of her fingernail, a nasty habit she'd never indulged in until that very moment.

"Angel wanted to know why you looked like her mother. She was very surprised."

Her heart pounded. "What did you tell her?"

"We sat down with her and explained there are always going to be people who remind us of the ones we love. For now, she seems content with that explanation."

Jenna blew out a breath she hadn't been aware of holding. "I'm happy to hear that. Too bad you couldn't tell her I'm her sister."

"Baby steps, Jenna. Now, back to the reason I've called. Once a month we have a family day where our residents' families and friends come out. We have a big barbeque and games for the kids."

"Do you think I should come?"

"I was hoping you would. How do you feel about face painting?"

Jenna laughed. "Why, do you want me to wear a disguise?"

He chuckled. "Not exactly, but we thought it might be a good idea if Angel thinks you're here for a reason, like face painting."

"Me? I don't know. I've never done anything like that..." Silence permeated the phone line. As hard as she tried, she couldn't come up with one reason not to do it. "I guess I could give it a try. How hard can it be?" she chattered nervously.

"That's great. We'll have everything you need here. All you need to bring is yourself."

His approval of her decision to try brought a smile to her lips. "When is this family day?"

"Oh, I guess you need to know that, don't you? Tomorrow afternoon, I know its short notice, but—"

"No, of course I'll be there! Thank you for the invitation. I'm looking forward to it."

Jenna hung up and smiled to herself. Jack was right. She did need to be here if she wanted to establish any kind of relationship with Angelina. She padded over to the flowers and feathered the delicate yellow petals of a chocolate-scented daisy. "I love you."

Her nose twitched at the sweet fragrance, and she rubbed her nose to chase away a sneeze. Behind her, Edna cleared her throat. Jenna looked up to find her entering the room with tray in hand. The rich aroma of coffee overpowered the floral ambrosia.

"Mmm, that smells heavenly. Thank you."

"You are most welcome. Charles asked if you'd like to join him for breakfast this morning."

Jenna smiled—the oppressive melancholy had been lifted away by the flowers and Daniel's invite to the ranch "Please tell him if he can wait until I've had a chance to shower, I'd love to join him."

Charles sat on the back deck, coffee in hand. He hoped her silence after Jack left meant she agreed it was the right decision for him to go on without her. There was no doubt the two would miss each other like crazy.

As promised, he'd looked into Daniel Meed's background for Jack, and as far as he could tell, the man was telling the truth. His recourses were limited in that he didn't want Jenna to catch wind of anything amiss. Luckily, most birth records were accessible, and he managed to track down his birthplace as Austin, Texas. For good measure, he traced Howard's birthplace. Ten years older than Daniel, he was born a Canadian, from Toronto, Ontario.

That didn't mean he was satisfied there wasn't a

connection between the two men. He didn't believe in coincidences like this one. Just in case, he'd beefed up security around the estate and even hired someone to keep an eye on the ranch. There was no such thing as being over-cautious when it came to Jenna's well-being.

The fresh scent of shampoo wafted to him and he turned. Jenna, hair still damp from the shower, stepped outside.

"Good morning, kiddo. I hope you slept well."

"Like a rock, and good morning to you, too." She sat at the small table set for breakfast and took a drink of juice, then smacked her lips. "There's nothing like fresh-squeezed orange juice to wake up the old taste buds."

"I'm happy to see you've taken Jack's decision to go home alone so well." He smiled warmly.

"Even though it's the right course of action, I'm not going to lie and say I'm happy about it." She reached for a blueberry muffin from the basket, putting it under her nose and inhaling deeply. "Mm, I think I've gained ten pounds since I've been back."

Charles chuckled, pleased to see the old Jenna back in true form. "So, tell me about your visit with Angelina? Does she look like you at all?"

Jenna shrugged. "Jack sees my mother's eyes in her. She definitely has the trademark red hair. It's darker than mine though." She slathered her muffin with whipped butter and popped a piece in her mouth.

"What kind of ranch is it she lives on? Didn't you say it was a home of some kind?" He made sure to appear in the dark about any of the details pertaining to Angel—careful not to slip up somehow and awaken any underlying suspicions she might have about Daniel Meed.

"It's a beautiful horse ranch. The residents all

have disabilities of some kind. Angelina has Down syndrome." She wiped her mouth with a napkin and shook her head. "Some of those kids broke my heart. One little girl they call Sweet Pea is the tiniest little thing, her hands all gnarled. Yet, you never saw a bigger smile than hers."

"I don't know much about Down syndrome. Is she physically disabled in some way?" He watched Jenna's posture straighten as she put on a brave front.

"Daniel says there are many different types of afflictions those with DS could have. He said Angel is one of the lucky ones. Her biggest challenges are being partially deaf and in processing information. I guess she doesn't react well to change, which is why we're being extra cautious not to rush her when it comes to me."

"Excuse me." Grace poked her head around the corner of the doorway. "There are two officers at the door who want to speak to you. Shall I bring them out here?"

"Oh my. Of course, yes, Grace." Jenna wiped her mouth. "You don't think it's about Jack do you? Maybe he got into an accident on the way home."

"Slow down. Try to control that over-active imagination of yours." Jenna had always been one to over-dramatize events throughout her life.

He got up from the table and offered his hand to the first officer. "Good morning. What brings you out here?"

"Good morning. I'm Officer Dixon and this is my partner, Officer Walker."

"What's wrong? Is somebody hurt? Is it Jack? Did he make it home okay?"

Officer Dixon put a hand on Jenna's shoulder. "I'm sorry, Ma'am, I didn't mean to alarm you. No, there's been no accident and nobody is hurt."

Jenna blew out a rush of air and flopped back in her seat. "Thank God."

"It seems a woman drove past the estate early this morning and saw someone hiding out in the bushes, watching the house through a pair of expensive binoculars. Unfortunately, by the time we got here, there was no sign of the culprit."

"Did she give you a description? How did she know they were expensive?" Jenna asked, twisting a cloth napkin in her hand.

Charles sat back and listened, seething beneath the surface. *I paid good money to have this house watched for something like this. Just wait until I get my hands on the idiots in charge of security.*

"The woman who called in happens to be an avid bird-watcher and recognized them as high-powered, expensive binoculars. It could be some reporter trying to get a story in relation to your father's death." He bowed his head solemnly. "Please accept my condolences on behalf of the police force."

"I hope you guys plan on keeping a lookout for this guy." Charles couldn't help the accusatory tone to his voice.

The officer arched a brow in response. "Of course. We'll have a car drive by at regular intervals for the next couple of days. Hopefully, the sound of sirens scared the guy off and he won't be back."

"Thank you for letting us know." Charles shook both men's hands in turn.

"Of course, you're welcome."

Officer Walker spoke to Jenna. "Please be careful when you leave these grounds. It might be a good idea to have your driver take you wherever you need to go for the time being."

Jenna nodded, but remained seated as the officers left them alone. "What the hell was that all about? I bet it's that disgusting excuse for a man, Howard Meed." Her cheeks stained pink, and her eyes ablaze with anger.

"You let me worry about that. Do as the officers suggested and have John be your chaperone for the next few days. If Howard is behind it, I'll find out and promise it won't happen again. It will be kind of hard for him to look through binoculars with two black eyes."

Jenna laughed and threw her napkin across the table. "My bodyguard."

"You bet I am. You don't have to worry about a thing, okay?" Charles returned to his seat across from her. "Besides, maybe it was a nosy reporter trying to get a story."

She smiled. "Yes, that is very possible." Jenna returned to her muffin, taking a huge bite.

Thankfully she seemed content with leaving any further action to him.

First thing, he'd check out the tapes from the security cameras around the estate. *If it is Howard, he'll wish he'd never tangled with me. I've had just about enough of his obsessive bullshit.*

Chapter Nineteen

The weather couldn't be more perfect for Family Day at the ranch. In the short time since arriving, Jenna garnered a new appreciation for the hard work and dedication of the staff. One couldn't help but get caught up in the very real sense of family. Something from her childhood she missed terribly.

She sank her teeth into a perfectly charred burger and caught the drips running down her chin with a napkin. "Mmm."

Daniel chuckled as he straddled the bench she sat on. "I take it you approve?"

Heat rushed to her cheeks. "Best burger ever."

A lady waved at him from the other end of the tent. "I'm sorry, duty calls. Will you be okay here on your own?"

Caught with yet another mouthful, she offered a weak smile and thumbs up.

"Enjoy."

With that, he took his leave, allowing her to finish her burger in peace. Jenna popped the last morsel in her mouth when she spotted Angelina staring at her from where she sat a couple of tables away. This time, she didn't appear to be upset or confused, only curious, openly checking her out.

Without making a big production of it, Jenna offered a smile and went back to eating the macaroni salad on her plate. A few minutes later, she chanced another glance, disappointed to find her sister no longer at the table.

She sighed resignedly as she left the tent. *Baby steps.*

FACE PAINTING was drawn with brightly colored markers on a poster-board hanging at the front of her station. Several kids had formed another line at her table.

I guess I'm not doing too bad of a job after all.

Before long, she was back in the groove, thoroughly enjoying the special kids. No matter their affliction, all had a big smile for her; some even clapped their hands and jumped up and down after she held up a mirror for them.

Jenna painted yet another butterfly to match Sweet Pea's other previously painted cheek. The little girl seemed to have taken a liking to her, never straying too far from her table.

"Who's next?" She looked up to find Angelina standing before her. Her heart started beating so fast she feared a heart attack right then and there. "Please, have a seat." A surplus of emotions ran rampant within her. She prayed her sister didn't sense anything amiss.

Angelina sat and eyed her curiously.

"My name is Jenna. What would you like me to paint on you today?"

"Can you paint an angel? That's my name, Angel."

Jenna tittered nervously. "I've never done one before, but I'll give it a try. Where would you like it?"

Her sister turned her face and touched her round cheek. "Right here, please."

She fumbled with the paint brush, dropping it on the ground. *Oh my, how am I going to keep my hand steady enough to paint her lovely face?*

Angelina picked up the brush before Jenna had a chance to and passed it back to her. She patted Jenna's hand. "It's okay. Don't be scared."

Jenna blinked rapidly. Angel's eyes were filled with compassion for her.

She let out a calming breath. "Thank you. Now, let's see if I can do this." She pictured the angel on the top of a Christmas tree. The familiar scent of lily-of-the-valley made keeping her emotions in check that much more difficult. She focused on a steady hand to paint a triangle for the body and a circle for the head, filling them both in with white. Angel's eyes reflected the sparkle of a glitter pen as Jenna attempted to draw a halo and steadily outline a pair of wings. She realized it wasn't just the eyes of her sister she looked in—her sister shared the same beautiful green eyes as their mother's.

Jenna held her breath, using one hand to steady the other, in order to finish off with green dots for eyes and red for a mouth. She hesitated before putting the paint brush in water and used the excess red to add a little color to the hair.

"Well, it's certainly not as beautiful as you are." With trembling hands, she held the mirror for her sister.

Angel's jaw dropped, followed by the most beautiful smile Jenna had ever witnessed in her lifetime.

"Oh, you did a *really good* job." She reached over and patted her on the back. "You did a good job, Jenna. Way to go."

Jenna's heart swelled, and she chuckled at her sister's enthusiasm.

Angel's brow creased, and the smile vanished from her mouth. "Why do you laugh at me?"

"Oh, I-I wasn't laughing *at* you." Jenna stammered, recognizing a melt-down when she saw one.

Angel stood, her bottom lip quivered. "You shouldn't laugh at people."

Before she could respond, her sister ran away, disappearing around the side of the barn.

Jenna jumped up. "Oh, my word. What just happened?" She stood dumbfounded, watching in horror as all the kids who waited in line disbursed except for Sweet Pea.

"Why did you make Angel cry?" She rubbed at the butterflies painted on her cheeks. "You are not my friend no more." She spun and ran clumsily to the tents.

Utterly mortified, Jenna scanned the grounds to find Daniel jogging toward her. "Thank God you're here. I've upset Angel. She thought I was laughing at her and ran to the barn...and then, then Sweet Pea..." She dropped to her chair and buried her face in her hands.

"Don't worry, Jenna. Pull yourself together, and I'll go find her. It's important the other children don't see you upset. You can use the bathroom in my office." He took hold of her shoulders. "Look at me. Stay in my office, and if I can get Angel to understand, I'm going to bring her to you. Okay?"

She nodded, not trusting herself to speak. She picked up her purse and followed Daniel's instructions as he ran off in search of her sister.

I can't believe what just happened. Did I ruin my chances of having my sister in my life? She surveyed the barn in passing. *Please, oh please understand. I'd never do anything to hurt you, Angelina. You're my sister and I love you.*

Chapter Twenty

The walls of Daniel's spacious office closed in on her. The clock on the wall ticked louder with each passing second. Now that she'd washed her face and took at least twenty deep breaths, she reflected on what just happened.

If she had any hope of salvaging some kind of a relationship with her sister, she'd have to become ever so mindful of everything she said and did. She'd learned in her research that some didn't understand the concept of laughter as an emotion. *Of course she felt like I was laughing at her.*

Her breath hitched with the opening of the door. In walked Daniel with her sister stuck to his side, seemingly a little leery to be in her presence again. Jenna watched him seat Angel next to him. The fear of saying something wrong kept her silent.

"I think things got off to a bad start. Angel is upset because she feels you were laughing at her."

Jenna shook her head. "No. I'm sorry if you thought that. I really wasn't laughing at you. I was just so happy to be spending time with you...I guess my happiness burst out."

Her sister sat still, eyes downcast.

"If it's okay with you, Jenna, maybe we can start over? How does that sound?" Daniel stroked the side of Angel's face.

"I'd love nothing more than to have a second chance." She pleaded

Her sister slowly raised her head and whispered. "Okay."

Daniel clapped his hands. "Wonderful. I'm so happy we could work this out."

Jenna rolled her shoulders back and held out her hand. "Hello, my name is Jenna. It's nice to meet you, Angel."

The corners of her sister's mouth twitched, quickly blossoming into a smile. She shook her hand. "It's nice to meet you."

"There we go. Now, doesn't that feel better?"

Angel nodded. "Yes." She looked at Jenna, waiting for a response.

"Yes, much better."

"I think we've all had a long day," said Daniel. "Angel has something to ask before you have to leave us."

Her sister peered up shyly. "Maybe you can come back and we can go for a horse ride?"

She wanted to pull her sister into her arms and jump for joy. "I've never been on a horse before. You'll have to teach me."

Angelina's face lit up. "I will teach you." She rubbed the top of Jenna's arm. "You don't have to worry."

Thank you, God. I am truly blessed to be given a second chance.

"Thank you. I won't be scared if you're helping me. When would you like me to come back?"

Daniel cleared his throat. "We can clear Angel's timetable on Wednesday afternoon. Does that work for you, Jenna?"

"Yes, Wednesday is perfect. Thank you for inviting me, Angel. I think we're going to be great friends."

Jack set the last puppy back with his mother. They'd doubled in size and were more and more active every day since their eyes opened. In another week or so, he'd introduce solid food to their diet. Hopefully, they'd be fully weaned by the time they reached six weeks old. Then he could begin their training for the harness in preparation for the sled.

The pups kept him super busy during the daylight hours, but at night, when all was calm, he missed Jenna so bad he couldn't even sleep in their bed alone.

Jack slipped on his gloves and climbed on his quad. There was no way in hell he'd last another four days without hearing her voice. He twisted the throttle and flew across the fields toward town.

The firehouse was quiet when he stepped inside. He made it to the chief's office without notice and rapped on the door.

"Hey, Jack. Come on in." Chief Dawson closed the book he'd been reading and set it on his desk. "I didn't think I'd see you until the weekend."

He shrugged. "What can I say? I've never been any good at waiting."

The fire chief smiled knowingly. "I suppose if I had a pretty lady like Jenna across the border, I'd be a little low on patience myself."

Chief definitely had a sweet spot for Jenna. It began the first time he came out on one of his random visits to check up on him. She had him under her spell the moment she flashed one of her winning smiles, just like me.

"I'd appreciate the use of your phone."

Chief stood and rounded the corner of his desk. "Any word on how long it's going to take to get service out to your place?"

"Probably not for at least a week or two." Jack took the chief's place in his chair.

"I'm going to head for the kitchen and see what I can scrounge up to eat. Be sure to tell the little lady I said hello."

Jack took a couple steadying breaths before keying in the numbers. He was a little nervous about talking to Jenna. *I miss her like crazy, but I have to convince her I'm doing okay on my own. She needs to bond with Angel, I totally get that.* If she suspects for one moment he wasn't faring well without her, she'd come home...and one day resent him for it.

"Hello?"

"Hey, Charles. It's Jack calling."

"Well, hello there. How are things out there in the middle of nowhere?"

He chuckled. "I'm keeping busy. Is Jenna around?"

"No, I'm sorry. You just missed her. She's gone shopping."

"Oh." He tried hard not to show his disappointment. "How is she doing?"

"From what I can see, she's doing okay. To be quite honest, I haven't seen much of her the past few days."

"How are things going with Angel?" He found himself hoping it was her sister who'd kept her so busy. Funny, he wasn't normally the jealous type, but not knowing what she was doing, or who she was with, drove him a little crazy.

"I guess they had a bit of a rough go of it earlier today, but they managed to work things out. In fact, Angel invited Jenna to go horseback riding on Wednesday. That's where she went, to buy riding boots."

That's great!

His taut muscles relaxed for the first time since being

separated from Jenna. "I'm happy to hear it. Can you tell her I called, and I'll phone again Saturday morning?" He made a concerted effort to appear unscathed at having missed Jenna. Not wanting to chance her catching wind that he wasn't happy.

"She's not going to be very happy about missing this call."

"Okay, well, I best be getting back to the dogs." The line grew quiet. "Can you tell her I love her for me?"

"Er, um, will do. Take care."

Jack set the phone down and leaned back in the chair. He pushed his fingers through his hair and let out a heavy sigh.

Oh Jenna, I wish I could've talked to you.

She went shopping...sounded like she was settling back into her old way of life. *Not sure if that's a good thing, or bad?* Of course he wanted her to have fun, but he wondered how she'd fare coming back here after being reminded of all the luxuries she'd be leaving behind?

And then there was building a relationship with her sister. Could she really leave her behind to come home to him?

Jack shook his head and got up from behind the chief's desk.

Why do I doubt the strength of our commitment to each other? Jenna loves me, and no person, or amount of money can keep us apart.

He left the office and made his way out of the firehouse, purposely avoiding any contact with the chief or other men. Once outside, he looked up at the star-filled sky and swallowed hard in an effort to squelch the rising insecurities within him.

"You will come home to me Jenna...won't you?"

Chapter Twenty-One

Jenna cut the engine of Charles' Mustang. She hadn't planned on taking his car, but John was delayed taking Grace grocery shopping, and she didn't want to risk being late for her riding lesson with Angelina, especially after the fiasco of the last time at the ranch. Though the officers strongly suggested for her not to go anywhere alone, she'd be damned to allow the incorrigible Howard Meed dictate where she could or couldn't go.

She swung her legs out of the car and adjusted her new riding boots. In her closet filled with shoes, sandals and boots in every style and color, not one pair deemed suitable for horseback riding. Hopefully, she chose appropriate clothes, opting for jeans and a white, button-down shirt, wearing a T-shirt under it in case the weather turned hot.

Please let today go well, and make it so I don't stick my foot in my mouth.

She had to remember how sensitive Angel was, how sensitive all of the residents were. Sweet Pea...maybe she could steal a moment with the precious little girl to smooth things over.

Oh how I wish you were here Jack. Jenna looked up at the blue sky and fluffy, white clouds. A wave of sadness came over her at having missed his call.

The front door of the ranch opened, and Daniel stepped out. He welcomed her with a warm smile that lifted her spirits.

"Good morning, Jenna." He waited for her to close the car door before clasping her hand in his. "It looks like you're all ready for your riding lessons."

"Ready? Well, that's debatable." She grinned. "Is Angel ready for *me* might be the question to ask."

"Your sister has talked about nothing else. She was up at the crack of dawn making sure your horse was brushed and the saddle oiled."

Jenna smiled. "I can't tell you how grateful I am to you for intervening the other day. I had no idea how sensitive she is."

"You'll find all of the residents are sensitive when it comes to their *differences*—even more so with the older ones who've had a taste of how the outside world reacts to them."

"I'm scared I'll do or say something to upset her again." It was like being on an emotional rollercoaster, up one hill to happiness, down the next filled with fear.

"The best advice I can give you is to treat Angel, and the others, with the same compassion and kindness you would a struggling friend. They just want to be treated like they're *normal.*"

"Thank you. So, where is my sister now?"

He held up a finger and arched a white brow. "Rule number one of Angel's riding lesson routine. All riders must have a good breakfast." He offered his arm. "Please, allow me to accompany you to the dining room."

She giggled and placed her hand on his forearm. "Lead on. We mustn't keep the teacher waiting."

Happiness encompassed her as she stepped into the dining room to find Angel flashing a huge smile in her direction.

"Good morning, Jenna. Please sit down."

"Thank you, Angel. I'm very happy to see you again." She sat next to her sister at a table filled with enough food to feed the entire ranch. "This looks delicious."

Angel beamed. "I wasn't sure what you like to eat."

Jenna smoothed a napkin across her lap and rubbed her hands together. "Where should I start?"

"I helped squeeze the orange juice myself." Her sister poured a glass and set it in front of her.

She raised the juice in a toast. "Here's to a great day together." The sweet nectar titillated her taste buds, and she drank down the entire glass, smacking her lips. "Mmm, now that was good!"

Angel made it her job to see that Jenna tried a little bit of every dish on the table. Quite some time later, she waved a white cloth napkin in surrender.

"I can't eat another thing." She rubbed her belly. "I hope my horse has a strong back, I think I just gained ten pounds."

Her sister tilted back her head and laughed whole-heartedly—a melody Jenna would remember for the rest of her life. Her laughter exuded genuine happiness and joy. If it could be bottled, what an amazing world it would be.

The hostess began clearing the table.

"You don't have to do that, Angel. Cook will be more than happy to." Daniel put his hand on hers.

She frowned and continued stacking dishes. "Cook works too hard. She's not getting any younger you know."

Jenna suppressed the urge to burst out laughing. Angel's expression was completely serious, so instead, she stood and followed suit. "I'll help you."

"I'll help you, too." A petite woman with beautiful olive skin and Italian accent came out of the kitchen. She held out her hand to Jenna. "My name is Twyla. It's nice to meet you."

She shook the woman's hand. "I'm Jenna. Nice to meet you as well."

Angel put her hands on her hips and scowled at Daniel. "See, they know what I mean. You're a man, no wonder you don't *get it*." She used finger quotes around the last two words.

"She's right. Why don't you go and do whatever it is that men do?" Jenna winked.

Her sister held up a hand to high five her. "Amen, Sista."

Jenna's breath caught at her choice of words, but noticed Twyla kept her eyes downcast, not once looking directly at Daniel as she helped clear the table.

I wonder why?

"Okay, okay," he replied. "I can take a hint. I'll meet the two of you at the stables."

Jenna loved seeing the feisty side of Angelina. It made her feel better knowing she could stand up for herself. She'd seriously underestimated her sweet sister. Angel was definitely stronger than she'd first thought.

What goes on behind those enchanting green eyes of yours?

Jenna smoothed her hand down the side of the jet-black mare she'd be riding. A twinge of sadness returned when she realized it was the same horse Jack had been drawn to on the first visit to the ranch.

"Don't you like her?" Angel searched her eyes.

She startled. "Oh yes, yes I do. She's beautiful. I'm sorry, I must've been daydreaming."

Angel visibly relaxed and smiled. "She's very gentle. My mother used to ride her whenever she came to visit."

Mention of their mother sent her already fragile emotions into a tailspin. Jenna struggled to maintain the façade of a calm exterior. "I promise to be extra careful with her."

Angel mistook her reaction as one of fear and rubbed Jenna's back. "Don't be scared."

Daniel sauntered into the stables. "Let's get this show on the road."

The man always seemed to be in the right place at the right time. His timely entrance stole her sister's attention long enough for her to gather her composure.

Angel spent the next twenty minutes going over everything one needed to know about horses and riding them. It was a well-rehearsed lesson she appeared to take great pleasure in reciting.

She instructed Jenna where to put her foot to climb on Midnight. Once up in the saddle, it didn't seem as terrifying as she'd imagined. "You're a great teacher, Angelina."

Her cheeks stained pink. "Thank you. You can call me Angel. Now you can both follow me to the trail, please."

The path was littered with signs of nature awakening in all its bounteous glory. Spring buds blossomed, bathing the countryside in a kaleidoscope of color. Once barren tree branches now sprouted new leaves.

The air filled with a sudden scream unlike anything she'd ever heard. She frantically looked around just as Angel's horse reared up on his hind legs in slow motion. All she could do was watch in horror as her sister flew back and crashed to the ground. The larger than life animal hovered over her, clawing at the air before coming down with incredible force on Angel's arm.

"Angel!"

Jenna's stomach heaved at the sickening crunch that sliced the eerie quiet. She twisted in her saddle to find Daniel already had a hold of the horse's reins, leading the spooked horse off to stand with his at the side of the trail.

"How do I get off this thing?" she shrieked before swinging

her leg over and sliding down the mare's side, not caring when the horse then cantered off to stand with the others. She fell to her knees beside her unconscious sister. "Oh, my God." Angel's right arm lay at an unnatural angle, and blood gushed from the back of her head.

"Daniel? We have to get her some help." Fear paralyzed her. She'd never felt more helpless.

He already had his cell phone out. "Try and stop the bleeding." He covered one ear and tried to explain where they were.

Jenna ripped off her over-shirt and folded it into a pillow, gently lifting Angel's head enough to slip it under her skull. She used the sleeves to tie it tight in hopes of stopping the flow. Her heart sank. In the few seconds it took to tie a knot, her white shirt stained red.

She cupped the sides of her sister's face with trembling hands. "Angel? Can you hear me? Please blink if you can hear me."

Her gaunt face remained motionless, eyes closed.

I'm begging you, God, let her wake up!

"Please, you have to be okay. I just found you...I can't lose you now," she cried out.

Daniel crouched to check Angel's pulse. "Hang in there. Help is on the way."

Chapter Twenty-Two

The caller display flashed the hospital's name, and Charles gripped the side of the table. Visions of Jenna in his Mustang wrapped around a pole left a sour taste in his mouth. Hesitantly, he answered the phone. "Hello?"

"Charles? Angel...the horse...and then her arm. There was so much blood."

"Jenna?" *Thank God it's you.* "You need to calm down. I can't understand a word you're saying. Did you say Angel is hurt?"

"She's unconscious. Oh my God... I can't lose her."

"I'll be there as fast as I can. Is there someone there with you?"

"Daniel is here."

He sensed her anguish through the phone line, and he prayed Angel would be okay as John drove him to the hospital.

Half an hour later, he rushed into the emergency entrance and made his way to intensive care. He'd barely made it through the doors when Jenna ran from a white-haired man's embrace and flung herself into his arms, trembling uncontrollably as she cried against his chest.

The man stood behind her, looking a little lost. He ushered them over to a waiting area.

Jenna clung to Charles, her tears dampening his shirt. He remained silent, giving her the time needed to get it all out. Once she'd regained her composure, he held her at arm's length. "Can you tell me what happened now?"

She hiccupped and dabbed at her eyes with a crumpled wad of tissues. "One minute we were riding down a beautiful trail, and the next, her horse reared up and threw her. She hit her head on a rock and..." She swallowed hard. "There was so much blood, and the horse's hoof crushed her arm."

Charles pulled her back into his arms and smoothed a hand down her hair. "The doctors are going to take good care of her. Have faith she'll pull through."

The man smiled and mouthed the words, *thank you.* Then aloud he said, "I don't think we've been introduced, I'm Daniel

Meed, curator of the ranch."

Daniel Meed...of course. He should've known it was him consoling Jenna.

Charles made a concerted effort to hide the suspicious nature in which he regarded him. "Charles Wylder. It's too bad we have to meet under these circumstances." He shook his hand. "What does her doctor say?"

"They want to operate on her arm, but they can't put her under until they know what's going on in her head."

"Has she regained consciousness?"

Jenna pulled away, sniffing into her tissues. "No, but hopefully the CAT scan will give us some answers."

As if on cue, the doctor approached and offered a tired smile as he sat down. "We ran a series of tests, including a CAT scan, and there doesn't appear to be any serious damage to Angel's skull or brain."

"Thank God," Jenna said hoarsely. "So, will you be operating on her arm?"

He sighed. "Well, yes she needs surgery. The horse broke several of her bones. Unfortunately, until she regains consciousness, putting her under is just too risky. We've immobilized the arm in case she wakes up agitated and causes further damage."

"How long do you think it will be before she comes to?" Daniel leaned forward and rested his elbows on his knees.

"I wish I could answer that. Her vitals are strong, and there really isn't any reason why she shouldn't wake up soon."

"Can we see her?" asked Jenna.

Jenna splashed cold water on her face and held the sides of the basin. She closed her eyes and took several measured breaths before looking in the mirror. "Oh my." Thank goodness Charles insisted she take a minute to herself before going in. If her sister came to and saw her puffy, blood-shot eyes, she might scream with fright.

The only time she'd ever been this scared was when her mother died...and after Jack dropped her at the post office so many months ago. Before the night she ran out of her father's birthday party, she prided herself on being in complete control of her emotions. It seemed ever since then, she cried at the drop of a hat, and she hated being this way.

Jenna soaked a paper towel with cold water and pressed it to her swollen lids. What a cruel twist of fate it would be to lose her sister after spending most of her life in the dark of her existence.

"No." She straightened her stance and sifted through her purse for her facial powder. "You will be strong for your sister," she told her reflection. Quickly, she touched up her face before hurrying to Charles, who waited in the hallway.

"Much better." He smiled warmly and took her hand in his. "Angel's room is just up here. Daniel is in there with her now."

Jenna heaved a sigh. "I can't believe this is happening."

"Sometimes life just isn't fair, but that doesn't mean it's all bad." He squeezed her hand reassuringly. "Let's hope once she hears familiar voices, she'll wake up."

"Yes, you're right."

Jenna braced herself before entering the room. Daniel sat holding her sister's hand. The pain etched in his expression was almost her undoing. With a nod, he took his leave so she could be at Angel's bedside.

Angelina's arm was strapped in a sling of sorts, her head bandaged. Despite the obvious, her face showed no sign of trauma. It was as if she slept peacefully without the influence of intravenous drugs pumping into her.

Her sister's hand was cool in hers. "Angelina, can you open your eyes for us, honey? It's Jenna." She cupped the side of her face. "Please wake up." Angel's eyelashes fluttered, and she struggled remain calm. "That's it. Keep trying."

The room grew silent as Angel blinked a few more times before her eyes slowly opened and she looked up at her.

"Mother?"

Jenna's grip on the bedrail tightened, suddenly faint at being mistaken for their mother, and overwhelmed with relief to see her eyes open. "It's Jenna. You're in the hospital."

Confusion clouded her eyes.

Daniel quickly moved in next to Jenna. "Angel, it's me, Daniel."

She shifted her gaze to him and visibly relaxed. "Daniel?"

"Yes, honey, it's going to be okay. You're in the hospital. The doctors are taking good care of you."

Tears spilled down her flushed face. "My arm hurts."

Jenna reluctantly stepped back as Angel reached for Daniel.

"I know it does, honey. The doctors were just waiting for you to wake up before they fixed it." He brushed the tears from her reddened face.

"I'll go find somebody." Charles, who until then had stayed in the background, left the room.

She fought the overwhelming need to have a good cry, feeling very much the third wheel in the room.

I'm glad Daniel is here for her, but God, how I wish Angel reached out to me for comfort. Stop it! Be positive. I will share a connection with my sister on an even deeper level one day.

"Can I get you anything, Angel?" asked Jenna

"Are the horses okay?"

She suppressed a chuckle. "The horses are just fine. You don't need to worry about a thing."

Angel's eyelids started to droop. "I guess I still owe you a lesson." Her voice trailed off as she fell back to sleep.

Chapter Twenty-Three

Jenna stretched out on her bed, answering the phone on the first ring. "Jack?"

He laughed. "Did it even ring?"

"Oh my God, Jack, it's almost noon." She pressed a hand to her chest to calm her racing heart. "Is everything okay? You had me worried."

"Aw, babe. I'm sorry for worrying you. I would've called a couple of hours ago, but before I left home, I did a head count and came up one pup short."

"Oh no, did you find it?" Jenna pushed the tears from the corners of her eyes with the pad of her thumb. The initial shock gave way to pure joy at hearing his voice.

"Little bugger had me searching for over an hour. I still can't figure out how he escaped.

Jenna held her stomach, his laughter made her so homesick. "Where was he?" She pushed her hair off her face and blinked away another threat of tears.

Whatever you do, don't give him cause to worry.

"You know the meadow behind the barn? Well, it seems he's taken a liking to wildflowers."

She laughed until tears came to her eyes. "I miss you so much, Jack."

"Not half as much as I miss you."

A knock came to the door, followed by Edna peeping in. "I'm sorry to interrupt, Ms. Jenna. John is ready to take you to the hospital."

"Hospital? What hospital? Are..."

Jenna put the phone to her chest. "Can you tell John I'll be there soon?" She waited for the door to close behind her before putting the phone back to her ear. "Jack?"

"I heard. Why do you have to go to the hospital? You're okay, aren't you?" His sincere concern had her swallowing a big lump in her throat.

"Yes. My sister took us horseback riding, and her horse threw her." Jenna shuddered; a flash of the horse standing over Angel filled her vision.

"Was she hurt badly?"

"The horse busted up her arm pretty good, and she was unconscious for a while from a nasty gash to the back of her head."

"I'm sorry, Jenna. You must have been out of your mind with worry."

"It was more like scared shitless." She shook her head. "I truly thought I'd lost her, after just finding her..." She coughed out the side of her mouth to mask the crack in her voice.

"I wish I was there for you, Jenna. I'm sorry."

Jack was making it very difficult to keep her emotions in check. She'd never met a man so in sync with her needs. He wasn't saying sorry, just for the sake of it. He was genuinely sorry he wasn't there for her.

"You have nothing to be sorry for. Nobody could've foreseen it happening. You can rest easy, Charles and Daniel took good care of me."

"I'm happy to hear that." He cleared his throat. "I guess you need to be going then?"

She sighed. "The doc agreed to discharge her today, and I kind of promised I'd be there to help her."

"Don't worry about having to cut this short. I'm the one who called late."

Her heart ached with longing. It was like someone shoved a hand in her chest and squeezed mercilessly. "If it was for any *other* reason, I'd make an excuse to get out of it, but..."

"Don't worry, babe, I get it." He failed to hide the edge of disappointment in his voice.

"When will you call again? I've got so much to tell you." *I will not cry...I will not cry...I will not cry...*

"How about I try for tomorrow evening?"

She sniffled. "Oh Jack, I love you. I'll be waiting by the phone for your call. I hate that I have to go."

"I love you, Jenna. Go be with your sister while you can."

Jenna held the phone to her chest and closed her eyes. "He's calling tomorrow night. That's not so far way." She set down the phone and ran to the bathroom where she washed her face in cold water and repaired her mascara. "Twenty four hours," she repeated, giving her reflection a nod before running out of her room and taking the stairs two at a time to the foyer.

Outside, John waited with the door open. "Good day, Ms. Jenna."

"Good morning, John." Every inch of the limo sparkled in the sun. He'd obviously made an extra effort. "The car looks like brand new! Angel is so excited to be going for a ride in a limousine."

The chauffeur tipped his hat and smiled graciously.

Jenna settled in the back and closed her eyes.

"Go be with your sister while you can."

She'd been so focused in forming a bond with her sister she hadn't given much thought to leaving her at some point. The backs of her eyelids prickled.

How am I going to pull this off without hurting someone?

After a lengthy discussion with Daniel, they mutually agreed now wasn't the time to reveal Jenna as her sister; it was too soon after the accident. Surely she didn't have to choose between Jack and Angel; there had to be a way to make it work so all parties involved got what they wanted.

Before long, John pulled up to the hospital entrance where Daniel stood behind Angel's wheelchair. Her sister gaped up and down the length of the limo. Her expression turned from awe to genuine excitement as John rounded the front of the car and opened the door.

Jenna climbed out and smiled. "Hello you two. Angel, you're looking so much better."

"I'm happy to see you, and happy to be going home today." She directed her gaze at John shyly. "Thank you for driving me home in your limousine."

He tipped his hat. "You can call me John. It's my pleasure, Miss Angelina."

Angel giggled behind her hand, and color flooded her cheeks.

Daniel stepped out from behind the wheelchair and hugged Jenna. "It's good to see you."

He kissed her cheek, his lips lingering longer than warranted. Jenna caught the fleeting look of disapproval from John, validating Daniel's tendency to be a little too familiar wasn't all in her head.

He stepped back and turned his attention to the chauffeur. "It's nice to meet you." He offered his hand.

John eyed him warily while clasping his hand firmly.

Jenna wasn't sure why Daniel's hug left her so unsettled. It was just a simple hug after all, wasn't it? Her fingers lightly feathered the cheek he'd kissed.

"Let's get you settled in the car, Angel." He offered his arm to help her to stand. Her broken arm, encased in a hard shell, rested in a sling knotted over her shoulder.

"Does it hurt very much?" asked Jenna

"Not too much." Her grimace as she got into the car belied her words.

Thankfully, John had the foresight to bring a couple of pillows for Angel's ride home. Daniel opted to sit in the front and talked cars with him. Oddly relieved, Jenna settled in next to her sister as she chattered on about the limo, and how excited she was to see her friends at the ranch.

Daniel ushered his ward inside to a thunderous cheer from the residents. A banner stretched across the width of the room, reading: WELCOME HOME, ANGEL. Her friends swarmed over to where he seated her, the younger ones being quickly reminded to be careful of her arm.

Jenna watched a young woman, who had the tell-tale characteristics of Down syndrome, run to Daniel, link her hands behind his neck and rise up on tip-toes to plant a kiss squarely on his lips. He jerked back and pried the girl's arms away, whispering something in her ear that instantly brought color to her cheeks before she ran off to join the others.

Jenna was careful not to make eye contact as his gaze darted around the room, and he swiped his mouth with the back of his hand.

What did he say to make the girl blush? The brief exchange left her confused and a little unsettled to say the least.

The excitement in the room quickly diverted her attention, and before long, she conceded to maybe misreading Daniel's intentions toward the young lady. It became abundantly clear they were one big, happy family here at the ranch. She could only hope one day Angel felt the same way about her.

Do I have the right to disrupt her life here? Maybe it would be better for everyone concerned if I simply went home to Jack.

"Jenna?" Angel waved her over. "Can you come with me to my room?"

"Of course." She threaded her arm through her sister's good one. "Are you sure you don't want one of your friends to take you?"

Angel cocked an eyebrow. "I thought *you* were my friend?"

She tittered. "I am. I am your friend." Jenna smiled, inwardly thrilled by the timely affirmation she hadn't been aware she so desperately needed. "I just thought you'd be more comfortable with someone you've known longer than me."

Her sister shook her head and led her down a hallway of polished tile floors. A series of Rockwell paintings lined the warm, mocha walls.

From the corner of her eye, she spotted Daniel with the same girl in tow. The two disappeared into what she assumed to be her room, and closed the door behind them. She almost walked right into Angel, who had stopped and opened a door.

"This is my room." She stood to one side for her to enter.

Angel's quarters complimented her personality. The butter-yellow walls lent the room a cheery atmosphere, and delicate, white sheers billowed at the open window.

"Your room is lovely."

"I don't know why I'm so tired." She yawned.

Angel sat in an armchair by the window, and Jenna took the matching chair next to her. "You just got out of the hospital. It'll take you a few days to settle in." Her breath hitched as her gaze settled on a photo of their mother on the bedside table.

Angel followed the direction of her gaze. "That's my mother. Everyone says I look like her."

"I can see why. She's beautiful." Jenna snatched a tissue off the table and quickly turned her head. She faked a sneeze, using the tissue to dab the moisture from her eyes, before addressing her sister again.

"You look like her, too." Angel eyed her curiously. "I think you must know my mother."

Oh God, give me strength.

She cleared her throat. "I'm going to get some water." Her purse fell as she stood.

Angel's jaw dropped as she took in the contents of her purse on the floor.

Jenna was rendered frozen in place as the sight unfolded before her.

Oh no.

Laying there for all to see was an old family snapshot. All she could do was watch her sister pick up the photo with trembling hands. She looked at Jenna and then back at the image of her standing with her parents when she was about fifteen years old.

Her beautiful eyes misted with confusion. "Is that you, Jenna?"

Bumps rose on her flesh with the sudden shift of emotions. *What should I do? If I lie, and Angel finds out, she'll never trust me again. Is she strong enough to learn the truth?*

She heaved a sigh and wiped her sweaty palms on her jeans.

"I don't understand. Why is my mother with you?"

Jenna summoned all the courage she could muster. "I'm just going to tell you the truth, okay?"

Angel nodded.

"The man in the picture is my father. He passed away a few weeks ago."

"I'm sorry. Are you okay?" Angel squeezed her hand.

Her sister's heartfelt compassion threatened her already fragile composure. "Yes, I'm okay. After he died, I found a box of old letters." She took a deep breath and blew it out shakily. "One of those letters told me I had a sister I knew nothing about." Jenna focused on gauging her reaction. "Her name is Angelina."

Her vibrant green eyes widened. "Your sister has the same name as me?"

"*You* are my sister, Angelina." Tears spilled over her lashes, no longer able to restrain.

"*My* sister?" Angel grew rigid and began rocking back and forth. She pulled her hand away and covered her mouth. Her gazed darted in every direction erratically.

"Angel? Are you okay?" Jenna reached out only to have her sister pull away.

"I want Daniel. Daniel! *Daniel,*" she shouted over and over again.

Jenna didn't know what to do and feared leaving her alone. Footsteps rushed across the tile floor outside her room. The door burst open, followed by a woman in nurse's uniform.

"Angel?" The nurse glared at Jenna. "What is going on here?" She made her way to kneel at her patient's side.

"My purse fell and she saw the picture....so I told her I'm her sister and she started calling out for Daniel." *What have I done?*

Her sister continued to rock as she grabbed a fistful of the nurse's uniform.

"I think you should leave."

"I'm sorry. I'm so sorry." She backed up to the door. "I'll find Daniel." She ran from the room and stopped a short distance away to press her back against the wall, gasping for air.

"Why didn't I listen? Look what I've done..."

Chapter Twenty-Four

Once again, Jenna sat in Daniel's office after upsetting her sister. It wasn't like she had any intention of telling Angel they were siblings today, but when she put her on the spot about the photograph, it felt like the right thing to do.

Jenna paced the office. "Idiot, idiot, idiot." *Why didn't I go to him first?* A flashback of Daniel and the young woman going into the room down the hall from Angel came to mind.

The office door opened and Daniel entered, only this time there was nobody in tow. She couldn't read his expression as he kept his head downcast until he reached his desk. He flopped into his chair and raked his fingers through his hair.

She sat at the edge of a chair across from him. "Well, is she okay?"

Daniel huffed. "Nurse gave her something to calm her down. She's resting now." He shook his head at her. "Honestly, what were you thinking? Didn't we just agree now wasn't the time?"

She let out an unsteady breath. "Yes we did. But one minute she said I looked like my mother, and then my purse fell and she saw the photograph of me with my parents." She threw her hands in the air. "What was I supposed to do? Should I have lied to her?"

"Listen, it's not going to do your sister any good playing the blame game. The truth is out, and we'll just have to wait and see how she handles things over the next few days."

Jenna took a deep breath before standing. "Maybe it would be better for everyone if I just left. All I've done since walking into her life is cause her pain."

She turned to the door, but hadn't taken more than a couple of steps before Daniel spun her around to face him. He held her firmly until she looked into his eyes.

"I'm not going to let you take the easy way out. You owe it to Angel to at least stick around until she's ready to talk."

Jenna shrugged his hands away and started to pace. "Stick around? Why, so I can screw something else up and really hurt her?" She came to a sudden stop, her hands clenched at her sides. "I shouldn't have disrupted her life." *Oh how I wish Jack was here.*

Daniel grabbed hold of her shoulders again. "Perfect. Angel went through hell when your mother passed. Go ahead and run off. I'm sure, after some major counseling and medication, she'll come to terms with her sister abandoning her, too."

Something inside of her snapped. All of the hurt and frustration since coming home rushed to the surface. Her knees buckled and she welcomed the support his arms offered.

Jenna wasn't sure how much time passed. She opened her eyes to find Daniel sitting beside her on the sofa, stroking her hair down her back.

How did I end up over here?

She pulled away and snatched a couple of tissues from the box on the table. "Oh, my goodness, I'm so sorry."

I've never felt so alone. What I wouldn't give to have Jack here with me now. To wrap his arms around me...

He tucked a lock of hair behind her ear and stroked the side of her face. "You have nothing to be sorry for. You've been through a hell of a lot these past few weeks."

Jenna inched back, a little uncomfortable with the gesture.

Dare I hope? Maybe, with Daniel's help, Angel will get through this unscathed. Maybe there's still a chance she'll see me as her sister.

He put a finger under her chin and tilted her face so she looked into his sky-blue eyes. "I'm just glad I could be here for you."

Before she had a chance to react, his lips met hers.

Jenna put her hands on his chest and pushed him away. "Wh-what are you doing?" She swiped the back of her hand across her mouth as she scrambled to her feet.

"I'm sorry. I thought..."

"No, you didn't think. If you did, you'd remember I'm in a relationship. You know, with Jack, whom you've already met?"

He stood to face her; she stepped back and eyed him quizzically.

"I know you're with Jack," he stated. "Honestly, Jenna, I just got caught up in the moment. I'm sorry."

He seemed sincere enough, but she needed to put some space between them, still unable to wrap her head around what had just happened. "I've got to go."

The memory of Daniel going into the young girl's room earlier flashed in her mind. Uncomfortable with her thoughts, she hurried to fetch her purse and rushed to the door.

Daniel appeared, blocking her path. "I can't let you go like this. Please, let's have a cup of tea and talk."

"Have a cup of tea? You can't be serious." She glared at him. "Step aside before I say or do something we both might regret."

He stepped aside. "I really wish you'd stay."

"I know, and I really wish I could turn back the clock and pretend that didn't just happen, but I can't."

Jenna ran from the ranch house to where John leaned against the front grill of the limo reading a newspaper.

He jumped to his feet and opened her door. "Is everything okay, Ms. Jenna?"

"Please just take me home, John."

Jenna unplugged her cell from its charger, and turned it off and on to make sure it fully charged before taking a seat at the window. Her gaze travelled around the room, coming to rest on the crackling fire. She sighed.

I wish I was home, snuggled in front of the fire with Jack.

A shiver brought goose bumps to her bare arms. She got up and pushed the armchair across the plush white carpet to the fireplace, and returned to the window to fetch the side table and her phone, checking it once again for calls. She yanked the folded quilt off the foot of her bed and wrapped it around her on the way over to the fire.

Jenna tucked her feet up under her, the chill quickly chased away. She rested her head back and closed her eyes. The emotional upheaval over the past few days had taken a toll on her. Upon her return from the ranch, the solitude of her bedroom gave her time to reflect.

She'd always prided herself on being a strong, confident woman, but she'd somehow lost her way since returning to the estate, what seemed a lifetime ago. Her gaze dropped to the phone on her lap and she flipped it over and frowned. *Still no calls.* There was one thing she knew for sure...

I love Jack, and my future is with him back at the cabin.

All she had to do was figure out a way to mesh her world in Thunder Bay with the one just over the border in Minnesota. *There has to be a way to do it without anybody getting hurt.* Jenna rolled her eyes. *Good luck with that, sweetheart.*

There was one thing in her favor...at least she hoped so. As much as it saddened her to see Angel so upset, the truth was out. Now all she had to do was gain her trust and garner a relationship with her.

Her "baby laughing" ringtone startled her. One hand flew to her chest and the other fumbled with her phone.

"Hello? Jack is that you?"

"Hey, pretty lady. It sure is nice to hear your voice."

She wanted to laugh and cry in the same breath. "Oh, Jack, how I've missed you." She put a hand over the phone and sniffled.

"Jenna? What's the matter, babe?"

"I'm just so happy to be talking to you."

"Are you sure you're okay? How did it go yesterday?"

Jenna relayed the entire day's events, minus the exchange between her and Daniel. No good could come of that, especially with Jack being so far away. *At least for now.*

"Well, nobody said the transition would be an easy one. I'm glad you're staying positive."

She shook her head. "How do you do that?"

He chuckled lightly. "How do I do what?"

"You have this uncanny knack of making everything seem less complicated."

"I miss you."

His sigh tugged at her heartstrings. "Do you know what I miss most?"

"I know it's not my coffee..."

Jenna blinked away the tears threatening to fall. "I miss you in bed next to me." She swallowed hard.

"Aw, babe. Me, too. I haven't slept in our bed since you've been gone."

She straightened in her chair. "Oh God, I'm so sorry, Jack."

"Don't be sorry. I can't help it if I keep reaching out for you and you're not there. I get a better sleep on the couch, lulled by the soothing serenade of Tito snoring."

She had to laugh at the vivid picture his words painted.

"This whole ordeal is so not fair to you." A deep breath kept her fragile emotions in check. She'd only make him feel bad if she gave in and cried like she wanted to.

"Don't you worry about me, I'm not going anywhere. You just concentrate on Angel so you can come home to me."

"I can't even venture a guess as to how long this is going to take." She chewed on her bottom lip.

"Listen, Jenna. The only promise I need from you is that you'll stop worrying about me."

She smiled despite the ache in her heart. "Okay, I promise...I'll try."

He laughed. "I love you, Jenna, but I kind of interrupted the chief and I told him I'd only be a minute."

It was so much harder not to cry than she'd thought it would be. "I love you, too. When can you call again?"

"How about Wednesday, same time?"

"Okay. Try and get a good night's sleep tonight."

"You betcha. I'll be dreaming of you."

Jenna set the phone on the end table and got up to stand by the window. Gazing at a star-filled sky always made her feel connected to Jack, even though she'd never been so conflicted in her life.

Her sadness slowly gave way to a thought formulating in her mind. A slow smile spread across her face. *Regardless of how things go this week, I'm going to surprise Jack with a visit for the weekend.* She wrapped her arms around herself and smiled up at the sky.

"I'll see you soon, my love."

Chapter Twenty-Five

Jenna flopped into an overstuffed armchair on the back deck. The estate grounds were spectacular, changing from one breathtaking view to another with the seasons. They had every luxury imaginable: indoor and outdoor swimming pools, tennis courts, and even a top of the line theater that seated twenty.

None of it meant anything to her.

"Hey there, kiddo. What are you up to today?" Charles stepped onto the deck and sat beside her.

"I have absolutely no idea. I think I'll go crazy waiting for Angel's decision to have me in her life or not."

"Maybe you need to find something to take your mind off things for a while."

"What exactly did I do around here to pass the time? I can count on one hand the times I remember actually swimming in our pools."

"I seem to remember your favorite pastime was shopping. Why don't you give Buffy a call? I'm surprised she hasn't pinned you down since you've been back."

Jenna winced. "Actually, she did leave a few messages. I haven't returned any of them."

He arched his brow. "There's nothing stopping you from doing so right now. Why don't you give her a ring and ask her to do lunch or something?"

"I think I will. What are your plans?"

He shrugged. "You know, I worked for your father for the past twenty years, twenty-four hours a day, seven days a week. That didn't leave a whole lot of time for socializing."

"Aw, that's kind of sad. Do you want to come and have lunch with us?"

He shook his head. "Oh no. I love you, but spending the afternoon shopping with the girls..." He chuckled light-heartedly. "I think I'll track down John and see what kind of trouble we can get into." He stood and offered his hand to pull her to her feet. "Unless of course you were thinking of having John drive you around?"

"No, you go ahead and spend the day with John. I'll get Buffy to pick me up with her driver."

Charles kissed her cheek and went off in search of John.

Jenna went inside to phone Buffy. After a few minutes of catching hell for not returning her calls, they agreed she'd come pick her up in an hour.

Upstairs, she stood in her closet looking at the vast array of clothes.

I definitely won't be shopping for something to wear. In fact, I can't imagine ever wearing ninety percent of these clothes again. At one time they obviously meant a lot to me, but I'm not that girl anymore.

"I *don't want* to be that girl anymore," she affirmed aloud.

Jenna smiled at her reflection, opting for a white, sleeveless blouse and jeans. A messy updo and silver hoops in her ears completed her *look*; one vastly different from the 'lunch with the girls' ensemble she'd have chosen before the accident. Buffy would definitely have something to say about it.

By the time she reached the front door, her friend's driver was just pulling the limo up. The car barely came to a stop when Buffy bolted from the backseat and practically threw herself at Jenna, knocking her back a few steps.

"Hey, easy girl." She laughed, having missed her friend more than she realized.

"It's so good to see you." Stepping back, Buffy put her hands on her slender hips. "I should be mad at you."

"I know, and I'm sorry. Once we've had a chance to catch up, you'll understand why I've been so distracted."

Buffy tilted her head sideways. Her brow creased as she stroked her chin. "There's something different about you?" She hmmed and hawed. "Are you actually going to leave the house without any make-up on?"

Jenna scowled at her childhood friend. "I'm wearing mascara...and lip gloss. What's wrong? Are you saying I need more makeup that badly?"

Buffed put her hands up in T formation. "Time out. Of course not. I've just never known you to leave the house without...more."

She shrugged. "I guess there's a first time for everything then."

Her best friend linked arms with her and led the way to the limo. "I made reservations at The Hub. We can catch up there."

As always, her girlfriend's upbeat personality and zest for life was highly infectious. They laughed and carried on like they'd never been apart, arriving at the restaurant in no time at all.

The Hub was *the* place for the elite. The dining area was almost filled to capacity with college students home for the summer. The *maître d'* led them to a window seat with a curved bench padded with plush velvety fabric.

"I forgot how beautiful this place is." Jenna slid over to the middle of the bench from one side and Buffy from the other end. Beautiful, maybe...but she'd never been more uncomfortable with such over-the-top extravagance.

"Margarita time?" Her friend rubbed her hands together. The sunlight caught the rings she wore on every finger, setting the diamonds and other gems alight.

Janna shrugged. "Sure, why not?"

Buffy ordered their drinks, flirting with the waiter as she did everywhere they went. Her friend was one of the most generous, fun-loving people she knew. Her silky blonde hair and long eyelashes attracted the attention of most men. She stood just over five-feet tall with killer curves; her short skirt and tight shirt left little to the imagination.

"So, tell me what's kept you so busy the past few months." Buffy took her hand in hers. "I'm so sorry to hear about your father. I would have been there for you, but I didn't hear about it until a couple of days after the funeral. How come it was kept so hush-hush? I thought your father would've wanted to go out in a big way."

Jenna heaved a sigh. "Oh, he went out in a big way all right." She shifted uncomfortably.

Her friend scooted along the bench to sit beside her. "What happened?"

"I got home literally minutes before he passed." She swallowed the lump in her throat. "Do you know what his last words to me were?"

Buffy shook her head, her eyes filled with worry.

"He said, 'you are dead to me.'" Jenna sniffled, not wanting to give her father the satisfaction in knowing how deep his words had cut.

"Oh no! What an awful thing to do to his only child." Anger tightened her delicate features. "The monster!"

Jenna welcomed the waiter's timely interruption. Once gone, she raised her glass. "I don't want to waste another second talking about him. Here's to best friends."

Buffy laughed. "I'll drink to that."

What she saw in a booth across the floor caused the tart drink to catch halfway down her throat, and she sputtered into a napkin.

Her friend patted her back. "Go down the wrong way?"

Jenna sat in stunned silence at the occupants of the booth at the back wall as Buffy turned in her seat to find whatever had caused her reaction.

"What is it?"

Jenna pulled on her arm. "Don't look," she whispered as loud as she dared.

Her friend's brow creased as she searched Jenna's face. "What the hell is going on?"

She glanced over once again to where Daniel Meed sat with a girl practically in his lap, his hand up the front of her *barely there* top. On the other side, *Howard Meed*'s hands roamed another woman's body. The lecherous drunk, who so desperately wanted to marry her, smiled devilishly at the woman before soundly kissing his more than willing date.

The threat of puking right then and there became very real. "I have to get out of here. I'm so sorry, Buffy, but we need to be anywhere *other than here...*"

"What? We've barely touched our drinks."

Jenna had already grabbed her purse and slid to the end of the bench. "Pay for the drinks. I really need to go, *now*." Without waiting for a response, she rushed away, not stopping until she stood in the lobby, well out of sight of the bar.

Apparently, Daniel *did* know Howard Meed. *What the hell is going on?*

Buffy burst into the lobby. "Holy woman! Do you mind

telling me just what the hell is going on with you?"

"I will, but let's get out of here first. It's kind of a long story."

Her best friend grabbed her hand and pulled her out the front doors. "If it's going to take a while, I'm definitely going to need another drink."

Chapter Twenty-Six

The bright sun shot daggers through Jenna's skull, and she pulled a pillow over her face. It had been quite some time since she'd had so much to drink. Now she remembered why.

They'd ended up going back to Buffy's house, where margaritas flowed endlessly. Once she got started sharing all that had gone on in her life, it was like the dam burst. She hadn't realized how much she'd missed having her best friend to talk to.

After spilling her guts, she still had no idea what the hell she was going to do next. The Daniel at The Hub that afternoon was the polar opposite of the man who cared so gently for his wards and adamantly stated to both her and Jack, he knew no *Howard Meed.*

Despite this latest revelation, it didn't change the fact the ranch was a beautiful haven for people like her sister...

Or is it?

Was the picture perfect setting a facade, like the ruse Daniel pulled off about his character? Had she made a huge mistake writing that check?

Is my sister's existence basis for blackmail?

A sudden rap at the door mimicked the merciless pounding in her ears.

"Jenna?" Edna's familiar voice called out to her from across the room.

She squeezed her eyes shut, willing the day to rewind an hour or two so she'd still be fast asleep.

"I'm sorry, Ms. Jenna, but I thought you'd want to know you had a call just now from the ranch."

"Angel?" She tossed her pillow aside and bolted upright, immediately regretting doing so. Her stomach churned precariously; she put her head in her hands and lowered it to her knees until the urge to vomit passed. "Oh, my god. Somebody shoot me."

Edna chuckled. "Angel is fine. Daniel asked if you would come out to the Ranch sometime over lunch hour for a chat. If that's not a good time, just call and reschedule."

Jenna groaned.

"I'll be right back with my *special remedy*. You stay put in that bed until I get back.

As curious as she was about a call from the ranch, she had no alternative but to stay in bed. In fact, at this precise moment, she doubted standing on two feet was an option.

Edna stepped back into the room with drink remedy in hand. "Remember, drink it all in one go."

Her hand trembled as she took the glass. Edna's remedy consisted of Gin, lemon juice, Tabasco sauce and a slice of chili pepper. The first time she awoke with a hangover, her caregiver suggested her *special remedy*. Jenna had thought it might be a shot of what she'd drank the night before, but it was actually the name she'd given her concoction.

Memory of how it tasted sent a shiver through her. Jenna closed her eyes and counted to three before bringing the glass to her mouth and tossing back the fiery liquid. Beads of sweat covered her face as the mixture blazed a trail to her stomach. "Wow." She squeezed her eyes shut and fanned her open mouth.

Edna giggled and took the empty glass from her. "Don't try and get up for at least five minutes." She waggled her finger at her on the way out of the room.

Jenna waved a hand and flopped back on her pillows. As promised, five minutes later, the fog lifted and she felt remarkably better.

Once showered and dressed, she went in search of coffee, only to find Charles sitting in the breakfast nook overlooking the grounds.

"Good morning." He raised his cup.

"Good morning. I'm so glad to find you here." She filled her mug and joined him.

"What's on your mind, kiddo?"

Jenna groaned. "I don't know where to start. What I do know is I need your help."

Over several cups of coffee, she brought him up to speed with what happened the last time she saw Angel, and the dilemma of seeing Daniel and Howard Meed at The Hub, having their own private orgy in the back booth.

Charles shook his head. "So, the guy has a social life outside of the ranch..."

Jenna cut him off, unable to believe what she was hearing. Her temper flared. "When I was upset, Daniel *kissed* me. His hands were all over me. Do you not see a problem with *that*?"

His eyes grew big and his hands clenched. "He did what?"

"You heard me. I was beside myself, and he totally took advantage of my vulnerability, even knowing I'm with Jack."

Her mentor wiped the sweat from his reddened face. "You didn't give me a chance to finish. Daniel being with Howard and what you've just told me changes *everything*."

"We need to get to the bottom of this. Something isn't right. I have to know Angel is safe there."

He arched a brow. "You don't think...?"

She shrugged. "I don't know what to think." She laid her hand over his. "Will you help me?"

"Of course I will."

"Daniel called this morning and asked to see me. Will you come with me to the ranch today? I don't know if the news is good or bad, but no matter what Angel decides, I owe it to our mother to make sure she's going to be okay, *and safe*, when I go home."

What she wanted to do was take Angel away from the ranch, but witnessing her meltdown with change of any kind, it could do more harm than good. In spite of everything, her sister did seem very happy living there.

"Maybe I should pay Howard Meed a visit?" His hands clenched to fists.

"Listen, neither of them knew I saw them together...maybe we should leave it like that for now."

Charles let out a long, slow breath. "I know you're right. That doesn't change the fact I'd like to deflate not only his bulging belly, but the asshole's swollen ego."

Charles enlisted John to drive them to the ranch. Based on facts alone, there wasn't enough dirt to bury the guy. However, coming on to Jenna when she was in an emotional state warranted a foot up his ass. Adding Howard Meed to the mix had him seeing red. His gut told him all wasn't as it seemed at the Rolling Hills Ranch. For Jenna's sake, he'd curb his anger. It wouldn't be easy, but he'd do it.

"Do you want me to go in the office with you?"

"I thought it might be the perfect opportunity for you to take a look around while he's busy with me."

He didn't blame her for being worried about him losing his cool. To be quite honest, he didn't trust himself being that close to the man. "I'm not crazy about leaving the two of you alone," he said.

"Look, your number is right here, all I have to do is push this button for you to come running, okay?"

John turned down the long stretch of entryway to the ranch. Charles watched Jenna tug at the bottom of her lip with her teeth, something she'd done when anxious since she was a little girl.

He put his arm across her shoulders and pulled her to his side, kissing the top of her head. "Don't worry, kiddo. Remember, you're not alone in this. I'll do whatever it takes to ensure Angel's safety."

She rested her head on his shoulder. "I love you, you know that, don't you?"

The emotion in her voice tugged at his heartstrings. "Right back atcha."

The ranch was just as Jenna described—picture perfect with its manicured lawns and pristine buildings. Nobody would suspect something amiss at first glance.

The limo stopped, and Charles squeezed her reassuringly just as John opened the door. She kept a tight hold on his hand crossing the parking area to the front doors.

Jenna paused and took a deep breath, letting it out slowly. "You okay?"

She nodded. "Let's just get this over with."

"Remember, if he tries anything, press that button."

Jenna rose on tiptoe and kissed his cheek before he opened the door and ushered her inside. Sunlight shone down the barren hallway, sending a shiver of unease up his spine. Suddenly, the door marked 'Office' opened and Daniel stepped out.

"I thought I heard a car pull up outside." His gaze shifted

about nervously.

Charles forced a calm exterior. "Good morning, Daniel." He clenched his jaw and offered his hand, noting the relief in his eyes at the gesture. *Don't be so sure, asshole...I know everything.*

Daniel eagerly shook his hand. "It's good to see you again."

Jenna openly cringed as Daniel put a hand to the small of her back. "Let's go in and have a talk about your sister."

Charles spoke up. "I think I'll go see if I can find a cup of coffee." He didn't wait for a response, giving her a knowing glance before walking toward the delicious aromas coming from the kitchen. A medley of tomatoes, garlic and peppers set his stomach growling.

He walked through the kitchen's swinging doors to find three women in pale blue and white uniforms in various stages of cooking. A woman with raven-black hair looked up from chopping onions. Moisture filled her chocolate-brown eyes, and he swallowed hard as she smiled at him.

"Can I help you?"

Charles found himself smiling back, entranced by her slight European accent. "I was told I might find a cup of coffee here." He moved closer. "The name's Charles Wylder. I came with Jenna to see her sister, Angel."

"Oh, Ms. Jenna. Please sit."

"Thank you. I'm sorry, but I didn't catch your name."

She wiped her hands on her apron, her cheeks flushing. "*'Scusa*, my name is Twyla Amaro."

He shook her small, delicate hand. "It's very nice to meet you, Twyla. That's a beautiful name."

She lowered her lashes. "*Gracie*, I was born *all' alba...oh, 'scusa*...at twilight. That's where my mother made the name."

He smiled at the pink tinge to her cheeks from mixing Italian with English. It had been a very long time since he'd felt an attraction to a woman. "Would you care to join me for a cup?"

The two women behind her giggled behind their hands as Twyla turned. "Is it okay with you if I take my break a little early?"

The older woman shooed her away. "Go on with ya."

Twyla poured two cups and led him out to the dining room, to a small table along a wall of windows where horses grazed literally a stone's throw away.

"This really is a beautiful place."

"Yes, it is." She kept her long lashes lowered.

"Daniel is pretty particular about appearances, isn't he?"

Charles caught the fleeting look of disapproval in her expression. "I guess so." She shrugged and feigned interest in her cup.

"How long have you worked here?" he asked casually, not wanting her to feel interrogated about her boss.

"Almost five years. Is everything okay with Angel?"

He briefly explained the situation. "She is having a hard time processing a sister."

"I think most would be a little shocked."

"Yes, I suppose so. Anyhow, Daniel called this morning and asked Jenna to come to the ranch and talk."

"Where is she now?" Twyla looked around the room and out the window.

"She's with Daniel in his office."

Her expressive eyes widened. "Alone?"

The worry in her tone had him straightening in his seat. "Is that a problem?"

Twyla's face reddened; she quickly stood. "No, I mean...'scusa. I really need to go back working"

Charles stood and put his hands on her shoulders. "Have I upset you?"

"I don't think I am to talk about this."

She scurried away before he had a chance to say anything more. He'd definitely find a way to smooth things over with her—getting to know the beautiful Twyla Amaro a little better would just have to wait—but right now, he needed to make sure Jenna was okay.

Chapter Twenty-Seven

Jenna's patience grew thin. Daniel took an *important* phone call seconds after the door closed behind them, several minutes ago. He now stood at the window with his back to her, speaking in hushed tones, laughing every now and then.

Enough is enough. Jenna stood and cleared her throat noisily. "Excuse me, Daniel? I don't mean to interrupt."

He turned and glared at her, his hand over the mouth piece. "Didn't I say this is an important phone call? What part of that don't you understand?"

Her jaw dropped, and her temper flared. "Pardon me? It was *you* who called me out here. Surely you can continue your conversation after ours."

He shook his head. "I'm sorry, doll," he said into the phone, "but it seems my next appointment is being a little selfish. Let me take care of her, and I'll call you right back."

Doll? He's talking to one of his lady friends? That's what is so important? She struggled to keep her cool.

Daniel stormed over to his desk and sat in his chair. "You know, Jenna, the world doesn't revolve around you and your sister."

She frowned. "Why are you treating me like this? You'd be wise to remember it's not too late for me to back out on the funding promised you."

"Go ahead and do what you got to do. The only ones you'll be depriving are your sister and the other residents. Besides, you made it very clear how you feel about me the last time you were here. How do you expect me to act?"

Oh my God, talk about the world revolving around you. It's all about his bruised ego. He can't handle the fact there's a woman who isn't attracted to him.

"I think if anyone has a reason to be upset, it's me."

A knock interrupted them. As he went and opened the door, his entire demeanor miraculously transformed to the nice guy she had first thought he was.

"Charles, you have good timing. I was just going to share the good news with Jenna."

Daniel shot her a warning look before returning to his desk. It took everything in her not to jump up and give her anger and frustration free rein in front of Charles. She kept her mouth shut for Angel's sake, and her sister's sake alone.

Charles settled in a seat beside her. He kept his gaze diverted from looking anyone in the eyes. His jaw clenched and unclenched, telling her there was more going on than just wanting to throttle the Ranch CEO.

"I have something exciting to report. Angel has finally come to fully understand you are her sister."

Jenna muffled a squeal into her hands, everything else pushed to the wayside by the good news. At least she hoped it was good news.

"Is she happy about it?" Charles asked.

"I think so, but she is being very guarded. She seems a little scared, like maybe she's afraid to have a relationship with you for fear she'll lose you like she did your mother."

"Nobody said the transition was going to be an easy one." Jack's words put things in perspective.

"I can understand that. Do you think she'd want to see me today?" Jenna purposely kept her gaze diverted. What she really wanted to do was run out of the office in search of her sister.

He leaned back in his chair. "Angel has been seeing the resident psychologist the past few days. Dr. Gilmore feels it's a little too soon. The reason I brought you here is to find out if you'd be willing to sit down for a session with the doctor and your sister."

"Yes, of course I'm willing. Name the time and place and I'll be there." *He could easily have asked me over the phone. What is his ulterior motive for wanting to see me in person?*

"Good, I'll talk to the doctor and set something up."

Charles was first to stand and shake Daniel's hand. "Thank you. Do you think I could use your facilities before we head out?"

"Of course." He nodded toward the restroom door.

The second they were left alone, Daniel rounded his desk to stand beside her.

"You would be wise to remember I am your only link to

Angel. I will do everything I can to bring the two of you together in return for the donation. But don't put me in a position to sever all ties with her," he whispered assertively.

Jenna opened her mouth to speak, but snapped it shut when Charles returned. She snatched up her purse and strode across the room, forcing a smile. "Thank you. I look forward to seeing Angel again." She left the office without waiting for Charles, not stopping until she was outside.

With a deep, steadying breath, she willed her heart beat to normal, hardly able to believe what transpired. If she told Charles there would be no holding him back, and she couldn't chance jeopardizing a relationship with her sister. As much as she hated it, she'd have to play by Daniel's rules, at least for now. She needed to find tangible proof Daniel wasn't the man he pretended to be.

...and then there's the issue of his association with Howard Meed.

I have to see her. Jack never had such an overwhelming desire to see someone.

The two students who watched over the dogs before agreed to come out after the pups were taken care of for the night. Unfortunately, they could only stay until the following afternoon.

He was pushing his luck driving over the speed limit, but the mountain roads were quiet, and he couldn't shake the intense need to be with Jenna. The two and a half hour drive took a little less than two hours before he pulled onto the estate grounds.

Only the housekeeper knew to expect him. He didn't want to get Jenna's hopes up and have his plans fall through. Edna opened the front door before he reached it, her housecoat buttoned up under her chin and a scarf of some kind covering curlers in her hair. She put a finger to her lips and stood aside for him to enter. Jack winked at her while slipping out of his boots. He took them with him as he mounted the stairs to Jenna's bedroom.

Once at her door, he stepped in and closed the door behind him. His pulse raced as his eyes adjusted to her darkened room. Moonlight illuminated Jenna's still form on the bed. He knew he'd missed her, but not until that moment did he realize how much.

Jack reached her bedside and gazed upon her. Her beautiful hair fanned the pillow like a halo.

My beautiful snow angel.

He watched her sleep peacefully as he undressed. Moving slowly so as not to startle her awake, he slipped between the sheets and inched over to her. He paused briefly to inhale her sweet scent before lightly pulling her hair back and kissing her neck.

Jenna stirred from sleep. She awoke with a sharp intake of breath as a body pressed against her back. She jerked her head to peer back over her shoulder; her confusion quickly turned to surprise.

"Jack? Is it really you?"

He shifted so she could turn over.

"Yes, it's me."

His body returned to hers, erasing the space between them as he cupped the sides of her face in a kiss so sweet it brought tears to his eyes.

"How did you get away?" She withdrew enough to look him in the eyes. "What about the dogs?"

"We can talk about all that in the morning. I had to come and make sure you're okay. I can't explain how, but I had such an overwhelming sense something was wrong."

"Oh, Jack." Her voice cracked. "I was planning a surprise visit to see you. You are *exactly* what I need."

Jack reclaimed her mouth. It wasn't a slow, dreamy kiss, but a hungry one that left her panting. His fingers lightly traced the swell of her breasts, and he kissed the tears from her eyes.

"Please don't cry, Jenna." He edged himself between her legs as his tongue explored her mouth, kissing her passionately.

My beautiful man.

Sometimes when they came together it was soft and sensual, but tonight, he handled her with insatiable hunger. He kissed her greedily, a kiss she was sure to leave her feeling long after tonight.

"God, I've missed you."

Jenna sensed growing need for release, his manhood hard against her inner thigh. "Please, Jack. I need you inside me...now."

"Are you sure? What about you? It will be over quickly."

The corner of her mouth lifted and she winked playfully. "What's the matter old man, you not up to going around the bases more than once?"

A groan escaped his parted lips. He kissed her deeply and positioned himself above her. "Hang on, babe..."

Chapter Twenty-Eight

"Jack? Jack?"

Jenna ran downstairs. She'd awakened totally naked and all alone. If it wasn't for her body still buzzing from their lovemaking, she'd think she'd dreamt it all.

Edna scurried out from the kitchen. "Ms. Jenna, it's okay. Jack is having coffee with Charles on the deck. You go ahead and join them. I'll bring some out to you."

"Thank God." She let out a rush of breath then chuckled at herself for such a dramatic display of emotions.

Her friend shook her head. "Kids," she mumbled on her way back to the kitchen.

True to Edna's word, Jack sat outside beside Charles, seemingly deep in conversation. She stood back and smiled. The two men she loved most in the world were at ease, as if they'd known each other for years.

I'm a very lucky woman.

She checked her housecoat to make sure she was fully covered before opening the door and joining them. "Good morning." She stooped to kiss Charles' cheek and then Jack's mouth. "This is a wonderful, albeit unexpected, way to start the day."

"Good morning. I trust you slept well." Charles grinned.

She flushed and shifted her gaze to Jack. "Better than I have in weeks."

Edna appeared with fresh coffee and a platter of breakfast snacks. Jenna took a blueberry muffin and tore off a piece of the top, promptly popping it in her mouth. "Mmm, I'm starving."

Jack gave her a knowing, lopsided grin, and the heat returned to her face. *I must be a brilliant shade of red by now.*

"I can't tell you how surprised I was to see you here. Who's watching the dogs?" she asked.

"The same two students who watched them last time I was here. Unfortunately, they have to get back to school this afternoon for an exam."

The blueberries soured in her mouth, and she forced them

down, placing the piece in her hand back on the plate. "You have to leave so soon?" She heard the tremor in her voice and forced herself to remain calm.

His brow creased. "I know. I wish I didn't have to. Is your sister okay?"

"Angel took the news of having a sister a little harder than we expected." Charles picked a bran muffin from the platter.

"Yes, but I'm meeting with her and the resident psychologist in the coming days to try and smooth things over." Jenna battled with how much of the story she should reveal. She wanted to tell him about Daniel and Howard, but knew, like Charles, he'd want to pay them both a visit, too.

Since Jack's time here was so short, no good could come of telling him everything. No, she needed to find something more concrete than her word against Daniel's before bringing Jack into the picture.

She stood and slipped onto his lap. "I know this is taking much longer than expected but—"

He put a finger to her lips. "I understand. As long as you're okay, take all the time you need."

Her heart swelled with love for this man, who never ceased to amaze her with his selflessness.

"Thank you. I'm so glad you get it. I really think, in the end, I'll have a relationship with my sister. The cat is out of the bag now, per se. It's just up to her to set the pace."

"Hopefully, after a couple of sessions with the doc, she'll come around." He rubbed her back. "Maybe you could bring her out to the cabin for a visit. I've seen how good she is with those horses, so I'm sure she'll love the dogs."

Jenna chuckled lightly. "Yes, I'm sure she would. Only problem with that is she'll want to take them all home."

"They must be getting big," said Charles.

"Yes, and full of mischief." Jack shook his head. "I swear the one is an escape artist. I've had to go search for him a few times now. I still have no idea how he's getting out."

Hearing him talk about the dogs made her even more homesick than she'd been before. "I can't wait to see them."

"Hey." He captured moisture on her eyelashes with the tip of his finger. "No tears, okay? It's going to be hard enough leaving you."

Jenna nodded and took a deep breath. "Yes, okay. How long do you have?"

Jack stood with her in his arms. "Long enough."

Charles cleared his throat gruffly and feigned interest in something on the opposite side of the deck.

She giggled. "I was hoping you'd say that."

Charles couldn't be happier about Jack's timely surprise. It was just what the doctor ordered. He hadn't seen that sparkle in Jenna's eyes for far too long.

It also gave him a chance to carry out his little excursion without any questions.

He hadn't been able to get Ms. Amaro off of his mind, so he phoned the ranch to invite her to lunch. When the receptionist realized who he was, she told him it was Twyla's day off. It took a little sweet talking to get a home phone number from her.

Charles gathered his courage to give her a call, which went out the window when she picked up the phone and said hello. He'd managed to stutter the invitation, of which she surprisingly accepted. He'd chosen the Mustang convertible because it was a two-seater, and the promise of a nice day might sway Twyla into going for a drive with him.

She didn't seem to be the type of gal who'd be very comfortable at some posh, high-end restaurant, so he phoned ahead to one of his favorite waterfront places. It didn't require a reservation, but he wanted to be assured of a table with a view.

Twyla lived just within the city limits, half the distance to the ranch, in a small, tidy bungalow with potted flowers and stark-white shutters. Before he put the car in park, she appeared in the doorway, even more beautiful than before with her dark hair falling in waves to her shoulders and a pretty, printed dress belted to accentuate a tiny waist.

He quickly checked his image in the mirror and laughed. *It's as good as it gets, ol' man.*

"*Ciao,* Charles." She smiled on her way to meet him.

His pulse raced getting out of his car to greet her. He

stooped to kiss her cheek before considering it might be too forward.

Twyla's cheeks stained a light pink, and she lowered her lashes.

"I'm sorry," he stammered.

"It's okay. Don't be sorry. I am not used to such a gentleman." She smiled, flashing pretty white teeth.

"You look very nice, Twyla."

"Gracie. It is good not to wear my uniform." She tittered, accepting the crook of his arm as he walked her to the passenger side.

"Che bella macchina." She looked up and down the length of it. "A '69 Mustang?"

"Yes, it is." He nodded, surprised and impressed, and opened the door, admiring a set of very sexy legs before closing it.

Easy does it, boy. You don't want to scare her away by drooling all over her.

He rolled back his shoulders and got in behind the wheel.

"So, where do you take me?" She tucked her hair behind a very kissable earlobe.

Down boy.

He coughed out the side of his mouth. "I thought we'd go to a great little place on the water. They serve the best fish in these parts."

"Perfetto." She put thumb and middle finger to her mouth in a kiss of sorts.

Charles beamed. "Okay then."

The short distance to the restaurant was pleasant. He learned her father collected miniature cars, which is how she knew about Mustangs. She'd moved here from a small town in Italy, barely speaking a word of English.

"Is there a reason you chose to live here of all places?"

"It is long story, my plans... e`caduto. How you say, fell apart. Diane, she give me a job at ranch and teach me the language." She lowered her face. "Many times, not so good."

"I'd say she is a *very good* teacher."

"Gracie. I still have problem with some words to musica on the radio."

He chuckled lightly. "Even I have trouble with today's teenager *music*."

The restaurant was fairly busy, but as promised, a table had been reserved on the deck overlooking the water.

Twyla smiled as she took in the view. "This is amazing. Thank you for taking me here."

Charles held out her chair. "The pleasure is mine."

"Good evening. My name is Denise and I'll be your server." Their server smiled a genuine smile. "Would you care for a glass of wine before dinner?"

"Lady's choice." He smiled at the waitress and then at Twyla, offering a small wink.

"Vino bianco...er, I mean white wine, not too dry," his date suggested shyly.

"Perfect. As you probably already know, Ontario is known for delicious ice wines."

"Yes, I'm a fan of them," Charles added.

"We have a light white, Chardonnay from the Colio Estate Wines on the Northern shore of Lake Erie." Her brow rose in question.

"Yes, that is good." Twyla nodded slightly before bowing her head.

He hadn't realized just how shy she was until now. He'd thought it was just him that made her uneasy.

Charles gazed out the picturesque landscape of Lake Superior. The night lights had just begun awakening the shoreline. "It sure is pretty out there."

She responded with the slightest of smiles and a dip to her chin.

Denise's return couldn't have been timed better. He chortled at the label of the bottle she held out to them. 'Girl's Night Out' flanked a graphic of a little black dress.

"Don't let the label fool you. I know you'll both enjoy this one." As proper etiquette dictated, she poured a splash in Charles' glass and took a step back in waiting.

He chuckled lightly as he swirled the wine, and took a sip. His eyes closed briefly. "Mm...perfecto!" He tried to imitate how Twyla did earlier.

She giggled behind her napkin.

The waitress beamed at his approval and proceeded to fill both glasses. She waited again for Twyla to taste the ice wine.

His date put the same two fingers to her far too sexy mouth and kissed them, taking them away with flourish. "Delizioso, grazie."

I could get used to her talking Italian to me.

The faint stirring of arousal made him squirm in his chair.

"If I could take your order, I'll leave you to enjoy your Chardonnay."

A brief discussion of the menu ensued, ending with him and Twyla agreeing to Denise's suggestion of a seafood platter to share.

"Thank you." She took their menus and left them alone.

Charles took a healthy swallow before steering the conversation to Angel and the ranch. "So, if you've been at the ranch for five years, you must know Jenna's sister, Angel, fairly well?"

"Oh yes. She is a good woman. Angel ask to help in kitchen many times."

"Jenna is really looking forward to having a relationship with her. Daniel has set up a few sessions with the shrink at the ranch."

At the mention of Daniel, her body grew rigid and she avoided further inquiry by gazing out the window.

How can I bring up the topic without making her feel like she's being pumped for information?

"Angel seems really attached to him. Are all of the residents so taken by the guy?"

Her gaze dropped to her lap, and she shrugged. *"Non lo so.* I mean, I think this is true."

"Is something wrong? Every time I mention your boss you get pretty uncomfortable."

She quickly glanced around, as if looking for anyone close enough to overhear. "Charles, I need my job, and I not think I can find more work very easy."

"If something's wrong, you can tell me. I promise I won't get you in trouble. You never know, maybe I can help."

Please don't tell me Daniel has harassed you. There would be no holding back if that were the case.

She sighed resignedly. "It is...I think maybe he is not a nice man like people think he is."

"Why do you feel that way?" He struggled to keep his anger in check.

Twyla shifted in her seat, scanning the area once again. "Daniel, he likes the ladies. He come to me when I first worked there, but I tell him I... *non sono quel tipo di ragazza.* Oh, I'm sorry, I tell him I am *not* that kind of girl."

"What did he do?" Charles grabbed the edge of the table; his knuckles turned white.

She dropped her gaze. "He told me to keep mouth shut or lose my job."

He put a hand on her arm. "I'm so sorry, Twyla. No woman deserves to be treated that way."

The scent of garlic and seafood stole their attention before Denise returned with a feast for the eyes. She set down a basket of warm buns and a vessel of whipped butter first.

"This looks amazing, Denise." Charles made a production of rubbing his hands together in anticipation, rewarded by Twyla's titter behind her napkin.

The waitress briefly described each dish as she set them on the table: King Prawns marinated with chili and coriander, Grilled Parmesan Oysters, sautéed Lake Superior Whitefish wrapped in bacon and Hot Smoked Salmon in a medley of Beetroot Salad with a sour cream and dill dressing. Baby spinach and watercress nestled small, halved new potatoes.

"And...your choice of Seafood sauce made with fresh horseradish and an orange dill sauce made from lemon zest and juice, dill and mustard."

"I think I will gain many pounds just looking at all of this." Twyla's eyes grew big as she took in the variety of dishes.

Charles' chuckle brought color to her cheeks. "Thank you, Denise. I'm sure we have everything we need and more."

A comfortable silence befell them as they tasted and fed each other samples of each dish in turn. He fanned his mouth seconds after she popped in a chunk of Hot Smoked Salmon.

"Wow!" He grabbed his water and took a big drink.

Twyla laughed...a sound he'd remember long after the night ended.

"You think that's funny, do you?" He narrowed his gaze on her.

"*Si.*" She dabbed at her eyes, still giggling.

The meal continued with the same sense of playfulness. Never had he enjoyed a woman's company as much as Twyla's.

Quite some time later, he leaned back in his chair and patted his belly. "I'm done."

Twyla wiped her mouth and dipped her fingers in a finger bowl with a slice of lemon. "Me, too. Done."

On cue, the friendly waitress appeared and cleared the table. "Would you like more wine, or perhaps a coffee?"

"Coffee sounds good."

"Yes, coffee please."

In a matter of seconds, they both had a steaming cup in front of them. Denise grinned, a devilish glint to her already bright blue eyes. "You don't get a choice for dessert. It's my treat, but have to ask if either of you have any allergy I should know of."

They both shook their heads, and Charles added, "I don't know if I can fit more in." His hand smoothed over the slightly strained buttons of his shirt.

"I think there is much room." Twyla winked at the waitress.

"I'll be back shortly."

Charles sat back and cast his date an inquisitive glance. One minute she seemed like she'd jump at her own shadow...and then she comes out with a zinger like that.

"You're quite a gal, Ms, Amaro."

Tiny lines appeared on her otherwise flawless forehead. "I hope this is good thing?"

A slow smile spread across his mouth. "Yes. Yes, it is a very good thing."

"If I tell you something, will you promise not to tell?"

He clenched his free hand under the table. "Of course, what is it?"

"I don't like how Mr. Daniel looks at the girls. I think he treats them...ina...inap, not good. Not the little ones, but like Angel's age. He touch them like a lover, not a leader."

He gritted his teeth. "You don't think he's...?"

Twyla shook her head. "I not know. Maybe I say too much."

He took her hand in his. "Look at me."

She slowly raised her head, her eyes glistening pools.

"Listen, I really like you, and I want to get to know you better."

The slightest of smiles lifted the corner of her mouth.

"Jenna and I also feel he isn't the man he appears to be. What you've told me only makes me more determined. If you can help us, I promise you will not lose your job. Even if you did, I can make sure you're okay."

Denise returned with a mouth-watering dessert. "Voilà! Raspberry Cobbler with Bourbon Sauce. I hope you enjoy it." She handed each a fork. "I hope you don't mind sharing." She winked playfully and promptly left them to eat.

Twyla was first to sink her fork into the decadent dish.

She closed her eyes. "Oh, my, goodness."

Curiosity piqued, Charles took a forkful of raspberries. "It had to be this good, didn't it?"

Twyla already had another mouthful and simply nodded in response.

I'll have to remember she has a sweet tooth.

Only half of the cobbler was consumed when Twyla dropped her fork on the plate with a clang and held up two fingers in a T formation.

He laughed and formed the Time Out sign as well.

Denise returned and refilled their coffee before taking the remaining dessert away and tucking the bill under his saucer. "Have a nice rest of the evening, folks. I hope to see you here again real soon."

"You're a star, Denise. Thank you." He waited a few minutes before picking up the conversation where it was left off.

"So, what do you say?"

Twyla cast him a sideways glance. "I say I am happy you come to find coffee at my work. I will help you."

Charles brought her hand to his lips and kissed it. "Thank you. You do know what this means, don't you?"

"No?" She furrowed her brow as her cheeks stained pink.

"You'll be seeing a lot more of me."
A smile erased the lines on her face. *"Perfetto."*

Chapter Twenty-Nine

Ribbons of fog whispered through the boughs of the mighty oak trees that flanked either side of the roadway leading to the ranch. Jenna shivered, not able to shake disarray at what the meeting with the doctor might entail.

John parked the limo and hurried around the front of the car to open her door. After closing the door behind her, he offered his arm, of which she gladly accepted.

At the front doors, she paused to close her eyes and summon the courage to move forward.

"Are you okay, Ms Jenna?"

She smiled at her driver, touched by his concern. "I'm just a little apprehensive."

"Understandably so." He opened the door and stepped aside for her to enter.

The halls were eerily quiet, adding to her unease. She glanced at her watch. *Lunch hour is almost over.*

John stepped in beside her and once again offered his arm.

She eyed him curiously. "You really don't have to, John. I'll be okay from here."

He shook his head as he took her hand and tucked it in the bend of his arm. "I have specific instructions to stick close by in case you need me."

"Charles?"

"Yes, Ms Jenna."

She chuckled quietly, but couldn't help wishing it was Jack's arm offered to her.

No, don't go there. Concentrate on Angel, and only Angel right now.

Jenna sighed resignedly and led him to a set of chairs against the wall directly across from the main office. "We can wait here. Lunch hour is almost over."

Within seconds of being seated, the door to the office opened, and Daniel stepped out. He eyed each of them in turn before settling on Jenna. "Good afternoon. I wasn't expecting to see you today."

"I got a call from Doctor Gilmore. He's arranged a session

with Angel in just a few minutes."

Daniel shook his head, seemingly annoyed. "This is the first I've heard of it. I'll give him a call and tell him you're here."

He didn't wait for a response before turning on his heel and ducking back into his office. Apparently the "big man" in charge didn't like things happening without his knowledge.

The click of shoes against the polished tile brought a small man with sparse hair and an ill-fitting suit walking toward them.

He smiled warmly and offered his hand. "I take it you're Jenna Blackburn? You're the spitting image of your mother." He shook hers heartily. "Why don't we go in my office and have a little chat before your sibling finishes her lunch."

Jenna smiled and followed the friendly man's lead. *Maybe this won't be so bad after all.*

The psychiatrist's office was very small in comparison to Daniel's, but it was a hundred times more comfortable. Knowing John was only a few feet away brought her comfort. Coupled with the doctor's pleasantness, her nerves began to settle.

"So, from what I understand, you had no knowledge of Angel's existence until recently?"

"That is correct. I learned I had a sister after my father passed. I was going through my mother's things when I came across some old letters."

"Your mother came here once a month faithfully up until her death. Didn't you ever question her time away from home?"

Jenna shrugged. "I guess not. My mother did lots of charity work. I guess I assumed she was off on one of her crusades." She chuckled lightly.

"I see." He closed the open file in front of him. "Angel learned about you not too long ago, after a photograph of you and your mother fell out of your purse?"

"Actually, my purse fell off my lap accidentally. That's when she saw it."

A light rap on the door set her heart racing. The door creaked open to reveal her Angel. Jenna clamped her hands on the arms of her chair to stop from jumping and hugging her tight. She opted for a friendly smile in hopes of calming her sister. Aside from her arm still being in a sling, she looked so much better than the last time.

"Come in, Angel. We were just getting to know each other while waiting for you to have lunch. I trust you enjoyed your meal?"

Her eyes remained downcast as she nodded her head. "Yes."

Doctor Gilmore got up from behind his desk and guided her to an empty chair beside Jenna. "You remember Jenna?"

She scowled. "Of course I do."

"Hello, Angel. It's lovely to see you again." She put her hand over her sister's, only to have her pull it away and clench it to her chest.

The doctor gave her a reassuring wink before settling against his desk. "Angel, can you tell me why you took your hand away from your sister's?"

Her gaze narrowed as she scrutinized Jenna. "How do you know she really *is* my sister?"

"You saw the photograph?"

"Yes, but that doesn't mean she's my sister."

"Do you trust me, Angel?" The doctor squatted to her level. "Yes."

"I have looked into it and she truly is your sibling. I've seen the records." He cupped the side of her face and looked directly at her. "Do you like Jenna?"

Angel's shoulders rose and fell. "Yes, I think so." She shook her head. "I'm confused."

"Would you like to see some pictures?" Jenna rifled through her purse for the small stack of snapshots.

Angel peered out the corner of her eye and shrugged.

"I think that's a great idea." The doctor took the photos from her and quickly flipped through them before handing them back. "I think you'll like these pictures, Angel."

The first one Angel turned to was of her mother and Jenna when she was only two or three years old. She pointed to the little girl in the frilly white dress. "That's me."

Her sister traced the outline of her face with a trembling

fingertip. "Mother." She slowly straightened in her chair and seemed to be enjoying the photographs as they were presented to her. Every now and then, she'd give her a sideways glance when given a childhood photo of Jenna.

"You look like my mother."

The statement instilled hope in her. Was she finally putting two and two together? She wasn't sure because Angel still referred to their mom as 'my mother.'

"How about if Jenna lets you keep those?"

The slightest of smiles came to her face. "Yes, I'd like that."

The doctor returned to his seat. "Do you have any questions for Jenna?"

Angel chewed on the inside of her lip for a bit before speaking. "Why didn't you come and see me with my mother?"

Jenna was terrified of saying the wrong thing, or worse, having it sound the wrong way. She faced the doctor for guidance.

"Jenna didn't know about you." The doctor leaned forward in his chair.

"Why didn't she?" Angel creased her brow, and the flash of anger in her expressive eyes didn't go unnoticed.

"I'm not sure if you'll understand this," Jenna began. "In fact, I'm not sure I do, but my father wouldn't allow our mother to tell anyone about you."

"Did your father hate me?" Her bottom lip quivered.

"No, it's not like that. My father didn't know you. If he did, he would have loved you, I'm sure."

Jenna noted the confusion in her eyes as she tried to process everything. How could she explain things so she understood?

Angel sighed.

"I think we've given Angel lots to think about." The doctor gave a definitive nod in Jenna's direction. "Why don't we set up another session in let's say, three day's time?"

She nodded her approval while Angel sifted through the pictures in silence. All she wanted to do was wrap her arms around her and tell her everything was going to be all right, but her sister needed to take the lead in her own time.

"It was very nice seeing you again. I'm happy you're feeling better after your accident." Jenna stood. "Thank you, Doctor Gilmore. I guess I'll see you on Thursday, same time?"

"Yes, this is a good time of day for Angel."

At the mention of her name, she gazed up at Jenna. "Thank you for the pictures."

"You are very welcome. Would you like to see more next time I come?"

She nodded and held out the hand not hampered by her cast. "That would be wonderful."

Jenna gently squeezed her fingers. "Okay. I'll see you soon."

"Yes, see you soon."

The wariness in her words heard loud and clear.

Chapter Thirty

Charles set the phone down. "That was John. They'll be here in less than an hour."

"That would be my cue to leave. Jenna would have a million questions for us if she came home to find me here."

Charles chuckled. "Jenna hates secrets. It's better for everyone's sanity if we don't let her find out we have one."

Jack stood and stroked his jaw. "I'm glad I'm not the one who has to see her every day and keep quiet."

"Yah, thanks buddy." He stopped at the back door.

"So, you'll get back to me on what we discussed?" Charles asked.

"You betcha. Expect a call late afternoon tomorrow." He put two fingers to his forehead in a wave of sorts. "Good luck."

Charles still heard his laughter after closing the door behind him. In that same moment, the front doorbell rang. "Now, who could that be?"

His heartbeat fluttered at the sight of Twyla at the door, wearing a yellow sundress. Her smile brought sunlight to his life.

"Twyla?" He leaned forward and kissed her cheek. "Is everything okay?"

She smiled brightly. "I guess Jenna never told you. After our talk, I tell her today I will help and she asked for me to a barbeque."

He put a hand on the small of her back. "Come in, this sure is a nice surprise."

She blushed. "I'm happy you think so."

Charles took her hand in his and led her to the kitchen, where the most mouth-watering aroma exuded. Edna helped Grace husk corn over a large garbage can. The silver-haired woman looked up and smiled.

"Hello." Grace wiped her fingers on her apron and rounded the end of a large island, offering her hand. "You must be Twyla. It's so nice to meet you."

Twyla smiled shyly. "Your kitchen smells *delizioso*."

"Why thank you. I just took buns out of the oven and

popped in a big ol' apple crisp for later. I hope you're hungry."

"How can I not be?"

"Why don't we sit outside." He opened a set of French doors leading out to the back deck. "It's a beautiful day out there."

Without exchanging words, they gravitated to the porch swing and sat.

"You look very pretty."

Her yellow halter dress complimented her small waist and shapely legs. The color showed off her olive skin.

"Yellow is one of my favorite colors." She smoothed a hand down her skirt.

"Can I get you a drink?"

"A glass of white wine would be lovely. That is, if it isn't too dry."

Charles stood and paused at her side. "I think I have something you'll really like."

Once inside, he asked Edna to prepare a tray with the drinks and he'd take it out himself, allowing him a moment at a mirror to wipe a hand over his bald head to check for stubble and brush his teeth.

He returned to the deck, tray in hand.

"This is an ice infusion from a local vineyard."

Twyla sipped from the crystal glass he handed her. "Mmm. It is *eccellente*."

"I thought you'd like it."

The doors opened enough for Edna to stick out her head. "Jenna is back."

"I hope her session with Angel went well."

Twyla's brow creased. "She was at the ranch today?"

"Yes. Her and her sister will be having a few sessions with the shrink to guide them through the transition to sisterhood."

"Hmm, well, that explains why Daniel and the doctor were arguing."

"What were they arguing about?"

"I couldn't hear everything, but from what I did, Daniel is angry the doctor does not tell him what they say. He shouted about, client... um, *riservatezza*? Client confi, confidently? I'm sorry, my English is not so good with big words." She blushed and carried on. "Daniel says bullshit. It was his ranch and he must know everything."

Charles rubbed her arm reassuringly. "I hope the good doctor didn't give in."

"No." She giggled. "The doctor stomped out of Daniel's office, only telling him it went well, and if he wanted to fire him, do it. Daniel slammed the door and I did not see him again when I left not long after."

"Control freak was probably having a hissy fit over not getting his way."

Twyla laughed. "I do not know this, hissy fit?"

Charles chuckled. "Temper tantrum."

She tilted back her head and laughed. "Like a baby." Twyla snorted, and her hand flew to her mouth, her eyes wide in surprise.

He reached over and squeezed her hand. "I love to hear you laugh."

"Did I miss a good joke?" Jenna stepped out onto the deck with a drink. "Hi, Twyla. I'm sorry I'm late. I saw a sign with horses for sale. I had to take a look. Glad you could make it."

"Ahem. Why didn't you tell me she was coming?"

Jenna shrugged. "I didn't want to." She winked at Twyla.

He waggled a finger at her. "I owe you one, kiddo."

"I love your dress. That color really compliments you." Jenna smiled.

"*Grazie*." Twyla lowered her lashes, seemingly embarrassed by the compliment. "How did it go with your sister?"

"I think it went pretty well. She's still very guarded, but I caught a moment or two when it seemed she was coming to terms with having a sister. The photographs I took in seemed to help."

"No trouble with Daniel, I hope?" asked Twyla.

"We saw him for a brief second when we arrived. He left us to tell the doctor we were there, and I didn't see him again." Jenna's brow wrinkled. "What did I miss?"

"Twyla was just telling me he was none too happy about being kept in the dark about your session."

Jenna sat in a lounger beside the swing. "I hope he didn't

give you a hard time, Twyla."

She shook her head. "Oh no, I just heard him shout at doctor."

Jenna chuckled. "Good, I'm glad Doctor Gilmore kept it from him."

Charles watched the two girls interact as if they'd known each other for years. Twyla fit into his life perfectly from all angles. He just hoped she felt the same way about him. Knowing she worked so close to Daniel wasn't something he liked very much, but he understood her need to earn a paycheck.

"What are you up to?" Jenna tilted her head sideways at him.

"What? Why would you think I'm up to something?" He frowned and diverted his attention to Edna, who came outside with a tray of steaks for the barbeque. "Mmm, thank you. I'll put them right on the grill."

Charles welcomed the timely interruption, making it possible to dodge the question while he attended to the barbeque. Jenna knew him all too well. He'd have to be extra cautious not to ring any warning bells.

As he grilled, Twyla told them about the set up at the ranch. On the main floor, only the older ladies around Angel's age had rooms. The upstairs was for the little girls, and the boys were kept in a shared basement room where they slept in bunk beds. Only the main floor had double beds of their own. This news was yet another reason to suspect something was going on behind closed doors.

"That's interesting. Tell me, do you honestly believe he is taking advantage of the main floor girls? I mean, the setup does give him the perfect opportunity, but is he actually capable of pulling it off without anyone knowing?"

Twyla shrugged and sipped the last of her wine. "Daniel is a very smart man. The girls all think he's a god. I don't know if he is close with them, *like that*."

Jenna clenched her hands. "I swear, if I find out he's done anything to Angel, I'll..."

Charles raised his long fork and pointed it at her. "You'll let *me* take care of him."

Chapter Thirty-One

Jenna pushed her empty breakfast plate aside and picked up her coffee mug. "I keep forgetting I don't have to ask permission to spend money. Wouldn't it be possible to hire a helicopter or something to go back home for a day or two?"

She noted the look of shock on Charles' face and how flustered he became.

"I guess I could look into it for you."

"What? You know how much I miss Jack."

He shrugged. "I guess I'm just a little surprised you'd want to leave here right now. I thought our number one priority was Angel and uncovering Daniel's ruse?"

She let out a heavy sigh. "Maybe you're right. There has to be a way to find out what's really going on there."

"That's the hard part. It's not like either of us can hang around the ranch without him knowing. What we need is another set of eyes in there." He put up a hand between them. "Before you say it, the answer is no. I won't allow Twyla to be put in harm's way by becoming more actively involved."

Jenna smiled knowingly. "It looks like somebody got bit by the love bug. I'm very happy for you, Charles. Twyla is a lovely woman." She sat up straight, excited as a plan came together in her mind. "What if we set him up? Put someone in there that can get close enough to him that he lets his guard down." The prospect made her giddy with excitement.

"It's a great idea, but just how are we going to pull it off? Who can we trust enough to help us?"

She began pacing. "What if someone who works there is called away on a family emergency? What if this somebody brings in a replacement, someone Daniel won't be able to refuse."

"Uh, oh. I know that look." He massaged his temples.

"I have to go out for a while." Jenna sprinted toward the door, keyed up by the budding plan. She paused briefly to glance back over her shoulder. "Don't worry about a thing. I'll fill you in over supper."

"Jenna..."

She didn't hear anything else, mounting the stairs two at a time. She had the perfect woman in mind. Daniel would be tripping over himself to welcome her to the ranch. No man could resist her charm.

In her room, she flopped into the chair and picked up her phone. She quickly brought up the number as she sat on the edge of the chair and bounced her leg.

"Hey you. How soon can you get over here?"

"Why, what's going on?"

"I need your help. Can you come over or not?" Jenna nibbled on her fingernail.

"Sure. Would you mind telling me what this is all about?"

"I'll explain everything when you get here." She tossed her cell on the bed and resumed pacing. Her plan was so crazy it might just work. With a little luck, they'd uncover the real Daniel, and ultimately keep her sister safe...and get *her* back to Jack where she belonged.

He knew Jenna had sent a message to Twyla through Edna, and Charles could hardly wait to find out what she'd been scheming behind closed doors.

Until then, apparently they were having guests for dinner in the solarium at six o'clock sharp. At least she'd dropped the notion of leaving for a couple of days. She was too damn inquisitive for her own good, which is why he needed to keep her close. So far, he'd managed to keep the secret surprise from her—mostly by sheer luck and a little quick thinking.

Edna had set a table for four, and a bottle of ice wine chilled in a bucket next to the table. He cocked his head to the side as the chatter of women grew closer. Someone laughed, and he straightened his stance.

I'd recognize that laugh anywhere.

As suspected, Jenna walked through the doorway first, closely followed by Twyla...and then *Buffy?*

Twyla walked straight to him. "We meet again." Her eyes sparkled as she reached up on tiptoes to kiss his cheek.

Boldly, he wrapped his arms around her in a hug. "It's good to see you, too."

Jenna coughed. "Let's pour a drink and take a seat. We

have lots to discuss."

He released Twyla and grabbed the bottle of wine. "Can I pour you a glass?" he asked her, to which she nodded. "How about you, Buffy? You're looking pretty as ever. It's good to see you."

"Oh stop. You're going to make me blush," she tittered.

Jenna's childhood friend was dressed to the nines as always. A fitted, black cocktail dress hugged her curves. Her hair was worn up in a twisted bun to showcase the diamond chandeliers in her ears. As beautiful as she was, she didn't hold a candle to Twyla. Maybe his Italian beauty didn't have a designer dress or thousands of dollars in diamonds, but she didn't need any of it. The glint in her eyes far outshone any gem.

Jenna snapped her fingers only inches from his face. "Earth to Charles? Do you care to join us?"

He cursed the heat flooding his face and mumbled under his breath as he took a seat.

"Before I came here, I talked to Diane like you ask me to, Jenna. You can trust her and she will help if you can make up her paycheck. She will make up a family problem, and take Buffy to Daniel so she can work until she comes back." Twyla smiled.

"Why are you all so certain Daniel will agree to any of this?"

All three women looked at him in surprise.

Obviously I've missed something.

Buffy stood and swayed her hips. "Hello? How can he resist all this?"

Charles tilted back his head and laughed. "Of course, what was I thinking? You might want to leave all the bobbles at home, though."

"Don't worry about a thing. This role was made for me." She spun an imaginary hula-hoop with her hips.

He frowned. "I don't know. I'm not crazy about Buffy and Twyla out there alone with him. Besides, do you know how to make a bed or even cook for that matter?

Buffy winked playfully. "How hard can it be?"

Charles shook his head; definitely not as convinced she

could pull it off as all three of them seemed to be.

"Hey, if you can think of a better idea, I'm all ears," Jenna countered pointedly.

Just then, Edna breezed into the solarium pushing a cart laden with covered dishes. Charles silently thanked her for perfect timing. He looked out the corner of his eye to find Twyla staring at him, an inquisitive glint to her eyes.

"Would you like a refill?" He reached across the table for the chilling wine.

Her hand covered his and guided it back to rest on the table between them. "Don't worry for me. I am good to take care of myself."

He smiled with a slight nod and gently squeezed her fingers. "I didn't mean to imply you couldn't. It's just the thought of Daniel anywhere near you makes me so…"

"Jealous?" She gazed at him through lowered lashes.

He shifted in his chair to accommodate his body's reaction to her sultry response.

"Ahem. In case you two have forgotten, we can hear and see everything going on between the two of you." Jenna waggled her eyebrows, mischief in her tone.

"We'll finish this conversation after dinner." He shot Jenna a warning look, ending the subject.

The scent of prime rib and roasted potatoes set his belly grumbling as Edna set a plate in front of each of them.

"Would anyone like a little gravy?"

Jenna took the gravy boat from her. "We can take it from here. Please thank Grace for this amazing meal."

"Okay. Here's some fresh-baked rolls and whipped butter. If you need anything…"

Charles slathered a roll with butter, and dipped it in gravy. "We know where to find you."

Chapter Thirty-Two

Angel quietly flipped the pages of an album Jenna put together for her. Every now and then she'd ask a question or cast an inquisitive glance her way.

She isn't all freaked out like she was after seeing the photo from my purse. Dare I be hopeful?

"Maybe one day you can come to my home to see some of our mother's things?"

Her sister stared at her for a few moments. "I think I'd like that, one day."

"Of course, whenever you feel up to it."

The doctor sat back and said nothing for most of the session. Jenna smiled. His look of approval reaffirmed the session had gone as well as she thought it had.

"You know, I've been here a few times now, and I've yet to go on a tour of the ranch."

Angelina brightened. "I can show you." She looked at the doctor. "That is if it's okay with you?"

"I think that's an excellent idea. Do you want me to come along?"

Her sister shook her head. "I can do it by myself." She smiled broadly. "I'll show you our craft room first."

Jenna eagerly followed her sister's lead out of the office, and was thrilled beyond measure to have Angel reach for her hand to hold as they went on their way.

Angel came to a full stop, however, when Daniel's office door opened. He stepped into the hallway, closely followed by Buffy and a woman she assumed to be Diane from the kitchen.

True to her word, her friend had toned it down considerably. Jenna never thought she'd see the day Buffy would leave the house with minimal make-up and her hair in a ponytail. Even without all the extras, she was a natural beauty—and judging by the way Daniel ogled her, their plan was going well.

"Take as long as you need, Diane." Daniel kissed the older woman's cheek. "We'll miss you."

He turned to Buffy. "Let's go back in my office and we'll

take care of the necessary paper work." Not once did he take his eyes off of his *new employee.* He put a hand to the small of her back and ushered her inside, closing the door behind them without so much as a glance in their direction.

Her sister scowled after them. "Who is that?"

"I heard Diane was called away for a family emergency. I'm guessing that girl is her replacement."

"Hmph." Angel stomped her foot. "I don't like her."

"You don't even know her, Angel."

Her gaze narrowed. "I know enough."

Grinning, Jenna asked, "So, can you show me the craft room now?"

She shrugged. "I guess so."

"On second thought, do you think we could go out and see the horses?"

It was like a switch flipped, and she offered Jenna a brilliant smile. "That's a good idea. We can get a few apples from the kitchen to feed to them. Would you like that?"

Jenna linked arms with her, and they half-skipped their way to the kitchen to find Twyla alone.

"Can we have some apples for the horses?"

Twyla smiled. "Yes you can." She gave Angel a plastic bag. "Take what you want from in the cold room."

"I'll be right back." Her sister scurried out of sight.

Jenna took a quick look around her. "Are we alone?" she whispered.

"Yes, but not so long."

"Daniel will probably bring Buffy here soon. He seems more than pleased to meet her."

"This is good, ci?"

Angel burst into the room. "I got the apples. Come on, let's go to the stables."

Jenna chuckled, as did Twyla.

"You two have fun." Her accomplice waved from the door.

Angel practically dragged Jenna across the lawn to where the horses were kept. She had visions of her toppling over on her bad arm, but there was no stopping her. Her sister seemed to go off in her own little world whenever she interacted with the horses. Her face lit up, and her otherwise uneven gait, now smooth, almost *angelic*. One by one she touched each horse as a mother would a newborn child.

Jenna remembered reading that when someone loses an ability, another will surface and compensate for the loss. Her newfound sibling may have Down syndrome, but she truly had a gift—a special connection with the horses. *Would Angel have the same bond with the dogs and other animals?*

"Here." Her sister placed an apple in Jenna's hand. "Watch me. You put the apple in your open hand and hold it under the horse's mouth."

"Are you sure he won't bite me?" She was a little nervous about her hand being so close to the animal's large teeth.

Angel laughed. "No, the horse wants the apple, not your hand." She guided Jenna's arm, moving it slowly until the apple was close enough.

As promised, the horse didn't bite her, but it left a little more slobber than she would've liked. She grimaced at her hand. "Ew, gross."

Angel giggled.

"Oh, so you think that's funny, do you?" Jenna held her hand out as if she'd wipe it on her pretty white blouse.

Her sister squealed and stepped back.

She moved toward her playfully, and Angel walked backwards, step for step.

"No don't. I'll give you a towel."

She winked. "No, that's okay, you'll do just fine."

Angel screeched and ran out of the stable, laughing as Jenna followed, holding her sticky hand out in front of her. Next thing she knew, they somehow tripped over each other and fell to the ground, lying on their backs in the grass, laughing until they both held their sides.

"Oh my, you didn't hurt your arm, did you?" Jenna gasped for breath.

Unexpectedly, Angel turned on her side and stared into her eyes.

"I should have known better." Jenna reached for her. "Does it hurt?"

"I think you must really be my sister," she said in all seriousness, seemingly oblivious to her concern.

Jenna gazed at her through a veil of tears. "I think those are the most beautiful words I have ever heard."

Angel got up on her knees, prompting her to do so as well. When her arms awkwardly wrapped around Jenna, it was like the huge void her mother's death had left within her was suddenly filled with warmth.

"I love you, Angel." Her voice cracked.

Angel pulled back a little and hiccupped, her nose red from sniffling. "I love you, too, sister."

Chapter Thirty-Three

It warmed Charles' heart to see Jenna so happy. Angel's acceptance of her as a sister meant the world to her.

"She wants to come here so we can sort through some of our mother's things."

"That's wonderful, Jenna. I couldn't be happier for the two of you." He noted the glint in her eyes. "Okay, what's going on in that pretty head of yours?"

"You know me better than anyone." She fluttered her eyelashes. "I'm going to brighten things up around here. It still feels like a mausoleum the way it is now."

Charles winced. "That bad, huh? What exactly do you have in mind?"

She jumped up from the sofa and padded across the room to the heavy brocade drapes. "Well, for starters, get rid of these." Dust particles danced in a stream of sunlight let in when she parted the curtains.

"I'm with you on that." He winked. "What else?"

Jenna opened her arms. "How about we take down those tapestries? They're beautiful, and probably cost a small fortune, but they're not for here. I think a fresh coat of paint would breathe life back into this old place."

He held up his hands. "Okay, okay, whatever makes you happy. Design is definitely not my forte."

She stood behind his chair and planted kisses across his baldhead. "Thank you, thank you. Did I ever tell you just how much I love you?"

Charles brushed her hands away and wiped his head as he stood. "I'm outa here before the waterworks start."

She threw back her head and laughed. "You know you love me."

"I never said I didn't. Why don't you go look at paint colors or something?" He left the house with a smile on his face and walked toward the garages that housed his newly acquired antique cars. Just as suspected, John had the Rolls out, buffing the chrome.

"She's looking mighty purty, ol' man." Charles whistled

long and low as he looked up and down the length of his car.

"Yes, sir. She's quite the lady."

His phone buzzed in his pocket and he quickly answered the call.

"Charles." Twyla breathed heavily as if she'd been running.

He froze in place. "Twyla? What's wrong? Why are you out of breath?"

"I ran to my car, and I'm on my way home." She swallowed audibly. "After Jenna left, I take a tray to one a girl that is sick. Angel skips right to me and hugs me. She tells me she has a sister now."

"Well, that's good news, right?"

"Yes, it is, but then Daniel came out of his office with Buffy. Angel, she... sono impazziti...um, she go crazy."

"What do you mean by crazy?"

"She march over and stop so close, right in Buffy's face."

"Shit." Charles swiped a hand over his head. "Please tell me it didn't get physical?"

"No, Angel put hands on hips and shout at Buffy."

He splayed a hand over his rapidly beating heart. "Why don't we talk over coffee? I'd rather have this conversation in person."

"Yes, me, too."

"How about we meet at your place? We can discuss this more openly there."

"Yes. I be home in twenty minutes."

"Okay then, I'll see you in half an hour. Twyla? Is anyone in urgent need right now?"

"No. We have time."

"Okay, I'm on my way." Charles tucked his phone away. His heart beat somewhat back to normal. "I have to go out for a while."

John smirked. "Yes, I heard. Don't worry. If Jenna asks, I'll tell her you're on a date."

Charles stroked his jaw. "You know what? I never missed having a woman in my life, until Twyla came along. There's something mighty special about that lady."

"You better snatch her up, my friend. A gal like her won't

be available forever."

He waved a hand in the air. "Yah, I know. See you later. I got my cell if anything comes up and you need me." He hurried off to fetch his Mustang.

Out of all his newly acquired cars, Charles loved driving the convertible the most. Having the roof down made him feel young and alive.

As does Twyla.

A vision of her wearing her sunny-yellow dress flashed in his mind.

Maybe it's time to find out if she feels the same way.

His attention swayed to the reason he was headed her way, and an image of Buffy and Angel, nose-to-nose, flashed in his mind. "Shit." *What did Angel say to poor Buffy?* He sped up a little. *Why can't things go smoothly for a change?*

Twyla's car was already in the driveway when he arrived. She stood at the door, still wearing her uniform and visibly upset.

Charles stooped to kiss her cheek. "Nice to see you."

She squeezed his hand and led him through her cozy little house to the kitchen.

"You've got a real nice place here."

"Gracie. Coffee?" She opened a cupboard and glanced back over her shoulder.

"Yes. Coffee sounds good. So, are you okay?"

She smiled sweetly at him. "I am good, just worried." Twyla nodded her head in the direction of French doors. "We go sit on the back porch, okay?"

He left the table and opened the doors for her. His gaze narrowed on the swing of her hips, and he smiled, appreciating the fact she looked good coming *and* going.

The seriousness in her tone put his thoughts back where they should be. "You said Angel faced off with Buffy?"

"I never did see Angel angry before."

"Is Buffy okay?"

"Angel shouted to stay away from Daniel. She sprayed from her mouth in Buffy's face."

"Ouch. I'm sure I'll hear all about that."

"Buffy did not move. Her mouth is open like she does not

believe this happened." Twyla took a sip of her coffee. "Daniel stood in the middle, so Angel steps back." She shivered. "His eyes are black when asks what Angel is doing. He say it not good to talk to Buffy. He tells her to say sorry. But Angel cross her arms and sticks up her nose at Buffy. She says, 'Daniel is mine. Go away.'"

"Wow. Didn't they see you standing there?"

"No. I stand with my back on the wall." She shook her head. "Daniel's face is red, and he say Angel to go in his office and stay. She sticks up her chin and pushes Buffy out of her way to the office. Daniel says sorry to Buffy. His hand goes down her back and stop too low, touch her bottom two times. Buffy smiled and takes his hands away."

"I can just imagine what was going on in her head. Buffy did well." He was actually surprised she kept it together, normally a fire cracker, she'd be up one side of him and down the other in seconds flat.

"Daniel is not happy at this and does a... *hissy fit*? He points down the hall and tells her to go to kitchen and stay there." Twyla snickered behind her hand. "Buffy walked away. I saw her mouth say, '*asshole*.'"

Charles tilted back his head and laughed. "Now, that's more like the Buffy I know."

"I saw her one more time before I go. She tell me she will check to see Angel is good." She glanced at her watch. "She will phone me to say what happens."

Just then, several solar lights came on. The garden was beautiful in the coming darkness. They sat in amiable silence, watching the backyard transform from day to night.

Charles stood and offered his hand. "Come, take me on a tour of your amazing garden while we wait for Buffy to call."

Chapter Thirty-Four

Jenna listened to Twyla and Buffy recant their day at the ranch. It was a good thing they started off by telling her Angel was okay, because she could hardly believe they were talking about the same girl she'd left earlier.

"I don't know what went on in his office, but before I left, I found her in the craft room with one of the younger girls. She was laughing and carrying on." Buffy tucked her feet up under her on a deck chair.

"What do you make of it all, Twyla? You probably know Daniel better than any of us. Is he the kind of man who'd take advantage of girls like my sister?" She clenched her teeth together in wait of her answer.

"I don't know him that way. He keeps...er, private? The one time I say no to him, he never try no more after." She heaved a sigh. "The girls on main floor try hard to make him happy. Is it sex? I say no, not with little girls. Maybe the big girls, but I never see this."

"All I know is that it was crystal clear Angel felt I was a threat. In her eyes, Daniel belongs to her." Buffy picked up her drink. "I seriously thought she was going to hit me."

Charles put his feet flat to stop the swing from moving and cleared his throat. "I hate to play the devil's advocate, but isn't it possible she thinks of Daniel as a father figure? Maybe after her mother passed, she became a little obsessed with not losing him, too."

More confused than ever, Jenna didn't know what to think. "I pray that's true. Nothing would please me more than being proved wrong about things."

He put his arm across Twyla's back and rubbed her shoulder with the pad of his thumb. "Are you cold?"

She snuggled to his side. "No, this is good."

Jenna smiled. It warmed her heart to see her dear friend finally find someone who thought he was as wonderful a man as she knew him to be. As happy as it made her, she couldn't stop a twinge of jealously; Jack wasn't there to comfort her.

"I don't know about any of you, but this working deal has

me all tuckered out." Buffy stood and stretched her arms above her head. "I'm going to crash here. So, what's the game plan?"

"Well, I think if you two ladies keep an eye on things on the ranch, I'll try to see if I can get my sister to tell me how she really feels about Daniel."

Charles left to drive Twyla home, and Buffy took the guest room next to her bedroom. Alone on the back deck, Jenna tried to make sense of everything. She wished Jack was there so she could lose herself in him, even for only a little while.

We need to get to the bottom of things quickly so I can go home.

Her phone buzzed and skipped across the beveled glass of the side table. Jenna startled. "Who could be calling at this hour?" Her jaw dropped upon seeing Jack's name flash on the screen.

"Jack?" Her heartbeat raced.

"Hey, Jenna. I hope I didn't wake you."

"Why is your name on my screen?" She heard the tell-tale tremor in her voice and made a concerted effort not to break down.

"What, you're not happy to hear from me?"

"Oh, Jack, of course I am. I just didn't think there were towers close enough to catch a signal from our house."

He snickered. "Well, there's a tower now. It's funny what a little money and persistence can do."

"It must have cost you a fortune!"*Dammit! I should've taken care of this long ago. I'll have to find a way to make him let me pay for it.*

"Don't worry about all that right now. How are things going there?"

"Angel wants to come here for a visit, so I've hired a crew to brighten up the place."

"That sounds encouraging."

"Yes, I'm pretty sure after a couple more sessions with her psychiatrist I'll be able to come home."

"I know you're excited, but be careful not to rush things. Make sure your sister is in a good place before leaving her."

Jenna frowned. She thought he'd be excited to see the end in sight. It was like he wasn't remotely happy about it.

"Aw, shit," he growled. "The dogs are going nuts out there. I hate to cut this short…"

The dogs' frenzied barking came over the line loud and clear. "It's okay, I can hear them. What do you think got them all riled up?"

"There have been a couple of pesky raccoons hanging around the past few days. I bet it's them."

"I guess you better go see." She tried to hide her disappointment, but she was actually on the verge of tears.

"I'm so sorry, Jenna. Do you want me to call you back after I've seen to them?"

"Don't worry, it's getting late. Now that you have a phone, you can call anytime. Why not call me in the morning?"

"I can think of no better way to start my day."

The noise level increased tenfold. "I love you, Jack. You better get out there."

"I love you, too. I'll see you in my dreams, baby."

She stared at the phone after he hung up.

Were things a little weird between us? Or is my insecurity working overtime?

Suddenly, she felt exhausted.

Maybe I'm just over-tired. That must be it.

Tired or not, now more than ever, she was committed to wrapping things up quickly.

I need to be home to rekindle the fire between us…my being away is so unfair to him.

Charles threaded his fingers through Twyla's. "Do you mind if I don't take you straight home? There's something I want to show you."

"Yes, but don't forget, I have work early in morning." She smiled sweetly.

"You know, you wouldn't have to if you stayed up all night." He wiggled his brows.

She feigned interest out the window, but he caught the lift of her lips, and it made his heart swell. He squeezed her hand.

"Where are we going?"

"We're almost there." He turned the corner where the road yawned to the lakefront. A full moon illuminated the rippling water. Once he parked the car and shut the engine down, only night sounds could be heard.

"Questo è bello."

"Come on, let's take a closer look." He hoped his voice didn't belie the trembling going on inside of him.

He helped her out of the car, and they walked hand in hand along the beach. He stopped to take off his shoes and socks. "I love the sand between my toes."

"I think me, too." She giggled and slipped out of her own shoes.

Ahead, a large formation of boulder-size rocks jutted out to the water, and he guided her to climb to the top, where they sat staring out at the vast expanse.

"I like to come here at night to think."

Twyla nuzzled closer to him. "I can see why. Molto bella."

"Molto bella, what does that mean?

"It means very beautiful."

Charles tipped her chin up with a finger and gazed into her eyes. "It's not the only thing that takes my breath away." He heard the hitch in her breath. "I know we haven't known each other very long, but it's only fair to tell you that I am falling madly in love with you."

Twyla's eyes filled with moisture and her lower lip trembled. "Yes, me, too."

He wiped his brow dramatically, his heart beating the path of a racehorse. "Phew! I was hoping you'd say that." His shaky hand dipped into his jacket pocket and he pulled out a small ring box.

Twyla's jaw dropped, and she searched his eyes for understanding.

"I'm not asking you to marry me today...unless, of course, that's what you want." He winked playfully. "But will you wear this ring, Twyla? I want every man who crosses your path to know you're mine."

She twirled a lock of hair around her finger. "So, do you want to marry me, or does this mean I am your girl?"

He found her light-hearted teasing sexy as hell.

Charles opened the box to reveal a stunning solitaire. The moon's rays cast prisms off the exquisite diamond. "I am asking you to marry me."

Her fingertips gently feathered the diamond. "*Molto bella.*"

"Is that a yes?" It was becoming increasingly difficult to keep hold of his faculties.

Twyla shifted so she could clasp her hands behind his neck and gaze up at him. "*Ci.*"

Charles laughed and pulled her to sit on his lap, where he proceeded to slip the ring on her finger. A perfect fit.

"I'll spend the rest of my life showing you just how much I love you. How do you say it in Italian?"

She looked into his eyes. "*Ti amo.*"

All thoughts of making it an early night tossed to the wayside as he drew her into his arms.

I'm not sure what I did to deserve a woman like this, but I can't chance losing her.

He gazed down into her glistening eyes. "*Ti amo.*"

Chapter Thirty-Five

Sitting outside Doctor Gilmore's office, Jenna whispered into her cell phone as loud as she dared, "Do you really think calling me while I'm here is such a good idea?"

"I thought you'd want to know, Daniel called Twyla to his office," Buffy replied in equally hushed tones.

"Any idea what it's all about?" She glanced up and down the hall.

"I don't know, but she's been gone..."

"Buffy? Are you there?"

"I should have known."

Jenna's mouth went dry. "Daniel?"

"Busted."

The phone disconnected. "Oh shit."

Footsteps suddenly ran across the tile floor, and Twyla turned the corner and hurried outside. Mere seconds passed before Buffy followed, her face red like she'd been crying.

Daniel rounded the corner to face her, his eyes ablaze with anger.

"What is going on here? Why are Twyla and Buffy so upset?" She looked past him. *Should I run out and see if they're okay?*

"I'd like to see you in my office," he snarled.

"I-I'm waiting to see the doctor and Angel." An uncomfortable mixture of fear and anger consumed her.

"I *strongly* advise you to do as I ask. That is, if you ever want to see your sister again," he hissed.

His threat challenged her own anger and she stood. "I only have a few minutes."

He nodded and stormed to his office.

How dare you threaten me.

A little voice in the back of her head told her not to go, even as she stomped down the hall and threw his door open; she left it slightly ajar. "First off, I want to know what you said to Buffy and Twyla."

Daniel sat at the edge of his desk, shaking his head. "Did you really think I wouldn't find out about your team of spies?

Nothing goes on around here I don't know about." He glared at her. "And I mean *nothing*. Got it?" He narrowed his steely gaze on her. "Now, would you mind telling me just what the hell you're trying to do?"

"I know there's more to you than the phony smiles and practiced lines. I'm not leaving my sister here without finding out exactly what kind of man you really are."

"I've been running this ranch for almost twenty years. Do you seriously believe I've had something sinister going on for that long without raising suspicion?"

"You seem to forget, I've been at the brunt end of a less than admirable side of you. If you've so much as thought about my sister inappropriately, I swear I'll see you behind bars."

Jenna spun on her heel, so angry she needed to put some distance between him and her, before things escalated any further.

A slight breeze whispered across her skin and a jolt of white lightening pierced her upper arm.

As if in slow motion, she fell into a black abyss of nothingness.

As the town came into view, Jack turned on his headlights and stroked his freshly shaven jaw. He'd been surprised to see the ATV approach the cabin with a stranger riding it, and even more surprised by the cryptic message Jenna had couriered to him.

Meet me in the middle. You won't regret it. Love Jenna

The note gave an address and directions to a motel in a small border town. He shivered in anticipation, and shifted in his seat to contain his growing desire, picturing Jenna in sexy lingerie, lying on a bed in wait of him.

He laughed at the deep, guttural groan that escaped his lips. "Me caveman."

Like a beacon in the night, the flashing lights of the Starlight Motel urged him forward. Once he parked and popped a breath mint in his mouth, he stopped at the main desk where he was given a key to Unit Seven, as promised.

From this day forward, the number seven will be my lucky number.

His key slid in the lock easily, and he creaked open the door. "What the..."

Two bodies were in the bed, but the room was too dark to discern if one was Jenna or not. He ran his hand along the wall next to the door until he found the light switch and flicked it on, bathing the room with light.

The man lying next to Jenna bolted upright and reached for his pants on the floor beside the bed. "What the hell do you think you're doing?"

Even though her face was covered, red hair fanned out over the other pillow. *Jenna.*

"You can start by telling me what the hell you think you're doing with my girl? Be very careful of your answer." Jack snarled, clenching his fists.

"Easy there, buddy." The man stepped into his pants and pulled them up. "I didn't see no wedding ring, and she sure as hell didn't mention a boyfriend."

The whole deal seemed surreal. Jenna still slept, softly snoring. Her bare shoulders told of her nakedness.

"Listen. I don't want any trouble. I'm going to give you and *your girl* a little privacy." The man quickly gathered the rest of his things and slipped past Jack. The door slammed shut behind him.

Jenna moaned.

"Jenna?" Jack spoke sternly. "Is this your idea of a joke? You need to wake up and start explaining. My God, if you wanted me out of your life, did you have to be so cruel about it?" With shaking hands, he braced himself against the wall, his mind reeling in disbelief.

Her head lifted and fell back to the pillow. She shielded her eyes and blinked rapidly. Her gaze travelled to the now empty side of the bed, and she moaned again, turning her back to him and placing the pillow over her head as if to block out the light.

His mounting anger fueled his path across the room to stand at the bedside, putting his hand on her shoulder and rocking her. "Wake up. I need some answers here. How could you do this to me?" He couldn't stop his voice from cracking.

She tossed the pillow behind her and squinted. "Jack?" Her voice was hoarse, and her breath reeked of stale booze.

"What's going on?" She looked around the room as she slowly sat upright, baring her naked breasts. "Where am I?" Her eyelids drooped like she was fighting to stay awake.

"Perfect. You don't know where you are? Do you at least know the guy you were sleeping with?" An excess of emotions exploded, like being sucker-punched in the gut.

Jenna's breath hitched, and her hand flew to her chest. Her head bowed, seemingly surprised to find herself naked, and she quickly pulled the sheet up to her chin. "Jack? I don't know what you're talking about. I don't even know how I got here."

He searched her eyes for a trace of truth, but all he saw was confusion, inevitably brought on by either a blackout or pathetic attempt to cover her ass.

He shook his head, disgusted. "You know, I was actually excited to get your invite to a rendezvous." He began pacing. "Is he the real reason you haven't come home yet? I'm such an idiot, envisioning how beautiful tonight would be." He choked on the threat of tears.

"Jack, please...I'm telling you the truth. I don't know how I got here, and I definitely have no clue as to what invitation I supposedly sent you. Where are w—"

He held up a hand to halt the lies spewing from her mouth. "Enough! I can't stand here and listen to anymore lies. I got a long drive ahead of me." He stormed to the door, ignoring her pleas for him to stay.

Jack stopped at the door and fisted the angry tears from his eyes. His heart shattered in a million pieces at his feet. "To think you actually got me to believe in love again." He took the invitation from his inside pocket and blindly flung it toward the bed before opening the door. "Good bye, Jenna."

Chapter Thirty-Six

Jenna sprung out of bed and immediately fell to the floor, holding her head in her hands as she dropped to her knees. *Oh my God, what is happening?*

Collapsed there, she wasn't sure how much time had passed since the man she loved walked out of the room and her life. Her teeth chattered as cold seeped in, making her aware of being naked on the floor next to the bed.

Why can't I remember anything? Jack said I sent him an invitation? Her gaze travelled over the unkempt room, coming to rest on a tangle of sheets where he had woken her.

Had another man really been in bed with me? Her stomach lurched, and she carefully stood, using the wall to stop the room from spinning. As quickly as she could move without falling, she made her way to the bathroom and fell next to the toilet, spewing every drop of anything that was in her stomach until only dry heaves ripped the lining of her throat.

Jenna lay down on the linoleum floor, pressing her face to the cool tile until the threat of vomiting again passed. Never in her life had she felt this way. It was definitely not like any hangover she'd ever experienced.

I have to get out of here. I have to find Jack.

In her present condition, it was impossible to do so on her own. She wanted to wake up and find it all to be a horrible nightmare; she needed help.

Buffy.

Tears returned to her eyes as she wobbled out of the bathroom. The phone sat on an end table, and as she keyed her friend's number on the phone, she realized she had no idea where she was. Panic ensued as she tore the room apart looking for a clue. Finally, she found a business card where she should have looked first—in a drawer of the same table she'd found her phone.

Buffy was relieved to hear from her at first, and then laid into her for scaring them all half to death.

"Buffy?" she interrupted her friends' tirade, her words

nothing more than a ragged whisper. "Buffy, please....please just come and get me..." Her voice cracked as tears flowed freely down her face. She managed to give her the address on the card before she succumbed to full blown sobbing.

"Jenna? I hate to ask this, but...were you raped?"

She froze in place. *Raped?* "Oh God, please just get here." She ended the call while Buffy still talked, and stumbled to the bathroom where she ripped open the tattered shower curtain. Once the water ran as hot as she could take it, she stepped under the stream, putting two hands flat against the wall for support.

Raped?

She teetered on the brink of hysteria as she frantically searched her mind for even a thread of memory. She turned her face upward and shouted her anger and fear. The water started to cool and she turned up the hot water.

Get a grip, Jenna. If I had sex with a man, wouldn't I feel it?

Jenna slid down the shower wall, remembering the morning after the last times her and Jack made love. She'd clung to every glorious sensation for the next couple of days. Her fingers followed the curve of her lips, while her hand tentatively slipped between her legs. There was no sensation of being raw, or bruised.

I can't feel anything to validate being raped.

Her gazed darted around the shower stall for soap. There was nothing, no soap, no shampoo...

"Ahhhh!!"

Her fingernails raked every inch of her body, trying to rid herself of the sense of violation that had all but consumed her until the water ran cold. Her teeth chattered uncontrollably as she stepped out of the shower. Her emotions, so fragile, had her almost sobbing with relief after finding a clean, folded towel.

As if in a daze, she patted her body dry and wrapped the cloth around her hair before venturing out in search of her clothes. Her stomach flip-flopped at the sight of the bed, and seeing one of her socks peeking out from under a bunched sheet. With two fingers she pulled it out.

Jenna returned to the bathroom, and put the lid of the toilet down to sit on while she slowly dressed with shaking hands. She hadn't looked in the mirror once since opening her eyes to this nightmare. The skin of her legs prickled from being scratched by her fingernails as she pulled on her jeans.

After she'd taken a couple deep breaths and closing her eyes, she raised her face to the mirror. *Oh God, please don't let me see any marks left by the stranger in my bed.* She was almost completely convinced there had been no sexual interaction. To find something now would definitely be her undoing.

She squeezed her eyes tight one more time before opening. Her shoulders dipped in relief. Other than looking seriously hungover and a little red from being scrubbed, she saw nothing to validate the question of being raped.

How long has it been since I phoned Buffy? It will probably take her an hour to get here.

She straightened her stance and took a couple of steps toward the bathroom door. The mere thought of seeing that bed again sent her stomach churning, and a cold sweat broke out across her brow. Her head shook violently from side to side as she stepped backwards, to return to sit on the toilet and wait for her friend. She wrapped her arms around herself and started to rock.

For as long as she lived, she'd never forget the expression on Jack's face. He'd left the room a broken man, and apparently, it was all her fault.

A knock came to the door.

Her heart pounded beneath her hand. "Buffy? Is that you?"

The door opened, and her best friend came inside, two extra-large coffees in hand. Her eyes grew big as she faced Jenna sitting on the toilet.

"Why are you sitting in there?" Buffy set down the coffee and hurried to kneel at her feet. "Thank God you're okay. We've all been worried sick about you. What's going on here? You didn't make much sense on the phone."

Her best friend's genuine concern for her as she searched her eyes set her body trembling and the threat of sobbing rose to the brink.

Buffy rubbed Jenna's upper arms briskly—the first warmth even the shower hadn't given her. "Never mind all that for now. Let's sit by the window."

Jenna nodded, thankful for the hand offered. Her friend led her out of the bathroom, leaving her to stand alone while she pulled two chairs over to a small table by the window.

"Come sit here." Buffy took her hand in hers and walked alongside her to be seated.

Jenna gratefully accepted the coffee in her trembling hands.

Buffy reached over and tucked a lock of her unkempt hair behind her ear. "You look like shit."

Intense heartache and anger rendered her immobile, stuck in a cesspool of self-loathing and confusion. She shook her head and closed her eyes, unable to hold back the tears any longer. "I don't understand any of this. Jack said I sent him an invitation, and that there was a man in bed next to me? I can't remember any of it!"

Her friend rubbed her back. The attempt to comfort her had the exact opposite effect, making her queasy. "Maybe we should phone the police and get you to a hospital. We can talk on the way."

Panic rose up in her and she grabbed her friend's hand, squeezing hard. "Oh God, please no. I checked everything in the shower, and I seriously doubt I had sex last night. Besides, I can't face a hospital...I need to find Jack..." Jenna set her cup down, sloshing coffee up the sides. A pathetic groan escaped her dry mouth as she tried to keep the very real threat of puking again at bay.

"Okay, okay, if you're sure you weren't....that you didn't have sex, we'll find Jack first. I'm not sure what's going on with you, but we'll get through this together." Buffy shook her head and took her cell from her pocket. "Try and drink some of that coffee. I promised Charles and Twyla I'd call once I found you."

Buffy got up and opened the door to stand just outside and make her call. Her voice muffled as Jenna held her coffee between both hands and sipped at it. Slowly, the caffeine worked its magic, and she regained some appearance of being in control over her emotions.

Her friend returned to sit at the table next to her. "What the hell did you do last night?"

"I don't remember anything before Jack waking me up."

Buffy sat quietly, listening to her, but her gaze kept going to Jenna's arm. Then her eyes opened wide and she practically jumped to the edge of her seat, reaching over to grab Jenna's upper arm and turn it gently. "You know what? I don't think you were drunk at all."

"How can you say that? Trust me, this is about as bad as a hangover can get." She shrugged at the faint bruise her friend showed her. "So, I probably banged into something."

"Look closer." Buffy tapped a red-polished nail in front of a tiny dark speck in the center of the bruise. "That's a needle track. Unless you got a flu shot yesterday, odds are you were drugged."

Jenna gripped the arms of her chair, and closed her eyes to stop the room from spinning. She trudged through the murky recesses of her fragmented memory.

I was standing in Daniel's office...

She broke out in a cold sweat.

A slight breeze...

"Daniel!"

Her hand flew to her chest, and she swallowed the sour bile that threatened to choke her.

"*Daniel* drugged you?" Buffy took her hands and squeezed them reassuringly.

Having her so close was nauseating, and she pulled her hands away and waved a hand in her face, feeling like she might faint. "Please, I need some air."

Her friend got up and scurried behind her to open the window. Jenna breathed in deeply. With each breath, the nausea passed and the oppressive weight lifted.

"I was in his office after Twyla and you tore out of the ranch. He said he knew I was up to something..." She grabbed a corner of her shirt and wiped the sweat from her face. "He said he wasn't going to stand back and let me ruin his life."

Buffy jogged to the bathroom and returned with a damp face cloth. She moved in to wipe her face, and Jenna stopped her, taking the cloth from her hand. "Thank you, but I'm feeling a little claustrophobic and need some breathing room."

"Of course, I'm sorry."

The last thing her best friend needed to be was sorry.

"Did you see the needle?" she asked and returned to her seat on the opposite side of the table.

Jenna pressed the cold cloth to the back of her neck. "No, but I remember something, like a bee sting on my arm...and then everything went black." The cloth quickly grew warm as she rubbed her nape and chest.

"The bastard set you up! He did all this so you'd lose one of the most important people in your life...Jack!" Buffy balled her hands and shook her fists. "We really should call the cops."

Jenna gently covered her fist with a hand. "No way. I don't want to have to explain all of this..." Her cheeks burned as she turned her head to look around the disheveled room. "They'll think I'm some psycho drug addict or worse."

Despite the marching band in her head, and the dredge from the bottom of a sewer that threatened to fill her mouth, she got up, a tad too quickly and swayed.

"Oh God, somebody shoot me and put me out of my misery."

"Let's get out of here." Buffy stood and picked up both coffee cups. "If you don't want to call the cops, or go to the hospital, where do you want to go?"

"For starters, I'd like to go home and get out of these clothes, and then I'm going to do what I should've done a long time ago." Jenna put a hand on Buffy's shoulder on the way out of the room.

"And that would be?"

"Tell Jack *everything*."

Jack drove around aimlessly for quite some time before swerving to the shoulder of the road, spewing gravel as he came to an abrupt stop, and pounded the steering wheel.

"What the hell am I doing?" He looked back over his shoulder for oncoming traffic. The second the coast was clear, he shot back onto the asphalt and peeled a U-turn, filling the air with smoke and the stench of burned rubber.

None of this makes any sense. If Jenna wanted to end

things between them there was no way in hell she'd be so manipulative and hurtful. *Yes, I know I saw a man in bed with her, but I also saw the hurt and confusion in her expressive eyes. No, there's definitely more to this story.*

Less than an hour later, he sat on the back deck of the estate, nursing a hot cup of coffee Twyla brought out for him before leaving them alone to talk.

"Buffy called shortly before you arrived, so I know what's going on." His mouth set in a grim line before proceeding. "Jenna doesn't remember anything. Did you really find a man in bed with her?" His big hands opened and closed, clenched so tight, his knuckles turned white.

"I'll never forget turning on the light and finding her in bed with another man." He paused and took a few deep breaths. "Jenna was out cold, and the guy shot out of bed and jumped into his jeans pretty fast."

"Please tell me you landed a fist in his face." Charles' face turned red with anger as he clenched his teeth.

"No." Jack shook his head, pissed at himself for missing the chance. "I was in shock. I couldn't speak never mind deck the guy."

"What was Jenna doing before he left the room?"

"I had to wake her up. Like I said, she was out cold. It took her a few minutes to realize I was even there. All I could smell was stale booze, and what I saw... You know, looking back, I didn't see a shred of guilt in her expression. All I saw in those green eyes of hers was fear and confusion. But all *I* saw was red. I didn't even give her a chance to talk." He raked his fingers through his hair.

Charles got up and started to pace. "I'd lay money on Howard or Daniel, maybe even both of them being behind this somehow. Besides, do you really believe our Jenna is capable of something like that?"

"Ugh!" Jack hit the deck with his fist. "In my heart I know Jenna wouldn't do this to me...but I can't dismiss what I saw with my own two eyes."

"And that's exactly what *he* wanted to happen." Jenna stepped out onto the deck and rushed to kneel at his feet.

Jack searched her tortured expression for a clue as to how

he was supposed to feel. His heart wrenched seeing her in such a sick-looking state.

"I was drugged," she stated breathlessly as she pushed up the sleeve of her shirt and pointed out the puncture mark. "Daniel drugged me and set it up to look like I was screwing around on you. You *have* to believe me."

"Oh God, Jenna, do you remember anything at all? Did that guy...." His words caught in his throat.

"No, I don't think so." She bowed her head, but not quick enough to hide the pain that darkened her eyes.

Jack lifted her chin and gazed into her tear-filled eyes. *Could I be any bigger of a jerk?* He gathered her in his arms and pressed his lips to her damp cheek. "Oh God, Jenna... I'm so sorry I doubted you... doubted our love." He swallowed the huge lump in his throat as he helped her up and held her at arms' length so he could see her face to face. "Please, can you find it in your heart to forgive me? You have every reason not to...it's just...I was so excited to get your invite...and then I opened the door...and..." His voice cracked as he drew her to him and captured her lips in a heartfelt kiss. He pulled back and took her tear streaked face in his hands and looked into her beautiful green eyes. "I'm sorry. I'm begging you for the opportunity to make it up to you, each day...every day, for the rest of my life."

Jenna furrowed her brow as she listened to Jack apologize, so intensely; his fear of losing her was almost tangible. This man, who only a short time ago walked in on her in bed with another man...

"Please Jack, you have nothing to be sorry for. Any man would've reacted the same way, perhaps even worse. You didn't go home...you came here?"

He shook his head solemnly. "I drove for awhile trying to makes sense of things before I turned around and came straight here. *Any* man doesn't share the love we have between us. How could I think for one second you'd do something like that to me?"

"Um... hello people!"

Jenna glanced past him at Buffy. Twyla went straight to Charles open arms, and her best friend looked from them to her and Jack and scowled.

"Let's try to have a little compassion for the only one flying solo out here."

A fleeting moment of dead silence preceded a burst of explosive laughter, shattering the wall of tension. Jack sat on a deck chair and pulled her down to sit on his lap, squeezing her hand so tight, like he feared if he let go she'd run away.

The aroma of chocolate chip cookies, straight from the oven wafted out to them. Charles was quick to offer Edna a helping hand with a tray laden with fresh coffee and cookies.

As much as she loved Edna, and her baking, if the delicacies came any closer to her, she'd be spilling her own cookies right then and there. She held up a hand to ward off the plate being passed to her, shaking her head while holding her tummy.

Jack rubbed her back. "Are you still feeling poorly?"

She feigned a smile. "That's putting it mildly."

Edna cupped the side of her face in her weathered hand: her eyes brimmed with moisture as she kissed her cheek. "Thank God you're okay. I'm glad you're home."

She pressed her lips firmly together and nodded, for fear if she opened her mouth to speak, she'd let loose the torrent of tears that lingered precariously on the edge of her already tattered emotions.

The housekeeper pressed a damp hanky to her mouth and retreated back into the kitchen.

"So, I guess the question is, where do we go from here?" Buffy grabbed a cookie and sunk her teeth into it as she flopped back in a lounge chair.

"Before we do anything, there is so much I need to tell you." Jenna tugged her lip with her teeth.

She turned towards Charles. "Please, can you help me? Jack needs to know everything... and I mean everything."

While he sipped at the much needed dose of caffeine, Charles filled him in about their troubles with Howard Meed and Daniel.

Jack hardly believed all that had gone on without his knowledge. "Wow. Why did you keep me in the dark?" His gaze narrowed on Charles. "Why didn't *you* let me know what those two jokers were up to?"

He raised his hands in defense. "I'm sorry, but I couldn't break Jenna's trust, and she didn't want you to worry about her, not with you being so far away. She feared you might hunt them down and do something that might land you in trouble."

"Both of those assholes could use a good foot up the ass." He released Jenna and clenched the arms of the deck chair, grinding his teeth. Jack caught Charles' sideways glance, a smirk plastered on his face.

His body relaxed and he laughed at Jenna. "Okay, *maybe* you had a point."

"Jenna was just looking out for you. In case you haven't noticed, she's crazy in love with you."

Jack wrapped his arms around her and nuzzled the crook of her neck. "The feeling is mutual."

Charles eased back in the swing next to Twyla, cookie in hand.

"I vote we pay Daniel and that weasel Howard Meed a visit." Jack curled his lip in a snarl.

Jenna set her coffee mug down heavily. "And that's exactly why I didn't tell you anything. I didn't want you behind bars for beating the crap out of them, even though both deserve it."

Jack's snarl turned to a grin. "Okay, I get it." He took her hand in his and gently stroked it. "We have to do *something*. The guy can't get away with this bullshit."

"I agree. The two of them need to pay dearly for what happened at that motel. But let's not forget Angel is still living on the ranch. Her well-being has to come first before anything," Charles added as he brushed the crumbs from his shirt front.

"Yes, Angel needs to be safe. The problem lies in that she's a very perceptive lady. It may take her longer to process different situations, but there's no denying she's very smart. The poor girl just found out she has a sister, and soon will have to deal with losing Daniel." It worried her to think of how her sister would react to losing him.

"Getting your sister away from Daniel is the best thing for her." Jack took a sip of his coffee. "Unfortunately, God only knows what's been going on in that facility over the past twenty years. Least of which is having those girls brainwashed with some kind of hero worship of the guy."

Jenna put a fist to her mouth and gagged. "It makes me sick to my stomach just thinking about it. I pray we don't uncover the worst case scenario."

Twyla reached across Jack to hold Jenna's hand. "Diane got my job there, and she worked there many years before. She would never be quiet if she saw him do this to the girls."

Jenna smiled. "Bless you. I so needed to hear that."

"She's right. What if we're looking at this from the wrong angle? What if sex has nothing to do with any of it? What if it's all about the money? It's possible he's manipulating those girls in a *loving* way as a ploy to get what he's really after?" Jack suggested.

"You might be on to something. Maybe my mother wasn't the only one paying cash. I mean, it's possible my father isn't the reason behind that arrangement."

Jenna welcomed the security of being in Jack's arms. Something she thought she'd lost forever only a short time ago. She glanced over at Charles, who appeared to be entranced with Twyla, and loving every minute of it.

He must've sensed her gaze on him for he looked up and smiled her way.

"You did good, my friend. She's a keeper."

He grinned sheepishly and held Twyla's hand up for all to see the stunning sparkler on her ring finger.

"Oh my God!" Jenna jumped to her feet and threw her arms around the newly engaged couple. "I'm so happy for the two of you."

Buffy clenched her hands. "Screw Daniel. He's *not* going to ruin any more lives. If he wants to fight dirty thinking he'll win, he picked the wrong opponents."

"I suggest we try and get Doctor Gilmore over here first thing in the morning. That way, we'll all be on the same page and can try and figure out exactly where to go from here." Jenna looked at Jack, dreading the answer to her next question. "When do you have to head back?"

He winked and smiled suggestively. "Right *after* our meeting with the good doctor."

Heat rushed to her face and down to her nether regions. "I was hoping you'd say that." Her eyes filled with happy tears. *Thank God I didn't lose you.*

Jack stood and scooped her up in his arms. "And on that note, if you'll excuse us."

Chapter Thirty-Seven

Luckily, Dr. Gilmore was more than happy to come out to the estate before his work day at the ranch began. He walked into her father's library and right over to sit behind the desk. Once settled in the chair, he looked up at Jenna and his cheeks instantly turned red.

"I-I'm sorry. How presumptuous of me. I guess its force of habit to be the one behind the desk." He made a move to stand.

She put her hand out to stop him. "It's perfectly fine. Can I get you something, perhaps a cup of coffee?"

"Maybe later. I have to say I'm more than a little curious as to why you were so adamant I come out here rather than meet at the ranch."

Jenna took a seat next to Jack and gave Charles a nod to begin, having allotted him the task of bringing the doctor up to speed.

The psychiatrist listened intently as Charles told him of their quest to uncover the truth behind Daniel, and how Howard Meed fit in to the whole sordid ordeal. His face remained void of expression until he got to the part about Jenna being drugged. His posture grew rigid and his bushy eyebrows arched as he stroked his stubbly jaw.

Jenna shuddered and kept her gaze trained out the window in an attempt to keep her anger at bay.

"Well, that's quite the story."

"You don't seem all that surprised," Jenna said.

He leaned forward with his hands clasped on the desk in front of him. "I've always considered Daniel to be a very complex personality. I've been at the ranch for quite a few years now, and you can rest at ease, I don't believe he's sexually abusing any of the girls."

She drew in a ragged breath, struggling to keep it together. "Thank God."

Jacked sat on the edge of his seat. "Maybe he isn't, but he sure has those ladies wrapped around his little finger."

"Surely you've suspected something amiss. It doesn't take a PHD to figure that out," Buffy retorted brusquely.

Jenna smirked, repressing laughter at her friend's not surprising remark.

Dr. Gilmore shifted in his seat, totally dismissing her crass remark.

"I've kept my position at the ranch for that very reason. The older girls are very tight-lipped when it comes to their relationship with Daniel. I would've quit a long time ago if I based my decision solely on how that man speaks to me, but my job is to care for the mental well-being of the residents. I couldn't...and never will, abandon them. They've come to be my family in many ways."

"Thank you for being there for my sister and the others. Nobody is more relieved than me that there doesn't appear to be any sexual abuse going on. If that's the case, though, then what is that man up to? I still feel the older girls are being exploited in some way. Are they in danger of physical harm?" Jenna expelled a sigh of frustration. "The way those girls, including Angel, act toward Daniel isn't natural. It's like my sister believes Daniel is her *boyfriend,* for lack of a better word. What could he possibly have to gain by leading them on like that?"

"It's simple. The root of that man's evil is the almighty dollar. The sick bastard is greedy, money hungry, and he'll stop at nothing to get what he wants without jeopardizing the façade of loving curator of the Ranch. For God's sake, the man drugged you." Charles started to pace. "The question is, how do the girls possibly help him gain financially given their physical and/or mental limitations?"

"I'm not sure we're headed in the right direction, but according to Daniel, my mother did pay cash on her monthly visits. Maybe she isn't the only one? Isn't it possible he's using the older girls to get to their parent's bankrolls?"

Dr. Gilmore cleared his throat. "You've definitely given me food for thought, Jenna. I really should be leaving. I'm never late, and we don't want to draw any unnecessary attention to me. I think we all need to take some time to digest everything we've discussed. I will help in any way that I can."

"How do you think we should handle things as far as Daniel is concerned? I'm sure he is awaiting some kind of response after what he did to me." Jenna balled up her hands, beyond angry at how she'd been drugged and almost lost Jack because of his twisted mind. "For whatever reason, Angel is *very* protective of Daniel. I don't want her seeing me as a threat to him."

Dr. Gilmore stood. "I suggest you all do nothing for a few days before surfacing. I promise I'll keep a close eye on Angel. That way, Daniel will think his plan has worked, and it gives your sister time to settle after the threat Buffy posed working at the ranch."

Jenna couldn't help but titter at her best friend's eye roll.

"Now, I really need to be on my way." He shook Jack's hand, then Charles' before offering Buffy a slight nod and making his way out of the office.

"I'll walk you out to your car." Jenna followed him out of the library. Her mind swirled with every conceivable emotion.

Jenna sat on the staircase, balancing a clipboard on her lap, almost every item on her list checked off. Redecorating the old homestead kept her mind busy over the past few days of keeping a low profile. The heavy brocade drapes were being replaced with exquisite, hand embroidered lace. Full enough to ensure privacy, yet sheer enough to bathe the room in much needed sunlight.

The front door opened, filling the foyer with a crisp morning breeze.

"Hey kiddo, why are you sitting there all by your lonesome?"

She got up to give Charles a hug. "The new curtains are being hung as we speak. Come take a look."

Charles clasped her hand and followed her lead into the living area. He folded his arms across his thick chest, raising one hand to rub his jaw. "They sure do breathe new life into this place, don't they?"

She smiled. "That's exactly what I'm trying to do."

"Well then, I'd say, mission accomplished." He reached over and patted her back.

"Miss Jenna, do you have a minute?" a worker standing on a step ladder called out to her. He held a framed painting of her mother over the fireplace. "Is this where you want it?"

"Raise it up two inches on the left side...perfect." Jenna nod her approval. "This is how I like to remember my mother."

A local artist had been commissioned to paint the portrait just before she was born. Given all the secrets that lie beneath her smile... Her heart ached for all she must've endured being married to a man like her father. A stranger would never have guessed their marriage was anything but perfect.

Hell, up until she died, I thought it was, too.

"Do you think she'd approve of all the changes around here? I'm so looking forward to bringing Angel here one day, hopefully in the near future."

"I think your mother is very proud of the woman you've become, and pleased at what lengths you've gone to, to ensure Angel's happiness."

She swallowed hard. "Thank you, you're a very special man, and you've made a beautiful difference in my life." Her words came out all raspy, thick with emotion.

Charles turned his head to cough into a hanky he quickly pulled out of his pocket. His attempt to hide the dabbing of his eyes failed miserably.

"Excuse me. The dust in the air from all the renovations is playing havoc with my hay fever." He folded the monogrammed hanky back into his pocket. "I hate to change the subject so abruptly, but I wanted to fill you in on a couple things I discovered while doing a little investigating on my own."

"What investigating?"

As if on cue, a shadow darkened the room as a billowing cloud blocked the sun's rays. Today was the first day in quite some time she didn't wake up with thoughts of getting even with Daniel for what he did to her. No matter how good of a day she had, or how hard she tried to block him out, he always found a way in.

"I'm sorry. I know he's the last person you want to talk about right now, but I did tell you I'd keep you informed. I wasn't able to identify the guy Jack found in the motel room, but I now know it definitely wasn't Daniel who booked the room."

Jenna frowned. "Of course Daniel is behind all of it. The coward probably hired someone to do his dirty work."

He held up his hand and gave her a stern look. "If you let me finish...the guy who runs the motel never heard of Daniel Meed, but, when he described the man who did book your room, it became very clear who his accomplice was."

Jenna arched her brows in anticipation. "Well?"

"None other than, *Howard* Meed."

Jenna literally felt the blood drain from her face as she sank into an over-sized armchair by the fireplace.

"It seems Howard is a regular customer, two or three times a week. He books a room for a couple of hours, a different girl on his arm every time. He uses the alias, John Dresser, and always pays very generously in cash."

"Oh God, please don't tell me Howard was guy in my bed." She gagged.

"Oh no, Jenna. I'm definitely not saying that. Unless Howard shed eighty pounds and grew a full head of hair, he's not even remotely in the running."

Her shoulders bowed with relief. The thought of that man next to her, seeing her naked, was enough to ruin her appetite for the rest of the week.

Charles walked over to stand beside her chair and squeezed her shoulder. "I didn't mean to upset you, but I did promise..."

She covered his hand with hers. "Yes, I know. I really do appreciate it. I'll just be glad when we have enough to put both of those assholes behind bars so I never have to think of them again."

"You and me both, kiddo." He gave her shoulder another squeeze before withdrawing his hand. "If you don't need me for anything, I'd really like to pay my fiancée a visit today."

The red tinge to his cheeks brought a smile to her lips. "I'm so happy for the two of you. You go ahead, and be sure to say hi from me."

Chapter Thirty-Eight

Now that all the workers were gone and Charles left to spend time with his new fiancée, Jenna felt very alone. She was really happy he found love, but it made her miss Jack even more.

She fetched the phone from her pocket and pressed HOME, smiling as she looked around at all of the changes. Even though the results were breathtaking, she realized it would never be her *home* again.

Home is with Jack and the dogs.

She frowned to hear the digital message service cut in.

Where are you, Jack?

A beep sounded in her ear. "Hi, Jack. It's just me, missing you. Give me a call when you get this message. I love you."

Jenna sulked and disconnected. "Now what am I going to do?"

Buffy. I've wanted to buy Angel something pretty to wear since noticing her wardrobe is pretty plain. It definitely doesn't reflect her vibrant personality.

Her friend's number connected on the first ring.

"Grant residence. How can I help you?"

Jenna recognized the housekeeper's voice. "Hi Gail, its Jenna calling. Can you put Buffy on the phone for me?"

"I'm sorry, but Buffy went on a shopping trip with her mother. I think they plan to be back sometime tomorrow. I'll tell her you called."

"Thanks. Don't worry about it. I'll call again tomorrow some time."

Jenna closed her cell and flopped back in her chair. She slapped her thighs and stood. "I'll just have to go without her then."

It was the perfect day. A bright blue sky being the perfect backdrop to a scattering of big, white, fluffy clouds. Since John was nowhere to be found, she took the less conspicuous Sedan into town.

Dina's Boutique was *the place* to go for cashmere. The woman stocked every color and style imaginable. She lucked out and found a parking spot a few shops away. A miracle in itself at that time of day.

The bell above the door announced her arrival, and Dina herself greeted her.

"Well, hello, Jenna. It's been far too long since you paid me a visit." The woman air-kissed both sides of her face.

"Yes, it has. I'm in the market for a couple of your gorgeous cashmere cardigans."

Dina's face lit up. "You've come to the right place. Please, follow me." The boutique owner's skirt swayed as she walked.

Jenna frowned. Across the store, Buffy's mother chatted with another woman over a printed dress in her hand. She surveyed the room and found no sign of her friend.

"I'll just be one minute, Dina. I see someone I'd like to say hello to."

She made her way through the maze of racks. Buffy's mother turned to watch her approach.

"Jenna? How nice it is to see you." The woman gave her a quick hug and stepped back. "You're looking wonderful, my dear."

"It's funny to find you here. I just called your house and Gail told me you were on a shopping trip with Buffy until tomorrow."

Mrs. Grant quickly looked away and laughed. "You know how Buffy can be. I can't keep up with her when she has her mind set on shopping. I came home, and she's still out and about."

Jenna eyed her suspiciously. The woman was obviously making up the story as she went along. "Where did she go shopping?"

Waving one hand, Mrs. Grant replied, "Oh, we went from one city to the next. I don't even remember where I left her." She tittered nervously, still unable to maintain eye contact. "You'll have to come over for tea soon, but there really is someplace I need to be." She lightly kissed Jenna's cheek and made a quick departure, giving her another wave at the door before she disappeared.

That was weird.

Her chance meeting with Buffy's mother took some of the

wind from her sails. She had Dina choose three new sweaters for her sister—one in hunter green, one in butter-yellow and one in a lovely shade of cranberry.

Happy with her purchases, she left the boutique and went to another store to find Lily of the Valley perfume with one of those spray pump attachments. She imagined her sister would get a kick out of it, especially when she recognized it as the scent their mother always wore.

On the way home, gray clouds rolled in blocking the sun, setting an even drearier tone to the day, totally mirroring the change in her mood since running into Buffy's mother.

Why did she lie about the shopping trip?

The whole situation left her confused, and hurt by the deception. They'd been friends since grade-school, and as far as she remembered, never lied to each other.

"Why now?"

Chapter Thirty-Nine

Jack took his buzzing cell from the inside pocket of his suit jacket. "Shit, its Jenna."

Charles shook his head. "Don't answer it. You can call later when you get back to your cabin. If she so much as catches a whiff of what we're doing, it's game over."

He didn't like avoiding her calls, but nod in agreement and put the phone away. "You're probably right. She'd definitely have a ton of questions if she found out I'm here."

"Women have an uncanny way of knowing what we're up to without us having to breathe a word." Charles grimaced as he ran a finger under the collar of his shirt, and tugged on his tie.

Jack chuckled. "I hear you." Having never explored Thunder Bay, he had absolutely no idea where they were, however, he did notice they now drove through an upscale part of the city. "How much farther?"

"A couple of minutes." Charles rolled down his window. "You can almost smell the money in this neighborhood."

"I can't wait to meet this guy." Jack clenched and unclenched his hands. It was hard to agree not to beat the crap out of the guy. He just hoped he could find the restraint. "Is he a very big guy?"

Charles snorted. "If you're worried about him in case of a physical altercation, don't be. The only exercise that moron gets is from tipping a bottle, and screwing anything in a skirt." He put the blinker on to make a turn. "In fact, he'll probably piss his boxer shorts when he realizes who you are."

"I still don't understand how Jenna's father could give her away to a man like that?"

"I suspect some kind of blackmail involving a whole lotta money." Charles shrugged. "We'll probably never know the whole truth, unless we get lucky and can get Howard to spill his guts."

Charles slowed down in a cul de sac, coming to a stop in front of a mammoth mansion that dwarfed the substantial homes on either side of it.

"He lives here? This whole place for him alone?" The place was even bigger than Jenna's.

"The prick needs a lot of space to fit his ego."

Jack laughed. "Well, let's see if we can take him down a notch or five." He reached for the door handle only to be stopped by Charles' arm across him.

"I know you're going to want to kick the shit out of this guy when you meet him. But remember, our plan doesn't involve going to jail because of his big mouth. When you feel like punching him, try to picture Jenna's face visiting you behind bars."

Jack briefly closed his eyes to get a grip on his rising anger. "This isn't going to be easy."

"You've never met this man. Trust me, it's going to be a whole lot harder than you can even imagine."

They got out of the car, and Jack followed him up a short stone path to the entrance, scanning the area for cameras.

"Isn't there some kind of security system in a place like this?"

"At the door, but don't worry, I booked an appointment." Charles put on a fedora.

"Are you telling me he actually agreed to see us?"

His friend smirked. "Not exactly." He winked at him before stepping up on a landing where a camera and intercom flanked one wall. He straightened his tie and positioned his hat low on his brow before pushing the button.

"Hello?"

"This is David Stern. I have an appointment with Mr. Meed."

"One moment please."

Jack tried to read his expression, but he wasn't giving anything away. Having kept out of the line of the camera, he chose to keep quiet in case they realized there were two of them.

A loud buzz startled him, followed by the distinctive click of the front door unlocking. The door opened to a man straight from the pages of a British Regency, dressed in full butler attire.

"Mr. Stern?" The man looked down his narrow nose at

Charles and then at him. "And you are?"

"Oh, Howard must not have mentioned I was bringing my business partner with me, Mr. Brian Swank."

The butler eyed them both, seeming to be assessing the situation.

Jack wished he'd known about their aliases before now.

"Very good, gentlemen, if you'll follow me."

If a home's décor reflected the personality of its owner, Howard Meed had the charisma of a rock. Not one painting or photo hung on the long hallway the butler led them down.

The man came to an abrupt halt, rousing him from almost running right into Charles' back. Jack's adrenaline surged through his veins, and he made a concerted effort to curb his rising anger.

Charles' pulled at the lapels of his suit jacket, and quickly exchanged a knowing look before the door was opened.

"Mr. Meed? David Stern and his partner, Brian Swank, are here to see you."

Howard sat with his back to them, pecking at a keyboard with two fingers. "Take a seat. I'll just be a second."

Jack hurried over to the phone on his desk as planned, and ripped the cord from the wall.

The man spun around in his chair. "What the fu—"

Charles slammed the laptop shut on his fingers. "Come on now, Howard, you can't be surprised to see us. You didn't really believe you'd get away with it, did you?"

Meed yanked his hands free and stood face to face with Charles. "I don't know what you're talking about. The two of you best get out of my office if you know what's good for you."

Charles pushed the man down to sit in his chair. "If you're smart, you'll keep your fat yap shut."

Howard turned his head to glare at him. "And just who the fuck are you?"

"Where are my manners? This is Jack Davis. I believe you know his girlfriend, Jenna Blackburn?"

His jaw dropped.

Jack had actually visualized lunging over the desk and closing his mouth for good. "So, you're the perverted dick Jenna's father expected her to marry? What a joke!" Jack shook his head. "You can't be surprised to see us here. I mean, you must've known I'd want to meet you face-to-face, especially after the motel incident." He clenched his jaw, gritting his teeth.

"What motel incident? I don't know what you think I did, but I have no idea what you're talking about."

Before Charles could intervene, Jack had the moron by the collar, his face inches from his. "Wrong answer, asshole."

Howard pushed him away and quickly opened his desk drawer, but not fast enough. Jack grabbed him by the fingers and bent them back until he cried out in pain.

Charles opened the drawer and withdrew a hand gun. "And just what do we have here?" He turned the gun over in his hand before aiming it at the suddenly mute idiot's head. "Just what were you planning on doing with this?"

Jack put a hand on Charles' arm. Shooting the guy would land him in jail for murder. It would kill Jenna to see either of them behind bars.

The corner of his friend's mouth lifted as he lowered the gun and proceeded to remove the bullets, dropping them in a large fish tank beside the desk. "Now, you can either keep your mouth shut, or I'll have to find something to fill that big mouth of yours."

Howard raised his hands in defense. "Okay, okay, say what you have to say."

"I'm not going to pussy foot around. My girl, Jenna, was drugged the other night and set up in a motel room so I'd find her in bed with another man." The palms of his hands itched to wipe the smile forming on the asshole's fat face.

Meed chuckled. "Trust me, if Jenna spent a night in bed with me, she'd never leave."

Jack saw red, and punched him square in the face. Blood spurt from his nose.

"You asshole, you broke my nose!"

He grabbed him by the shirt collar and hoisted him half-way across his desk. "I'd love nothing more than to leave you laid out on the floor with a whole lot more broken than your nose."

Charles stepped in front of him, and pulled out a stack of

Polaroids from his suit jacket pocket. He then fanned them out across the desk.

Howard stared at the snapshots, his mouth agape, seemingly lost for words.

Jack rubbed his knuckles, enjoying the trail of blood dripping from the man's pocked nose. He and Charles had gone back to the motel to talk to the owner. When the man opened a drawer for his log book, Jack caught a glimpse of these photos. It seemed the owner had an obsession for taking pictures of his customers.

After a whole lot of talk and a few hundred dollars, they left with at least twenty images of Howard Meed with a variety of different girls. Six of whom were *very* young. Having sex with a minor carried a rape charge and stiff penalty that included a minimum of ten years behind bars.

"I strongly suggest you tell us the whole truth, beginning with Daniel drugging Jenna."

Chapter Forty

Jenna sat up in bed and stretched. The warm sun on her face held promise of a nice day.

Is this a good omen my visit with Angel will go well?

She'd wrapped her sister's gift with wrapping paper covered with pictures of horses on it. One of them looked like the black one Jack had taken a liking to.

Jack.

Even a fleeting thought of him made her heart hurt from missing him so much.

Nobody knew of her plans to visit Angel today...not even Jack. In fact, he'd called the previous night, and she'd painfully let it go to voice mail. If she talked to him, there was no way she wouldn't have told him. She wasn't going to let anyone change her plans...not even him.

Daniel doesn't know I'm coming so he'll have had no time to orchestrate another sinister ploy. I won't put myself in danger. In fact, I hope to visit my sister without anyone being the wiser.

"Knock, knock!"

The aroma of coffee accompanied Edna into her room, where she set a steaming mug and toasted bagel with cream cheese on the small table by the window.

"I swear you have psychic powers." Jenna laughed as she got out of bed and slipped into her housecoat. "How did you even know I was awake?"

Edna winked playfully. "I have my ways." She walked over to the wrapped gift. "Who is this for?"

"It's for my sister. I bought her cashmere sweaters."

She nodded. "I see. Do you have any idea when you'll be able to see her?"

Jenna quickly dropped her gaze and shrugged. "I'm hoping sooner rather than later."

Her dear friend meandered over to her and raised her chin to look into her eyes. "What are you up to?"

"Please, Edna, don't ask me that question."

"You can't be planning on going to the ranch alone?"

She huffed resignedly. "No, I plan on taking John with me."

Edna shook her head. "John's not here."

"Where is he?" Charles was out with Twyla; Jack was probably chasing after the escaped puppy again, and now John. Uneasiness settled upon her. "Has he found love as well?"

Edna blushed. "You could say that. I believe his name is Michael."

"You mean Michelle." She chuckled.

"No, I mean *Michael*."

Jenna's gaped. "Are you saying our John is gay? How did I not know this?"

The housekeeper shrugged. "It's been a well kept secret. If your father had found out...well, you know what would've happened."

"Yes, my father would not have hesitated to fire him." A slow smile came to her lips. "I'm so happy he doesn't have to hide it anymore. Everyone deserves somebody to love."

"Speaking of love, does Jack know what you're up to? I highly doubt he'd approve."

Jenna frowned. "Don't you have something to do other than interrogate me?" She waggled her eyebrows. "Please."

Edna threw up her hands. "Okay! Have it your way, but don't come crying to me when Jack or Charles find out."

She got up and put an arm across Edna's shoulders, ushering her to the door. "He's not going to find out from you...right?"

The housekeeper mimed zipping her lips and throwing away the key.

Jenna kissed the top of her head as she left the room, and closed the door behind her. Feeling like she was racing against the clock now, she dressed in jeans, a black silk blouse and riding boots. She thought about straightening her hair, but seeing as her sister didn't take too well to change, she opted not to.

A guilty conscience led her to call Jack, and she breathed a sigh of relief when he didn't pick up. She left a short message and headed out to get her car.

Walking past the empty bay reserved for the Rolls told her John hadn't come back yet. Jenna grabbed the keys for the Sedan and set Angel's gift on the passenger seat before backing out of the garage and setting course for the ranch.

The entire drive out there, she had the should-I-or-shouldn't-I battle, of which she declared a tie upon riding under the Rolling Hills Ranch sign. She looked in all possible directions before parking and getting out of the car. There were several empty spots reserved for staff, including Daniel's.

Dare I declare the asshole isn't even here?

With her confidence rejuvenated, she grabbed the present and crossed the parking lot. Her heart pounded in her chest as she paused briefly before rolling back her shoulders and opening the door.

Barren hallways and an unsettling silence greeted her. She caught herself tip-toeing past Daniel's office and laughed.

She reached Angel's room, totally excited to see her and give her the present. "Angel? It's me, Jenna. Can I come in?"

Silence ensued, prompting her to turn the handle and push open the door. She froze.

What in God's name is going on here?

Everything was gone...not one trace remained of Angel living there for the past twenty-odd years.

Goosebumps covered her flesh as she dropped to the mattress and set the gift beside her before putting her head between her legs until the nausea passed.

Flashes of Angel at the mercy of Daniel quickly chased away her initial shock, and she darted from the room, coming to an abrupt stop at Dr. Gilmore's office. The half-open door revealed the room had also been cleared of any sign the doctor had ever been there.

Jenna darted down the hall to Daniel's office, bursting through the door only to stop dead in her tracks. The decorum had changed, and the black man behind the desk definitely wasn't Daniel.

"Can I help you?" The man towered above her.

"Can you help *me*? How about telling me who the hell you are, and what you've done with my sister?"

The man put a hand up between them. "I think we need to

start again." He held out his hand as he left his place behind the desk. "I'm Damon Knolls, acting CEO of Rolling Hills Ranch"

Jenna dismissed his hand. She grabbed a corner of the desk, suddenly light-headed and weak in the knees.

Knolls grasped her arm—her pale complexion a stark contrast against his dark skin.

"Please, have a seat. Can I get you a glass of water?"

Jenna waved him off.

He returned to his chair behind the desk and opened a leather-bound ledger in front of him. "Now, let's see if I can help you, Miss...?"

"Jenna Blackburn." Her patience grew thin.

"Miss Blackburn? Your sister's name is?"

"Angelina Freeman." She blinked rapidly and straightened in her seat. The barrage of events and emotions in her head slowed down enough to think reasonably straight. "Where's Daniel?" Jenna wanted to scream, frustrated beyond belief.

Damon raised his head. "Mr. Meed has taken an indefinite sabbatical, for personal reasons."

"No way." She shook her head. "Daniel would never leave his position here willingly."

"Yes, it's true. I came to take over his duties the day before yesterday."

"What about my sister? All of her things are gone from her room." *Please don't let her be alone with Daniel.*

He shifted his attention back to the ledger; his finger travelled from line to line. "Here it is...Angelina Freeman was discharged at approximately the same time Daniel took his leave."

Jenna sprang to her feet. "What do you mean by *discharged*? Where the hell did she go, and exactly who discharged her?"

"Let me see...it appears Daniel signed her out just before he left."

Panic kicked in full speed. "Did Angel leave *with* Daniel?" *Please say no, please say no, please, please...please God.*

The black man shook his head "I'm sorry, Miss Blackburn. I don't have any answers for you. I wasn't here when she left.

See for yourself, here's Daniel's signature."

Jenna lunged from the chair to his desk and gaped at his uneven scrawl. Anger consumed her. "Now you listen to me, Mr. CEO. You had no right releasing Angel to anyone but me." She balled up her hands and smacked the desktop. "I suggest you pick up that phone and find out where Daniel took my sister...now!"

"Take it easy. Losing control and name calling won't make it any easier finding answers."

"Forgive me, *Mister Whoeveryouare*, but at this precise moment in time, I don't care whose feelings get hurt." She fell back into her chair and covered her face in her hands.

Angel must be scared out of her mind. I swear, if he hurts her...

"I'm sorry. Do you want me to call somebody for you?"

Jack! "I need Jack. Call Jack, please." She choked on the words. The tiny bit of composure she had left hung by a tattered thread as she hit HOME on her cell.

If only I reached out to him from the beginning, none of this would be happening, and Angel would be safe. It's my fault. I'm so sorry, Angel.

Jenna wiped her eyes before putting the phone to her ear. "Jack?" Her voice cracked and she gave her tears free rein.

"Jenna? What's wrong? Are you crying?"

The compassion in his voice snapped something inside of her. She shook so bad, she had to hold her phone with both hands. "Angel is gone." She managed to tell him about Daniel's sabbatical and the new staff at the ranch, and how her sister's room was cleared out, and so was Dr. Gilmore's.

"Come home, Jenna. We can handle things from here by phone."

"I-I can't leave. What if Angel tries to contact me?"

"Listen to me. You'll have your phone, Mr. Knolls will be at the ranch, and Edna or Charles will always be at the estate. You're not alone, Jenna. It's time to come home."

Her shoulders sunk with relief. "If you are sure we can find Angel with me there...yes, I want to come home."

"You go pack a bag. I'll make sure we have every angle covered, including calling the police. Don't worry, baby, we will find your sister."

"I love you, Jack. I'll head out to the estate now."

"I love you, too, Jenna. I'll arrange for a car to pick you up at the estate in...let's say an hour from now. Now, put the director on the phone."

"Mr. Knolls? Jack wants to talk to you. I need to head back to the estate." She fished her car keys from her purse, and realized she'd left Angel's gift back in the room. "I'll be right back."

Upon her return, the new CEO of the ranch stood outside his office and handed back her phone. "I don't think you should be driving. Why don't you let my secretary drive you home? We can figure out the rest later."

"No, I'll be fine." Jenna suddenly felt desperate to be with Jack. She knew he'd move heaven and earth to find Angel for her. "I trust you've arranged with Jack to call if you hear anything from Angel?"

"Yes. Please drive safely."

Jenna offered a weak smile and left his office.

I'm going home...

Angel sat in the corner of a cold, damp room, her knees drawn up to her chest. Her otherwise vibrant green eyes, now bloodshot and puffy from crying. Her breath hitched and she began shaking uncontrollably as the footsteps drew nearer.

"Well, my dear Angel. There's nothing to stop us now. I'm going to take great pleasure in teaching you what goes on behind the bedroom door, between a man and a woman in love. You do know how much I love you, don't you, Angel?"

She opened her mouth and screamed...

Jenna's eyes flew open, her hands covering her ears. Her heart pounded so hard, she feared it might actually jump out of her chest. She sat in a helicopter beside the big window. *It was all a bad dream. I must've dozed off.*

It was too dark to tell exactly where they were, but the mountains grew closer ahead of them. Her breathing slowed back to normal. The arrangements to hire this mode of transportation took longer than she'd wanted, but her frustration ebbed with the realization she'd be home very soon.

Jenna leaned back in her seat and gazed at the star-filled sky.

"Keep her safe, Mother. We're going to find her."

Chapter Forty-One

Every nerve ending in his body sparked in unbridled anticipation of Jenna's return home. During the entire drive to the precinct, he mentally prepared himself to carry out their cleverly orchestrated ruse, knowing Jenna would understandably be upset about not knowing Angel's whereabouts. All he had to do was make the half hour drive home without spilling the beans.

Luckily, they were able to hire a helicopter and the chief gave his permission to use the landing pad on the precinct roof. Jack was a little nervous about having to lie to Jenna about searching for Angel. No, he wasn't crazy about that part of their plan, but she would have wanted to be an active participant in Howard and Daniel's demise. There's no way in hell he'd put her life at risk for anything, or anyone.

Surely when she sees for herself what we've been up to, she'll understand and forgive all of us...right?

The door leading up to the landing pad opened, ending his attempt to justify their actions. It was too late now. He took a deep, steadying breath as the pilot stepped through the doorway and held the door open for Jenna.

His heart clapped the rhythm of a racehorse on the last lap...and then their gazes met. Even from the distance between them, he saw tears rolling down her flushed face. She rushed to him, and he whisked her off her feet, kissing her so intensely it left them both breathless once he set her down.

Jack held her at arm's length. "It's so good to see you."

"I'm sorry, but I didn't know what to do. All I could think of was talking to you." Jenna linked her hands behind his neck and laid her head on his shoulder.

"You have nothing to be sorry for." Jack hated being the reason behind her tears. *Just a little bit longer...* "Come on, let's go home."

"Has there been any news about Angel?" she asked as they left the precinct heliport.

Jack shook his head—inside, he could hardly contain his excitement. "We got the best of the best looking for her. Trust me; it's just a matter of time."

Jenna picked up a suitcase from a cart, and he quickly took it from her. "Is this the only one?" He remembered the size of her closet on the estate.

"Yes, thank God. I have no need for a bunch of shoes and fancy party dresses out here."

Her change in priorities surprised, and more than pleased him. He lifted her suitcase into the back of his newly acquired truck and padded over to passenger side to let her in.

"Whose truck is this?" she asked as she climbed up onto the passenger seat.

Jack closed her inside quickly, and took the long way around the back of the truck to give him a few extra moments to compose himself. He opened the door and slid in behind the wheel, leaning across the seat to kiss her softly and hold her hand.

"So, whose truck is this?"

He smiled. *I should have known she wouldn't forget she'd asked me.*

Jack closed the door and turned his key in the ignition, bringing the new vehicle to life. "It's our truck. You're going to see a few changes to the old homestead. I thought it was high time I conformed to modern society and indulged in a few of life's niceties."

"Such as?" She looked sideways at him.

"You'll find out soon enough." He knew she was still looking at him, but he didn't trust himself to face her.

"I hope you didn't spend a ton of money you don't..." Her hand covered her mouth. "Oh God, I'm so sorry. I didn't mean to imply..."

Jack brought her hand to his lips and kissed it. "You didn't imply anything. I never said I didn't have money, I just chose not to spend it on things like this truck and... Well, you'll see soon enough."

For a short distance, they drove in amiable silence. If he could read minds, he'd bet money she was trying to figure out what he was up to. He totally sucked at keeping a lid on things.

"You're acting a little weird. Is there something going on I should know about?"

He flicked his high beams on outside the city limits. "You know, you really need to learn how to have a little patience."

"I'm sorry, but I'm just so damned worried about Angel. You can't begin to imagine the horrific dream I had about her on the way here." Her voice cracked, and she turned her head to cough into her hand.

"Try not to worry, Jenna. I promise you she's okay."

Shit. Way to go, like she isn't going to be even more suspicious with a promise like that.

He chanced a look her way. Even in the dark, he saw the confusion that lined her brow and clouded those beautiful green eyes.

"Let's just get you home. We can sit down, and I'll fill you in on everything that's going on." He squeezed her hand reassuringly. "Okay?"

Jenna nod, and managed the slightest of smiles in response. She turned and gazed up at the star-filled sky.

A short time later, he turned onto the new gravel road leading home.

"We have a road now? That must have cost a fortune."

He immediately saw the regret in her expression.

"I'm so sorry, Jack."

"Stop saying you're sorry. How were you to know I had a few bucks tucked away?" He winked.

"I'd say more than a few."

Jack laughed. "God, it's good to have you back."

"So, are you going to tell me what changes you've made to our place?"

Our place.

A sense of well-being encompassed him, and he knew without a doubt Carly would approve of what he was about to show Jenna—how he'd spent the insurance money. He slowed to a stop and put the truck in park.

"Why did you stop?"

"I want you to be surprised." He took a scarf from his jacket pocket. "I'm going to cover your eyes."

"Is that really necessary? I mean, it's pitch black outside."

"Humor me, okay?"

Jenna shrugged, and closed her eyes. "Okay, if you insist."

Jack covered her eyes with a bandana and tied it at the back. He put his mouth close to her ear. "I promise you, everything will make sense in just a couple of minutes." He kissed her cheek. It took everything in him not to laugh out loud.

She's going to freak out...in a good way...I hope...

Though Jack's excitement was highly contagious, Jenna couldn't help feel guilty for enjoying this while her sister was still out there...enduring God knows what. She tilted her head, having heard the click of headlights being turned on and off.

Is he signaling someone? Who could it be, and why?

The truck came to a stop and shut down. The silence that followed brought goose bumps to her skin, and she shivered in anticipation. Jack got out of the truck without speaking.

What's that? She strained to hear. *Is that what I think it is?* A horse whinnied in the distance. *Did Jack buy us horses? Is that my surprise?*

Her door opened. She kept what she heard to herself, not wanting to ruin things for him.

"Take my hand."

She did as asked, and he helped her out of the truck. "Can I take this thing off now?" The mounting excitement was driving her crazy.

"We're going to walk a few steps and then up three stairs."

After the three stairs, he walked her a few more steps and turned her to the position he obviously wanted her. "Sit here."

The sounds of breathing made it very clear they weren't alone. In fact, more than one person was sharing in the surprise.

"Are you ready?" Jack asked from behind her.

"How in the hell should I know?"

Several people joined in Jack's laughter, but one in particular caught her attention. Her mouth went dry, and her pulse raced.

I'd know that laugh anywhere.

"Jack? Is Angel here? Take this thing off of me." Jenna pulled the blindfold down.

All she saw was Angel, clapping her hands excitedly.

Her sister lunged forward and wrapped her good arm

around her. "Surprise!"

Jenna cried softly into her hair. *Oh my God, she's really here.* She looked past her sister at Jack who now stood in front of them. "What is going on?"

Angel stepped back and stroked Jenna's hair—her other arm still in a sling. "Don't cry, Sister. Aren't you happy to see me?"

Jenna huffed. "You have no idea how happy I am."

A whimper drew her attention downward, to a smaller version of Sasha at her feet. "Who do we have here?"

Angel knelt. "This is Chubby, and he's all mine!"

Jack shrugged. "Like I could say no."

Jenna wanted to sob in relief and dance with joy, but she had to rein in her emotions, not wanting to upset Angel if she didn't understand her confused reactions. Her jaw dropped as Jack moved aside to reveal a line of people.

Charles and Twyla, John and a man she'd never met before, and Dr. Gilmore, grinning sheepishly, his hands rest on precious, Sweet Pea's slight shoulders.

"What are you... How did you all... Why are you all here?"

She spotted someone peeking out from behind Charles. "Buffy? I don't know whether to hug you or strangle you to death."

Jack stepped between them. "Before you start swinging, there's more."

Her hand flew to her chest. "I don't know if my heart can take much more."

"Are you ready, Angel?"

"Ready!" Her voice came out of the darkness.

"One...two...three!"

Bright lights momentarily blinded her. She squinted, and as things came into focus, she gasped. "What have you done?"

Jack pulled her to his side. "Jenna, I saw your struggle—thinking you had to choose between me and Angel. I had already started making some changes when the whole Meed fiasco went down. I thought to myself, why not bring Angel to live here, with us? One thing led to another, and before we knew it, we'd come up with a plan to keep everyone together...and happy."

"Is it true? Angel is really going to live here with us?" Jenna struggled to wrap her head around it all. "Charles? Did you know about all of this?"

He grinned. "Yes, and I'm sorry I had to tell a couple of white lies. Shortly after you found Angel, Jack came to me with a plan to create all of this. I was sworn to secrecy while we figured out if we could actually make it work. We didn't want to get your hopes up until we knew, without doubt, we could pull this off."

"What about Daniel? I saw his signature on Angel's release form."

Jack snickered. "Once we confronted Daniel with the evidence we had against him, he was only too happy to oblige. We had him sign a waiver, handing Angel over to us, and step down as CEO of the ranch. He also agreed to move away and never take a job in the same capacity. If he tries, we'll happily hand him over to the police."

"What about Howard? I wouldn't put it past him to try and take Angel from me. We can't let our guard down, not even for a second."

"Relax. You don't ever have to worry about that man ever again. I guess you could say we gave Howard Meed a taste of his own 'blackmail medicine.'"

"I don't understand. What blackmail?"

Angel returned with Chubby dancing around her feet.

Jack pulled Jenna closer to his side. "We'll have plenty of time later to go over all the details, okay?"

"So, what you're saying is, it's over. Angel is really here to stay, for good?" She briefly closed her eyes, struggling to keep it together.

"Actually, we're all here to stay." Buffy added. "That is, if it's okay with you?"

Jenna looked at each of them in turn. "I don't quite know what to say?" Her attention was drawn to the spot where the shed they kept the pups in had been. In its place, a proper stable painted red and white, the carbon copy of the one at the ranch, undoubtedly done with Angel's transition in mind. Off to one side were several cabins in various sizes and stages of completion. The beautiful, wrap-around porch she stood on, substantially bigger than the step up into the cabin as before. She couldn't fathom what she'd find on the other side of the new door.

Jack lifted her chin to gaze into her eyes. "This can be a safe haven for people like Angel and her friends back at the ranch. Of course, we'll have to start small, and eventually take on more residents." He wiped the tears from her face. "So, what do you say? Are you in?"

Jenna took in the group now gathered around her. How blessed she was to have such amazing people in her life. "Are you sure about giving up your solitude?"

He kissed her softly before he held her face in his hands. "My life changed forever the day I uncovered my angel in the snow. You opened my heart to love again. I no longer wish to hide away from the world. I want to participate in life, a life with *you*, and everyone who loves you as much as I do."

Jenna threw her arms around him. "I love you, Jack Davis."

The porch erupted in cheers. Angel squealed in delight as she ran down the stairs with flashlight in hand. She stopped next to something covered by a large tarp.

Jack gave her two thumbs up, prompting her to grab hold of one corner of the cover. She stood proud. Spotlights in the ground shone up on the covered object.

"I'd like to welcome you all to our new home." She pulled the canvas off of a rustic wooden sign. Inset in the upper half's center were glass angel wings, and burned in the heavy wood beneath them...

Safe Haven
Where Angels Fly

ABOUT THE AUTHOR

Adelle Laudan lives in Southern Ontario with the last of her four children still under her wing. She is keeper of one little diva dog named ChaChi who always manages to make her smile. Adelle is a multi-published author, spanning many genres.

Adelle invites you on the many twists and turns of being a published author. Be sure to fasten your seatbelt, as it's sure to be a ride you won't soon forget.

"If I can evoke emotion from my readers, whether it be laughter or tears, I've accomplished what I set out to do."

www.adellelaudan.com

ADELLE'S BOOKS

Iron Horse Rider Trilogy
In Your Eyes
Heart of Steele
Killer Scents / Scent of a Killer
Angels In Red
Short Stories
Crucified
Serenity
Free Reads
Solidarity
Timeless Encounter
Women of Strength Series
Juliana
Rosa
Shani
Kat
Grace
Dani
Eva
* * * Adult Reads* * *
She Rides
Mystified

www.ingramcontent.com/pod-product-compliance
Lightning Source LLC
Chambersburg PA
CBHW071447170626
46811CB00007B/2500